KATE'S PATH

KATE'S PATH

VIVIAN MCDERMOTT

ISBN-13: 9780997055320
ISBN-10: 0997055324
Library of Congress Control Number: 2017913594
Vivian McDermott, Shelby, MT

ONE

Barb Jensen laid her red pencil down on the kitchen table and stood up. Stretching her arms up high and tilting her head from side to side she rolled her shoulders to ease the kinks in her muscles. Correcting papers was tedious and time-consuming, but well worth the effort, at least in her opinion. She was passionate about education, and the fact that she was using the curriculum she had designed made teaching English her dream job.

Five years ago, the school board had approved a one year trial period for her to use writing assignments as a vehicle to teach vocabulary, grammar and punctuation to her middle school students. As she had hoped, test scores improved dramatically, and now her writing program had been made a part of the curriculum. Because she believed that reading and writing were the basis for communication, she was even more delighted with the enthusiasm her students displayed for English, which most of them had previously considered to be boring.

Every two weeks, she gave a new writing assignment and each one became a little more difficult, until the last assignment for her eight graders would be a research paper. Her seventh graders were just getting started though, and the subject for the current essay was Halloween. Barb was quite pleased with the variety of essays. Some students described their search for the perfect costume while others reminisced about trick-or-treating or visits to the local haunted house in years past. A few presented details about the history of the holiday itself.

Barb circled mistakes when she read their first drafts, then each student corrected their own papers for grammar and punctuation citing page numbers from their textbook to prove they had looked up the proper usage. That was the strength of the program, in Barb's opinion. Most of her students didn't make the same mistakes in subsequent papers since looking up and documenting proper usage was so tedious. During the next few class periods, groups of four students swapped papers and provided feedback to each other on vocabulary, readability, description and content. Using the feedback from their peers, they re-wrote their essays and Barb gave each one a final grade. Next they presented their final papers to the class and received a group evaluation of their work. Both her grade and the group evaluation went into the grade book.

Barb filled the kettle at the kitchen sink and placed it on the stove, tidying the table and placing the corrected essays in her briefcase while she waited for the water to boil. Petite with a heart-shaped face, blue eyes, and thick dark brown hair curling softly around her face, her movements were brisk and efficient.

The kettle had just begun to whistle when Kate entered the kitchen. Kate and her mother shared the same heart-shaped face, blue eyes and dark hair, but Kate was several inches taller. She wore dangling silver earrings, had her long hair secured at the nape of her neck with a silver clip, and was dressed in black slacks, black sandals, a peach colored blouse and a black cardigan.

"She hates me, Mom." Kate said miserably as she slumped dejectedly onto a chair at the table.

"Who hates you, dear?"

"Charlie's mom." Barb remained silent as she added a tea bag to a second mug, poured boiling water over it and placed it in front of her daughter, then took her seat across the table with her own steaming mug.

"Do you want to talk about it?" she asked. Kate nodded, and with her hands cupped around her mug, she began to share the details of her evening.

"On the surface, everything was fine. Charlie's parents asked me polite questions, like if I had siblings, and about you and dad. You know the stuff you ask when you are getting to know someone." Barb nodded, and Kate continued. "But everything Mrs. Whitcomb said had an edge to it, like a double meaning." Kate paused and stared fixedly into her tea for a moment as if searching for answers in a crystal ball.

"Double meaning?" Barb prompted.

"Yeah, like when she asked what my favorite entrée was and I said the only time I'd eaten there was with Charlie on my birthday. I said I ordered the shrimp stir-fry and it was delicious."

"Entrée? I thought you were having dinner in their home." Barb interrupted.

"I did too, but we went to the country club instead. Thank goodness I didn't wear jeans!"

"I see." Barb said thoughtfully. "Go on."

"So, she raised her eyebrows and said, 'Oh, your parents aren't members, then?' as if that was a mark against your character or something." Kate exclaimed, indignantly.

"What did you say?" Barb asked curiously. Kate shrugged.

"I just said that we weren't members, and then Charlie's dad kind of laughed and told her to stop grilling me, and she said she was simply trying to find *something* we had in common so we could chat. But that wasn't what she was doing, Mom. I felt like she was deliberately trying to make me feel inferior. Why would she do that?"

"Maybe she isn't inclined to like the woman her son is dating." Barb suggested. "Or maybe she's just hard to get to know."

"Maybe," Kate said, doubtfully, "but I got the impression it was personal, that it was me she didn't like. I mean, she's involved in a lot of community work and charity events, so she must know how to be charming and pleasant, or at least polite. Instead, she was deliberately rude." Kate sipped her tea and then continued.

"Later on, she asked me what I was studying. I said I was working right now and saving money to enroll next semester to study business. So then she asked what kind of job I had and I said I was a waitress. She said she sure hoped I followed through, because so many young people never get around to going to school once they get a dead end job."

"Well, that's true enough, isn't it? Your dad and I have talked with you about that." Barb commented mildly, as Kate stared moodily into her tea cup. In fact, she and Kent had discussed exactly that situation with Kate in great detail, precisely because they knew from experience that life often takes unexpected turns.

Barb had been in high school when she got a job cleaning rooms at the Holiday Inn and began saving her money to pay for college. She worked hard and two years after graduation, she was a full-time sophomore and a part-time waitress, halfway to fulfilling her dream of becoming a teacher.

Then Kent sat in her section of the restaurant after his shift one evening, and ordered a sandwich. He was six foot two with wavy black hair, hazel eyes and a lopsided grin. Lots of police officers frequented the coffee shop where Kate worked, and quite a few of them were good looking and single, but there was just something about Kent. He noticed her too and came back the next evening and the one after that. Before long the two of them were dating and six months later they were married.

Kent supported Barb's dream of becoming a teacher, and she continued with her classes and her job until an unexpected pregnancy put her dream on hold. When their two daughters were in school, Barb juggled a part-time job, college classes, parenting and household chores for three years in order to finish her degree and her student teaching. Then she substituted in the local school district for another three years before she finally got a full-time position. Well, it had been worth it, she thought as she pulled her attention back to Kate.

"It wasn't what she said, Mom, it was the way she said it. Her mouth was smiling, but, well, she's blond with blue eyes, and her eyes were like chips of ice." Kate shivered. "I'm telling you, she hates me. What am I supposed to do about that?"

"I don't know, dear. You just keep trying, I guess, and hope things will change once she gets to know you better."

"Did Grandma Jensen dislike you when you first met her?" Kate wanted to know.

"Well no, but then Carol likes just about everyone. And my parents liked Kent right away too. Maybe we were lucky." When Kate finished her tea and went off to bed, Barb remained at the table with a second mug of tea, wishing she had better advice to offer. Unfortunately, she had no experience with the lifestyles of the rich and influential even on the relatively small scale that existed in Billings, Montana.

Both she and Kent came from blue-collar families who resided squarely in the middle of the middle class. Her mother, Vera and Kent's mother Carol were homemakers, skilled in cooking and sewing and living on a budget. Both were active in church and community. Barb's father, Ron Jacobs, was a printer, as his father and grandfather had been before him. After thirty years at a daily newspaper he became the manager of a commercial print shop. He had been good at the newspaper business, but he was passionate about office supplies. Although he didn't think of himself as an artist, he seemed to have a knack for helping his customers design logos for business cards and stationery.

Kent's father, Mike, got his training as a mechanic in the army. The man was a genius with engines. When people asked him why he didn't open his own repair shop, he smiled and explained that if he did that, he'd have to worry about inventory, accounts receivable, rent, and a whole lot of other things that would take time away from doing what he loved, which was fixing engines. He always said he was happier punching a clock in the shop at the car dealership and going home to his family at the end of the day.

Barb wondered why Charlie's parents had opted to meet Kate at the country club instead of their home. Maybe their kitchen was being remodeled, or perhaps Mrs. Whitcomb didn't cook. She was sure there was a reason, but it did seem odd to her. She reminded herself not to be judgmental since she didn't know very much about the Whitcomb family. She'd seen their names and pictures in the paper now and then, but given that Billings was a good sized city, she had never met any of them personally.

Her mind drifted back to the first time she and Kent met Charlie shortly after Kate started dating him. They had invited him to dinner as they had always done when Julie, their oldest daughter, was dating. It was a new experience with Kate because she hadn't dated much and they were anxious to meet Charlie. Over dessert, Kent had asked how he was related to the Whitcomb family who had the law firm. Charlie had hesitated for a fraction of a second before his dimples flashed.

"Well sir, my full name is Charles Whitcomb IV, but I don't answer to 'fourth' or 'Charles'."

"You aren't ashamed of your family, are you?" Kent asked, half jokingly.

"Oh, no sir! I'm proud of them and what they've accomplished." Charlie explained how his great-grandfather had started the Whitcomb Law Firm. Both of his sons, Charles Jr. (Chaz) and Levi, joined the firm when they completed law school, and in due course, Charles III, who started out as 'Chuck' but was now called 'Huck' and his brother Will also joined the firm as did Levi's sons Jeff and James.

"So, are you studying law?" Kent had asked curiously.

"Not a chance!" Charlie replied firmly. "Everyone in the family expected me to, of course, but I chose accounting instead." He'd made light of it, explaining that his brother George was planning to carry on the family legacy. Now, in light of Kate's meeting with Charlie's parents, Barb wondered if perhaps it had not been as amusing as he led them to believe. And as she thought about it, she also realized that Charlie had not talked about his family until

Kent brought them up, and he never mentioned them again after that. That omission and the fact that Kate hadn't met or spent any time with Charlie's family in the year she and Charlie had been dating now seemed rather ominous.

Well, she supposed mothers always worried about their children. She remembered that when her mother met Kent, she had immediately zeroed in on the daily danger he faced as a police officer.

"Every time he goes to work he will put his life on the line. How will you live with that?" Vera had asked with an anxious frown. Barb had replied that of course she worried about his safety, but Billings wasn't exactly a war zone, and she was very proud of Kent for wanting to make a difference. Worry for his safety hadn't stopped her parents from accepting Kent as a son, just as Kent's parents had welcomed her as a daughter.

Charlie had spent so much time in their home that Barb and Kent already considered him part of their family. As she rinsed her mug and put it in the dishwasher, Barb doubted that Charlie's parents, or at least his mother, would accept Kate in a similar way. No sense borrowing trouble, she chided herself. Kate and Charlie would make their own choices and live their own lives, and the future would take care of itself.

TWO

Charlie left campus after his morning class and drove downtown, parking a block away from the Sinclair Insurance Agency. Talking with Ben always helped him sort things out, and he really needed that right now. Ben's great-grandfather, Walter Sinclair, started an insurance agency in Billings at about the same time Charlie's great-grandfather started his law firm. The Sinclair and Whitcomb families had never been close friends, but they had been part the same social circle for three generations by the time Charlie and Ben met in middle school. The two boys hit it off immediately and were inseparable from the day they met, managing to keep in close contact even when they went off to different colleges. Charlie always felt comfortable with Ben's family and spent a lot of time in their home. By mutual, unspoken consent they avoided Charlie's house where neither the atmosphere nor Charlie's mother were warm or welcoming. Charlie was a frequent visitor to the office and he waved at Ben's secretary before he rapped his knuckles lightly on Ben's open door.

"Charlie!" Ben looked up and grinned, then leapt to his feet and came around the desk to shake hands and clap Charlie on the back. Both young men were six feet tall and had medium brown hair. There were differences, of course. Ben had hazel eyes. Charlie's eyes were chocolate brown, and he had dimples, but they looked enough alike that they were often mistaken for brothers; sometimes they didn't bother to clear up that misconception.

"How is the manager of the brand new Bozeman branch of the family business?" Charlie forced a smile as he teased his friend.

"Things are going pretty well. Pull up a chair! How have you been? Why aren't you attending classes?" Ben exclaimed. Ben had crammed four years of school into three by attending summer sessions and liked to lord it over Charlie that he was still in school.

"I had a ten o'clock and I've got a class this afternoon." Charlie replied still standing. "Uh, can you get away for lunch?" Ben frowned and looked more closely at his friend. This was not a social call, then. Since falling in love with Kate, Charlie had been a new man; happier and more relaxed that Ben had ever seen him. The man standing before him was the old Charlie with a tight smile and haunted eyes.

Ben nodded, snagged his jacket off the back of his chair, and told his secretary that he was going for an early lunch. The two friends were silent as they walked to a small diner on the next block and found a table in the back. Once they placed their order, Ben braced himself and waited for whatever bad news had erased Charlie's happiness, hoping it hadn't been a break up with Kate. Charlie clasped his hands on the table and got right to it.

"I introduced Kate to my parents this weekend, and well, let's just say that it didn't go well. Dad was okay, but Mom spent the entire evening asking rude questions, and went out of her way to put Kate down, probably because her family doesn't have buckets of money." Charlie shook his head in disgust. "Well, you know how she is."

"Nothing new, then. Is Kate okay?" Ben's hazel eyes were sympathetic. He didn't care for Charlie's mother. She had gone out of her way to put him down, too, the few times he'd been unable to avoid being around her. He knew Charlie had been worried about her reaction to Kate, apparently with good reason.

"She was pretty quiet, and we didn't have enough time to talk. My mother put the dinner off til Sunday night and I had to get back here. I'm sure she did that on purpose. Anyway, it's not something

I want to discuss on the phone..." Charlie's voice trailed off as he stared down at the hamburger the waitress had just put in front of him. He wasn't hungry. His stomach had been tied in knots since dinner at the country club Sunday night. His plan had been to introduce Kate to his parents on Friday or Saturday night, and then he and Kate would have had a chance to talk afterwards. But of course his mother had other plans.

"So, what can I do to help?" Ben wanted to know, taking a bite of his own hamburger.

"I'm going to ask Kate to elope. The sooner we get married, the better!" Charlie said. "And I want to make her the beneficiary to my life insurance policy. That's what I came to talk to you about. I just wanted you to know why." Ben put down his hamburger and wiped his fingers on a napkin. He studied Charlie across the table for a moment before he spoke, remembering the pact he and Charlie had made years ago to always tell each other the truth.

"Okay." Ben said slowly. "Making Kate your beneficiary is a good idea; we can do that after lunch." He paused. "But eloping is not a good idea, Charlie."

"Why not? Kate and I have been talking about getting married for quite awhile, and now that my mother knows I'm serious about her... well I want to get married right away. If we wait until I graduate, you and I both know Amelia will do everything in her power to screw everything up! She's probably already working on a plan to try and come between us." Charlie said, angrily. "At the very least, she will make our wedding a miserable experience for everyone."

"I know." Ben said, quietly. "But, well, let me tell you a story. Eat your hamburger." Charlie looked down at his as yet untouched burger and sighed.

"You remember when Genny and I got married?"

"Of course I remember!" Charlie said, impatiently. "I was your best man!"

"I know you remember that we had a wedding, but do you remember any of the details?" Ben persisted. Charlie shook his head.

"Well, it was an absolute disaster!" Ben exclaimed. Charlie looked startled, but Ben held up a hand to forestall any comments and continued.

"Just listen. And eat your hamburger." Charlie unenthusiastically picked up his burger and took a small bite.

"What happened was that Genny's mom took over the wedding and it got way out of control. Everything was super elaborate, and there were people on the guest list that neither Genny nor I knew. Genny thinks her mom didn't get to have her own wedding the way she wanted it and she went a little crazy. Normally, she's a wonderful person so something like that probably happened. But anyway, then my parents got all competitive and threw a huge rehearsal dinner and gave us a honeymoon in Hawaii." Ben paused and grimaced. "And Genny cried herself to sleep on the flight. I didn't know what to do. I was afraid she was already sorry she'd married me."

"She loves you!" Charlie objected.

"Yeah and I love her. That isn't the point." Ben shook his head and searched for the words to convey what he wanted Charlie to understand. "See, when it came to the wedding, I just did what they told me to do without paying much attention, because I wanted Genny to have what she wanted and I really didn't care about the dress or the cake or the flowers or the candles or any of that. I bet you don't either, am I right?" Charlie was listening intently and he nodded, chewing another bite of his hamburger. Ben leaned across the table and paused for effect.

"Women care about weddings, Charlie. A lot. When I finally got Genny to talk to me without crying, she said she didn't want to remember the beginning of our life together as a huge social event planned by our parents. She wanted" he used his fingers to make air quotes for emphasis "a meaningful memory."

"But the wedding was over. What could you do?" Charlie asked, looking bewildered.

"As soon as we got to Hawaii, I had a little chat with the concierge at the hotel. He recommended a pastor who was happy to bless our marriage, and the two of them helped us make arrangements for our own private ceremony on the beach. Genny wore a white sundress, I wore khakis and a white shirt, and we both went barefoot. We wrote our own vows and since we already had rings, we exchanged leis that the pastor had blessed. There was even a guitar player, and the pastor took a picture for us. Then we swapped our room at the hotel for a little bungalow on the beach and enjoyed the rest of our honeymoon."

"Seriously?" Charlie asked. "You basically did another wedding?"

"Not another wedding exactly – but we created a meaningful memory of the beginning of our lives together." Ben assured him. "Pictures of the elaborate wedding our parents gave us are in an album we seldom look at, but the picture taken that day on the beach is in a frame on the mantle. And we think of the vows we exchanged on that beach as the official beginning of our life together, or at least Genny does."

"What about you?" Charlie teased as he finished the last bite of his hamburger.

"In my mind we've been together since our first date." Ben grinned.

"Okay. So how does that translate to Kate and me?"

"Well, I'd say go ahead and ask her to marry you, but don't ask her to elope. Let her plan the kind of wedding she wants. Genny and I have gotten to know Kate pretty well, and I'm betting it will be just family and close friends." Ben advised. "But if it isn't and she wants a big elaborate event, you'd be smart to go along with it."

"What about my parents?" Charlie protested. "The reason I wanted to elope was so I wouldn't have to tell them until after we're married. I don't want my mother anywhere near Kate or our wedding!"

"You don't have to tell them or even invite them to the wedding if you don't want to – that's your choice. But you should talk to Kate about it and decide together." Ben said, shrugging. "I learned things like this from being married. Trust me." Charlie thought that over for a minute and then nodded to himself. The tension in his shoulders eased and he gave Ben a genuine smile.

"Okay, so if we end up having a wedding, will you be my best man?" Charlie asked, and Ben agreed. After lunch, they returned to Ben's office and filled out the paperwork to make Kate the beneficiary of the whole life insurance policy Charlie had purchased as a show of support for Ben when he joined Sinclair Insurance Agency. Charlie had been his very first client.

THREE

Charlie arrived at the Jenson home on Friday afternoon, knowing Kate was at work and Barb at school. He was relieved to see the patrol car parked in the driveway. Kent opened the door wearing his uniform and a questioning look.

"Charlie?"

"I know you need to leave for work pretty soon, but I'd like to talk to you first, please." Charlie said, in a rush.

"Sure." Kent said, ushering him past the wrought iron coat tree and into the living room. Charlie loved spending time in this house. Sunlight beamed through the picture window that offered a panoramic view of the front yard and the street beyond. The gleaming hardwood floor was partially covered by a faded rectangular area rug in shades of burgundy, cream and green. Bookshelves crammed with books, pictures and knick-knacks stood at one end of the room. Kent's hunter green recliner and Barb's sage glider chair and ottoman were separated by an end table. The overstuffed cream colored couch draped with a hand crocheted afghan sat on the other side of a square pine coffee table. The table often had a board game of some kind on its top; today it was covered with a half-finished jigsaw puzzle.

Kent took a seat in his recliner while Charlie sat opposite him, perched stiffly on the edge of the couch. He cleared his throat nervously.

"I want to marry Kate," he blurted. "And it would mean a lot to me if we had your blessing." Kent studied him.

"Of course you have my blessing, Charlie, and I know Barb will agree. We know you and Kate have been talking about getting married. But I thought you wanted to graduate first." He hesitated. "Is Kate pregnant?"

"Oh! No, sir, she isn't!" Charlie exclaimed. He should have known that an unplanned pregnancy would be the first reason for a sudden desire to get married. He ran his hand through his hair and tried to think how to explain. "Our family has a kind of unofficial timeline about getting married after college. A degree first, and then a big society wedding, you know, but, well…" He looked at the floor for a minute and then met Kent's eyes.

"I introduced Kate to my parents last weekend and as you probably already heard, it was a disaster."

"I heard. I'm sorry." Kent smiled in sympathy. He and Barb had agreed that the situation was none of their business and had vowed not to interfere.

"Obviously my mother isn't going to approve anyway, so waiting would just give her more time to try and break us up. I love Kate, and I want to marry her." Charlie said firmly. "As soon as possible."

"You don't have a job." Kent observed, mildly. Charlie flushed and looked out the window, his lips pressed into a straight line and his jaw tight.

"I graduate next spring and then I plan to sit for the CPA exam. I don't think I'll have any problem getting a job." He looked away from the window and met Kent's gaze. "And, uh, I have a trust fund."

"A trust fund." Kent repeated.

"Yes, sir. From my grandparents, so my mother has no control over my income. I'll get a disbursement when I'm twenty-five, but between now and then I get a quarterly allowance. Right now I'm using it for living expenses and school."

"I see." Kent said thoughtfully. "I've never met anyone with a trust fund before, Charlie, so I was curious how that works, but it isn't important to me. I try to judge a man by his character and not by his bank account." Kent smiled and extended his hand. "I will be proud to call you my son." Charlie let out the breath he didn't know he was holding as he reached out to shake Kent's hand.

◆ ◆ ◆

Charlie let himself into the stately two story house overlooking the golf course, feeling like a stranger though he had lived here for most of his life. The view was nice, and when he was younger, he had utilized the tennis courts and the pool, but those amenities would have been available to him anyway with his parents' country club membership. In his opinion, living on a golf course was extremely pretentious given that none of them played the game.

He glanced into the rooms he passed as he moved towards the stairs. He couldn't remember the last time the dining room with its mahogany table and twelve high backed chairs had been used. To Charlie, the table looked coldly formal with a basket of dried fall flowers in the middle flanked by a pair of burnt orange candles in silver candlesticks. Adjacent to the dining room, the kitchen sported all the latest appliances, uncluttered cream colored granite counters, pale birch cupboards, and a round glass topped table with bronze placemats and a display of small pumpkins and ornamental gourds. His mother used the coffee maker, but that was about it. He doubted anyone had eaten there all week, or would enjoy a meal there anytime soon.

In the formal living room across the hall, the only hint of color came from the peach colored walls and the pillows of the exact same color that adorned the couch. The carpet and draperies were pale gray; the upholstered furniture was white, and the mahogany end tables matched the spinet piano that nobody played.

The door to his father's study was closed. Beyond the study, under the curve of the stairs, was an enormous space called the family room, but it was a misnomer. Charlie used to wonder how a room could look so inviting and be so forbidding. One side of the room contained a pool table, a fully stocked bar, and a couple of high top tables and chairs. Chocolate brown leather couches, matching arm chairs and an oak entertainment center filled up the other side of the room. The furniture was luxurious, very comfortable, and brand new. Nobody ever sprawled there with their feet on the coffee table to watch the big screen television. One simply did not sprawl or put one's feet on the furniture in Amelia's house.

He took the curved stairs two at a time and went to his room, crossing over to the window and staring out at the street below thinking about his conversations with Ben and Kent, and planning how he would propose to Kate. A movement on the street below caught his eye. His dad's forest green sedan was turning into the driveway. Charlie glanced at his watch; it was not quite four o'clock, which seemed early for Huck to be home from the office. He stood, irresolute for several minutes. He loved his dad, and he knew that Huck loved him. When he opted for accounting over law as a career path, his mother had gone ballistic, but his dad had stood by him, quietly insisting that Charlie was entitled to make his own career choice. It was one of the few times he could remember his dad directly opposing his mother; usually he just worked around her. Huck had seemed to like Kate, but what would he say about Charlie's decision to marry her – before he graduated, and without a big wedding. Finally he lifted his chin, squared his shoulders and decided he would give it a try. He went back downstairs much slower than he had gone up, and walked across the hall to the door of the study, which stood open now.

"Charlie!" Huck exclaimed, turning from where he stood looking out over the golf course. He was tall and lean, like Charlie, with the same medium brown hair and chocolate brown eyes. "I saw your car outside. Mom has bridge club today."

"Yeah, I know."

"You must be home for the weekend?"

"I came to see Kate." Charlie said. Huck motioned Charlie towards one of the chairs in front of his desk while he lowered himself into the big black leather chair behind it and sat back comfortably. Charlie found himself on the edge of his seat for the second time that afternoon.

"I enjoyed meeting Kate, Charlie, and I'm sorry that your mom was, well, not very nice."

"What did you think of Kate?" Charlie asked, curiously, ignoring the comment about Amelia, mostly because he didn't know how to respond to it. It was unusual for his father to criticize his mother, even obliquely.

"I liked her." Huck said without hesitation. "She seems to have a good head on her shoulders, I think she loves you very much, and she's very pretty." Huck smiled.

"I'm going to ask her to marry me." Charlie hadn't planned to say that, or at least he hadn't planned to blurt it out, but then he hadn't expected his father to be at home. Nor had he expected an apology for his mother's behavior. Huck nodded but didn't reply, so Charlie plowed on.

"If I could choose, I'd elope this weekend, but if Kate wants a wedding I'll do that. Soon, I hope." He paused. "I'd rather Mother didn't know about any of this right now, and we might not invite her to the wedding." Huck sat motionless in his chair for several long moments before he spoke.

"Do you have a ring?" Charlie gaped at his father, disoriented by the question. He could not remember ever having an odder conversation with his dad. He had been expecting a mild admonishment for his comments about his mother along with a strong suggestion that he wait to marry until he was finished with college.

"Uh, no. I um, well, I thought we'd shop for rings together, so we can get something Kate likes." He stammered. Huck shifted forward in his chair, rested his elbows on the desk with his hands clasped under his chin and stared off into space deep in thought for a few moments before he appeared to come to a decision. Standing, he walked to the picture hanging on the wall behind his desk. It was a family photograph, taken several years ago at his parents' fortieth anniversary. The picture was memorable both because it commemorated a milestone and also because Amelia had actually attended the event and was included in the photograph. Normally, she avoided family gatherings and photos. Charlie watched as Huck swung the hinged picture to the side and twirled the dial of the combination lock on the wall safe until there was a soft click. Pulling the door open and reaching deep inside, he retrieved a maroon velvet drawstring pouch and returned to his chair.

"This is a family heirloom," he began, cradling the small pouch in his hand. "My grandfather gave it to Grandma Margaret, my dad gave it to my mom, and I gave it to your mother when I asked her to marry me." He smiled ruefully. "Grandma Margaret and my mom both wore it until their oldest son was ready to marry. But times change and everyone has different likes and dislikes. Amelia never really cared for it…" Huck fell silent, remembering Amelia's disappointment that the ring wasn't a large showy diamond. He should have paid more attention to that incident, but he had been blindly in love and so had ignored the warning. For perhaps the millionth time, he reminded himself that regardless of the state of his marriage, he had been blessed with two wonderful sons.

"Dad?" Charlie asked uncertainly as the silence stretched. Huck jerked his attention back to the present.

"Yes, well anyway, my first impression of Kate is that she might like it. If not, you can still go ahead with your plan to shop together for something she'll like better." As he and Amelia had done until they found the ostentatious diamond she wanted. He pushed that thought from his mind as he leaned forward and handed the velvet pouch to Charlie, who loosened the drawstring and reached inside. The ring was beautiful in its simplicity; the gold band had a lacy pattern etched around a single medium sized emerald cut stone in a blue that reminded him of Kate's eyes.

"Sapphire?" Charlie asked as he gazed at the ring, knowing instantly that it was perfect for Kate.

"Mined right here in Montana. Grandpa Charles bought the stone from a friend who mined it himself, and then had the ring designed especially for Grandma Margaret."

"Kate will love it, Dad! Thanks!" Charlie exclaimed. "I plan to ask her tonight." He stood and moved towards the hallway.

"Charlie?" Huck said softly. Charlie turned and waited. "If you and Kate decide to get married without us, I'll understand."

"Thanks, Dad." Charlie said soberly. After Charlie left, Huck walked to the window and gazed sightlessly at the golf course beyond the patio, his mind drifting back over the years. When he finally realized that Amelia didn't love him, though she enjoyed his family's social position, it broke his heart. Amelia's father was gone now, but he'd been a judge when Huck met Amelia, and Huck had assumed that they shared the same backgrounds and had similar goals. He had adjusted to the knowledge that Amelia had married him for reasons other than love, but he wasn't even sure she loved their children, or if she was capable of loving at all. For several years he wrestled with the question of whether or not to seek a divorce. As an attorney, he knew the odds were against him getting custody of the boys, and he wasn't willing to become a weekend father, so in the end he chose to stay married. With or without his wife, he spent time with Charlie and George, attending their activities, overseeing their homework, and trying to instill values and important life lessons. The rest of the time, he worked. Some called him a workaholic, and perhaps he was, but it helped him to stay sane and gave him a purpose.

For the most part, he and Amelia lived parallel lives and Huck was able to treat her with kindness and a modicum of affection reminiscent of the love he once felt for her. Occasionally, things could get quite tense between them. They had not spoken for several weeks when Charlie decided against becoming an attorney. Huck was not looking forward to the upheaval that would come over Charlie if he and Kate got married, but he would stand by his eldest son in this as he had done over his career choice. As always, he knew he would have the full support of his parents and his brother's family. Even so, he was not looking forward to the battle. He sighed and returned to his desk and the files he needed to review.

◆ ◆ ◆

Charlie had made dinner reservations at a small Italian restaurant because it was one of Kate's favorite places to eat, and also because he knew they would have the privacy to talk things over. He cast several sideways glances her way as he navigated the streets to their destination. She was unusually quiet and her hands were clenched in her lap. He needed to fix this, but not while he was driving.

They were seated immediately at a secluded table covered with a red and white checked tablecloth. The silverware gleamed in the glow from the fat red candle flickering in the middle of the table. One server delivered goblets of water and menus while another set a basket of warm breadsticks, butter, and a tray of antipasto on their table.

"We need to talk." Charlie began as soon as they were alone, but then he couldn't think where to begin and fell silent.

"Girls don't like to hear that phrase, Charlie. It usually doesn't end well." Kate said quietly, avoiding his gaze and struggling to keep her voice steady. She'd thought about Charlie and his parents all week. Amelia Whitcomb was the first person who had ever taken such an instant dislike to her, and she didn't quite know how to respond. It made her both sad and angry. Charlie hadn't mentioned it when he took her home after dinner, he hadn't called, and now she was beginning to wonder if he had decided that his mother was right and she wasn't good enough for his family. Surely if he was planning to break up with her, they wouldn't be out for a nice dinner at her favorite restaurant. At least she hoped not. Her hands twisted in her lap as she steeled herself to get through this meal and hear whatever Charlie had to say. She vowed not to cry, no matter what it was. As if Charlie could read her mind, he shook his head and quickly reached for her hand, entwining their fingers under the table.

"Nothing is wrong between us, Kate, at least not on my end. I'm just sorry my mother was her normal charming self last weekend." Charlie began. "I guess you can understand why I haven't introduced you to my parents before this. She upset you, didn't she?" Kate blinked at him in surprise. Whatever she had expected him to say, this wasn't it. She had been shocked by Amelia's attitude towards her, but Charlie didn't seem at all surprised.

"She didn't seem to like me very much." Kate ventured, uncertainly.

"I'm not sure she likes me very much either, so don't take it personally." Charlie said, grimly. "In fact, I can't think of anyone she actually likes, including my dad."

"Your dad seemed nice." Kate commented, still not sure how to have a conversation like this one.

"My dad is great. He's always been there for me and my brother, but he's a lot more reserved than your dad; harder to talk to." He paused, remembering the afternoon. "I did have a good talk with him this afternoon though, and he even apologized for my mother. He also said he liked you." They were interrupted by the waiter, ready to take their orders. Without a glance at the menu, Charlie opted for spaghetti. Kate had been so worried about her relationship with Charlie that she had barely eaten all week, and now that things seemed to be okay, her appetite had miraculously reappeared. She decided on lasagna, and both of them ordered salads.

"Will you marry me, Kate?" The words burst from him as soon as the waiter walked away. With a mental grimace, Charlie understood where the phrase 'pop the question' came from. He had planned his proposal to take place over dessert, and with a lot more finesse, including the romantic gesture of dropping to one knee. Kate momentarily looked startled and then she broke into a wide smile and squeezed his hand.

"Oh, Charlie! Of course I'll marry you!"

"I had a whole speech ready." Charlie said, ruefully, "I worked on it all the way home from Bozeman and now I can't remember a single word of it. I just know I love you. I want us to have a family and get old together."

"I think that's a great speech, Charlie. I love you too." Kate smiled again.

"What kind of wedding do you want?" When she hesitated, he coaxed. "Ben says weddings are important to women, so tell me what your ideal wedding would be."

"Won't your mother expect…" she began, but Charlie shook his head. "Never mind her; I want to know what you want." He insisted.

"I think I would like something small and meaningful, maybe an evening ceremony with family and close friends, and candles." Kate murmured hesitantly, and as soon as he heard the word 'meaningful' Charlie knew Ben had been right.

"Could it be soon?" Charlie asked eagerly. "Like maybe during Christmas vacation?"

"Next week is Thanksgiving Charlie! That would only give us a few weeks. I thought you wanted to graduate first." Kate was struggling to keep up with a conversation that had more unexpected twists and turns than a mountain road.

"I just want to marry you. The sooner the better and I don't want to invite my parents." Charlie asserted.

"Oh, Charlie!" Kate exclaimed. "Not invite your parents?"

"You saw what my mother is like, Kate. I talked to Dad about it today and he agrees. Crap! Where is my head? I almost forgot!" He pulled the velvet pouch from his pocket and handed it to her. As she loosened the drawstrings and took the ring out, Charlie watched her face, and knew immediately that he and his dad had been right; the ring was perfect.

"Oh, Charlie!" Kate breathed turning the ring in her fingers. "It's beautiful!" He took it from her and slipped it onto her finger, keeping her hand in his as he told her the history of the ring, including the fact that his mother had never worn it. He was actually glad that the ring hadn't been tainted by spending any time on his mother's finger, and while he had the thought he wondered if he should feel guilty for feeling that way. With a mental shrug, he decided that he didn't feel guilty at all.

At that moment, the waiter placed their food in front of them, and Charlie knew he would enjoy this meal a lot more than he would have if he had nervously waited to propose over dessert. By the time they finished their pasta, they had rudimentary wedding plans in place.

FOUR

Charlie spent Thanksgiving with Kate and her parents, both sets of her grandparents and her sister Julia, her husband and their two sons. It was a long-standing family tradition for each one to share something for which they were thankful over pumpkin pie. When it was her turn, Kate held up her left hand, flashed her ring, and announced their engagement. Charlie was already considered a member of the family and everyone was quick to congratulate the two young people.

During the next week, Kate and her mother got busy with wedding preparations. Within just a few days, they had reserved the church and the fellowship hall, ordered the flowers and the cake and arranged for a photographer. The ladies of the church volunteered to cater the reception.

Everything fell into place except finding a wedding dress, and that was starting to cause Kate to panic. She visited several bridal shops without finding a single dress that she liked. She was looking for inexpensively elegant when elaborately expensive seemed to be popular, she thought ruefully. Finally, she decided to enlist the help of her grandmothers, both of whom were skilled seamstresses. Grandma Vera had sewn several prom dresses for Kate when she was in high school.

Kate, Barb, and Barb's mother Vera met at Carol Jensen's house to compile a guest list and address invitations. As they worked at the kitchen table, Kate explained why Charlie's family wasn't on the rather short guest list.

"Charlie says his family isn't like ours. I met his parents, and his dad was really reserved, but seemed nice. His mother though, was, um, well, rude and condescending, is the best way to put it, I guess. I thought it was me she didn't like, but Charlie says she doesn't really like anybody, not even her own kids! He says she will probably do her best to cause trouble for us from now on, and we just don't need that on our wedding day."

"Life is never perfect." Grandma Vera commented. She was petite and slightly plump with vivid blue eyes, pink cheeks, strong opinions and a soft heart. She wore her snow white hair feathered around her heart-shaped face.

"I guess not." Kate agreed with a frown. "Charlie said if we tried to plan the wedding for after graduation, his mother would ruin the wedding and he would be distracted from classes this last semester. But to tell you the truth, it still bothers me that we're starting out with a rift between us and his mother."

"That isn't ideal, but you have to do what works for you and Charlie." Grandma Carol assured her. Five feet eight and still slender, she had thick silvery gray hair that she usually tied at the nape of her neck. Today with her hair up in a careless bun on top of her head, Carol radiated energy and confidence. She had an oval face and wide-set hazel eyes behind silver wire-rimmed glasses.

"I suppose some people will think I'm pregnant." Kate muttered. "But I'm not, so they can think whatever they want." When they finished the invitations, Carol served homemade vegetable soup and fresh rolls for lunch. Kate explained her fruitless search while they ate, and asked if it was possible to make a wedding gown in three weeks.

"I always hoped to wear your dress, Grandma, like Mom and Julia did." Kate lamented, smiling ruefully at Vera. "But I'm too tall!"

"You get your height from our side of the family." Carol Jensen agreed with a smile. Hesitantly, she added, "I still have my wedding gown."

"You do? Really?" Kate asked in surprise.

"I do, and you are welcome to try it on. If it isn't what you had in mind, or doesn't fit, it wouldn't be hard to make a gown if we can find suitable fabric, right Vera?" She looked across the table with raised eyebrows and Vera nodded her agreement. Kate wasn't paying attention, having zeroed in on the fact that she still had a chance to wear a family wedding gown.

"Can I see it?" She asked eagerly.

"Of course." Carol rose from the table and disappeared into the bedroom at the end of the hallway, returning with a large flat box. She placed it on the kitchen counter and stepped aside motioning for Kate to open it. Lifting the lid and peeling back several layers of tissue paper, Kate gazed down at a satin brocade gown the color of pale cream. Reverently removing it from the box, she held it up, gently shaking out the folds and then with sparkling eyes and a delighted smile, she hurried into the bathroom to try it on.

The gown was sleeveless with a high neck and a row of tiny fabric covered buttons down the back. Fitted through the waist and hips and gently flared from knees to floor, it fit Kate as if it had been designed especially for her.

"Oh, Grandma! It makes me feel beautiful!" Kate breathed as she reappeared in the kitchen and Barb stepped behind her to do up the buttons.

"It looks lovely on you. I'm glad you like it." Carol was so overwhelmed with emotion that she barely managed to keep her voice steady. She had sewn her wedding gown with some help from her mother and grandmother, but with only sons, had never considered passing it on.

"The right wedding dress is supposed to make you feel beautiful, dear, and that is definitely the right dress." Vera commented. "I wonder…" her voice trailed off and her blue eyes took on a faraway look.

"Are you thinking about the cape, Mom?" Barb asked. Vera nodded.

"Cape?" Kate asked.

"I think it would be perfect over that dress!" Vera replied.

"I do too!" Barb agreed. Turning to Kate, she explained their cryptic conversation. "Grandma's cape is made of midnight blue velvet. And it's lined, so it's nice and warm. I wore it once, to a winter formal. All the other girls were envious – and cold."

"Where did you get a cape, Grandma?" Kate asked.

"I made it." Vera smiled at the memory. "We were invited to a New Year's Dance the first year we were married, and of course I couldn't afford to buy something new to wear. I had a white lace blouse in my closet, so I made a long skirt out of blue velvet. I didn't want to wear my old winter parka so I decided to try and make a cape out of the velvet that was left." She smiled, remembering. "It turned out really well, and for the rest of the winter, capes were all the rage."

◆ ◆ ◆

On December twenty-eighth, Kent escorted Kate down the aisle of the church where she had been baptized and confirmed. She and Charlie exchanged plain gold wedding bands and repeated their vows in the glow of candlelight. Kate wore her Grandma Carol's dress and carried a bouquet of red roses, nestled amongst baby's breath and greenery. Kate's sister Julia served as matron of honor in a deep green floor length wool dress with a cowl neckline and long sleeves. She carried a bouquet of red and white carnations and greenery. The groom and his best man wore black tuxedos with white shirts and red rose boutonnieres in their lapels.

The six o'clock ceremony was attended by Kate's extended family and close friends, and Ben's parents and grandparents, whom

Charlie viewed as his surrogate family. The groom's family had not been invited, or indeed, even informed of the event.

The tables for the reception were covered in white tablecloths and graced with frosted evergreen boughs and red candles. A buffet supper of ham, turkey, scalloped potatoes, a variety of salads and warm dinner rolls was followed by a three tiered wedding cake and champagne toasts.

"Thanks for your good advice about having a wedding instead of eloping, Ben." Charlie said while everyone enjoyed wedding cake. "Where did you learn so much about women?"

"From Genny, and I have sisters, remember?" Ben grinned. "Three of them!"

When it was time to leave, Charlie settled Grandma Vera's midnight blue velvet cape around Kate's shoulders to keep her warm for the short drive to the honeymoon suite at the Holiday Inn where they were to spend the weekend.

◆ ◆ ◆

On New Year's Eve day, Charlie surprised Kate with reservations for a week at Chico Hot Springs. He chose Chico for several reasons. It was, first of all, historic, having been established as a resort in 1900 and Charlie knew that Kate loved Montana history. Chico was also close to Bozeman, and there were a few things he wanted to take care of, now that he was a married man.

In the middle of the week, Charlie suggested they drive to Bozeman for the day. The first place they went was to the bank where Charlie closed his accounts and transferred the money into new joint accounts in both their names. After lunch, they drove to the apartment he'd found for them, currently undergoing routine maintenance and updating including fresh paint, minor repairs and new carpets.

"It won't be ready until the first of February, but what do you think?" he asked eagerly. Kate loved everything about the partly furnished two bedroom space, midway between downtown and the MSU campus, and together they started a list of what they would need in the way of furniture. After strolling through the MSU campus, and touring Charlie's fraternity house, they ended the day at Ben and Genny's house for dinner.

"Have you told Charlie's parents?" Genny asked as she started making a salad to go with the roast beef that had just come out of the oven.

"No." Kate paused in the act of setting the table. "They left the day after Christmas to spend a month in Arizona. Charlie says he'll talk to them after they get back and see if they want to have a reception or something, maybe in the spring. Charlie's mother makes me very uncomfortable, to tell you the truth. We're going to stay at their house til Charlie goes back to school, and I'm even nervous about that. I hope I don't break anything!"

"I've met Charlie's mom." Genny said, frowning and shaking her head. She was five foot seven, like Kate, with shoulder-length dark blond hair and blue eyes. "She makes me uncomfortable too." She didn't say any more, but privately she doubted Charlie's mother would be at all happy to hear the news of their marriage. Much as her own mother irritated her sometimes, like when she had gotten carried away over the wedding, Genny was grateful that her parents and Ben's parents were loving and kind.

FIVE

On the tenth of February, Kent was at his desk in the police station trying to catch up on his share of the seemingly endless paperwork when his partner said they were wanted in the captain's office. He sighed. Nothing good ever came from a summons like that, he thought, as he stood up and moved into the hall. The captain looked up when they rapped on the open door, motioned them in and gestured towards the chairs in front of his desk.

"Bad news." He said grimly as they sat down. "We have a next of kin notification." He handed a slip of paper across his desk. Frank glanced at it, grimaced, and then handed it to Kent. Glancing down at the name and address, the blood froze in his veins and he heard a buzzing in his ears. Frank was half-way to the door when he realized Kent was still seated.

"Are you coming?" he asked impatiently. Everybody hated next of kin notifications, and Frank was no exception. He just wanted to get it over with. Kent sat as immobile as if he and the chair were carved from a single block of granite. Frank raised his eyebrows at the captain who was also watching Kent. Finally, Kent took a shuddering breath and spoke in an anguished whisper.

"Charlie -- Charles Whitcomb the fourth is -- was my son-in-law."

"Damn, Kent!" The captain apologized. "I didn't know! I'm sorry man, truly sorry." Frank retrieved a bottle of water from the little refrigerator in the corner and pressed it into Kent's hand, then laid a supportive hand on his shoulder.

"I'll get Crenshaw to go with me to see the Whitcomb family. Do you want someone to come home with you?"

"No, no. I'll be fine." Kent got to his feet feeling as if he'd aged fifty years in the last few minutes.

"You drive Kent home in his car and have Crenshaw pick you up there. Then you can go to the Whitcomb residence." The captain ordered. "Kent shouldn't drive right now."

◆ ◆ ◆

Barb was in the kitchen when she heard the front door open. She thought it was odd, because Kate had come in from her last day at work about ten minutes earlier to finish packing. Renovations on their apartment in Bozeman were finally completed nearly two weeks later than originally planned; she and Charlie planned to move over the weekend. Barb stepped to the doorway between the kitchen and living room to see who had come in. One glance at her husband and his partner standing grimly just inside the front door, and she knew they were the bearers of bad news.

"Where's Kate?" Kent asked in a somber voice, just as Kate emerged from the hallway on the other side of the room. She froze in her tracks, her glance skittering between her dad and his partner and her mother. And somehow, she knew.

"Charlie!" she whispered into the silence as the color drained from her face. Her mother rushed to her side and guided her to the couch, where her parents sat on either side of her and Kent explained as gently as he could that Charlie had been killed that afternoon in downtown Bozeman by an elderly man who had probably suffered either a heart attack or a stroke and sped through a red light, plowing into the driver's door of Charlie's car. The elderly man had also died at the scene. Kate sat motionless, staring blindly at the floor with her fingers clasped tightly in her lap. Frank squeezed

Kent's shoulder in silent sympathy and slipped out the door to go and notify Charlie's parents.

◆ ◆ ◆

Kate moved mechanically through the next few days like a robot. She wasn't hungry and couldn't sleep, and worse, she did not cry. She didn't feel sad, or angry, or horrified; she didn't feel any-thing, not anything at all.

When Kent offered to take Kate to the funeral, she stared at him for a long time before she said she guessed she should attend. Charlie had not told his parents about his marriage to Kate, and Kent understood his reasoning. But right now he was trying not to resent that omission because he thought it might have helped Kate gain some closure to be included in the funeral preparations. It was an odd situation to be in, and neither he nor Barb knew what to do.

Kate insisted they sit in the back of the church and slip out early, so they arrived only a few minutes before the services were to start. They had just hung their coats up when Amelia materialized in front of them, blocking their path. She was dressed completely in black, with flawless make-up and every blond hair in place, but her pale blue eyes were wild, her fists were clenched at her sides, and her whole body vibrated as if she could explode at any moment.

"You!" Amelia hissed. "Get out, you little gold-digger! You aren't welcome here!" Kent reacted instinctively, hugging Kate to his left side, while shifting his big frame protectively between her and a possible threat. Kate held fast to her father and gazed blankly in front of her as if she had heard nothing.

"I beg your pardon?" Kent said quietly, looking down at Amelia with his emotions masked behind his cop face. Hearing about Amelia Whitcomb had not prepared him for the reality of meeting her face to face. As they stood there with their eyes locked in silent combat, a young man strode towards them and firmly took Amelia's elbow. He was tall and slender with light brown hair, and Amelia's blue eyes.

"Mother. It's time to go in." He said quietly, casting a curious glance towards the two of them as he tugged Amelia firmly into the sanctuary. Amelia tossed a final threatening glare at them over her shoulder. The young man must be Charlie's brother Kent thought, but he had never met him and couldn't remember his name.

"Let's just go home, Dad." Kate said, wearily, and without protest, he helped her back into her coat and led her to the car, completely understanding at last, why Charlie had not invited his own mother to his wedding. He would bet money that she was mentally ill.

◆ ◆ ◆

Being kicked out of the funeral had broken through the numbness and plunged Kate into a sea of grief. Some days she dragged herself out of bed, but on other days she couldn't seem to make the effort and spent hours lying in bed staring blindly at the ceiling. She told her parents she was fine, but they all knew she wasn't fine.

She had become a widow forty-four days after becoming a wife. When she could think, her mind swirled with questions. She didn't know if she should continue to wear her wedding rings, and if so, on which hand – left or right? Maybe she should put them on a chain and wear them around her neck out of sight, but still close to her heart. Did the Whitcomb family engagement ring even belong to her? She didn't know. She also didn't know if she wanted to be Kate Whitcomb or go back to being Kate Jensen. What was legal? What was right? What should she do with the wedding gifts packed in boxes and stacked in the garage? Should she try to get another job or go back to the one she quit to move to Bozeman? Should she go to college? Between pondering the questions chasing each other around the inside of her head, she zoned out for long periods of time with her mind completely blank, sometimes coming back to an awareness of her surroundings as if waking from a drugged sleep.

She knew that both her parents were worried about her. The purple smudges under her eyes proved that she wasn't sleeping, and she was losing weight because even when she did manage to swallow a few bites of food, she couldn't keep anything in her stomach. One evening she passed out as she stood up from the kitchen table and Kent only just managed to catch her before she hit the floor.

"That's it!" he exclaimed in alarm. "You need to see a doctor!" Barb agreed and ignoring Kate's objections made the appointment and accompanied her to the clinic for a complete physical that same week. As she sat in the waiting room, Barb admitted to herself that although she usually preferred natural remedies to taking prescription medications, she was desperate enough to try whatever the doctor thought would help Kate; sleeping pills perhaps or maybe something for nausea. Neither she, nor anyone she knew had been to see a psychologist, but she wondered if they should check into grief counseling. What she hadn't expected, was that Kate needed prenatal vitamins.

◆ ◆ ◆

The knowledge that she was pregnant was a lifeline that Kate clung to as she was tossed about on the waves of her grief. Like the flicker of a lighthouse in the vast darkness of a storm at sea, the life she carried within her gave her something to focus on; she had Charlie's child to protect and nurture.

Kate didn't know if the soda crackers and dry toast helped her deal with the morning sickness or if it ceased on its own. Meditation before bed sometimes allowed her to sleep without having nightmares about the day Charlie died. As the weeks of her pregnancy passed, she struggled to regain her equilibrium, at first second by second, and then minute by minute.

Kent and Barb insisted she stay with them, and she agreed because she knew she couldn't survive without their support until she could put her life back together. But she vowed that living with them would be temporary. She would establish her own home as soon as she could so she wouldn't become a burden. As the weeks turned into months, she started to formulate a plan for her life. The plan included finishing her education, establishing her own home and becoming the best single mom in history.

◆ ◆ ◆

It was late April when Ben called and said that he was in town visiting his parents, and asked if he and Genny could stop by that evening. Kate assumed it was a social call, but when they were seated in the living room, Ben said he had some business to discuss with her. Then he explained about Charlie making Kate the beneficiary to his life insurance policy. When he had finished recounting the details of Charlie's visit to his office just before he'd proposed to Kate, she and her parents sat in stunned silence.

"Oh my God!" Kate exclaimed when she found her voice. "When his mother finds out, she'll try to have me thrown in jail."

"Why do you say that?" Genny asked, and Kate explained what had happened at the funeral.

"She called me a gold-digger!" Kate exclaimed.

"I've always thought there was something wrong with Amelia, like maybe she has some kind of mental illness, you know? But maybe I just never met anyone who was so callous and self-centered." Genny shrugged.

"I doubt Charlie's family knew about this policy and even if they did, he specifically designated you as the beneficiary, so there isn't anything they could do about it. The money is yours." Ben assured her. "Fifty thousand dollars will go a long ways towards paying for college, don't you think?" Kate admitted to herself that it would also pay for the expenses of her pregnancy, but she didn't want to share that news just yet.

As they prepared to leave, Ben took both her hands. "The happiest I ever saw Charlie was after he met you. You were the center of his world, and that makes you part of our family – Genny's and mine. We'll be staying in touch."

"Yes we will." Genny agreed. "And we want you to have this." She handed Kate a manila envelope and gave her a warm hug. Later that evening in the privacy of her room, Kate paged through the small photo album she found inside the envelope, poring over school pictures of Charlie as a middle schooler with braces and Charlie as a varsity football player. His high school graduation picture was there, as were several candid shots with Ben; floating the river, sitting around a campfire, and one of each of them as the best man for the other's wedding. The last picture in the album was of Charlie and Kate holding hands and smiling as they walked down the aisle after their vows. At last, Kate cried.

◆ ◆ ◆

As she straightened her room the following week, Kate found a stack of junk mail that had fallen down between the dresser and the wall. There were several catalogs and a padded envelope from a bank in Bozeman. Puzzled, she opened the envelope and found two boxes of checks for the joint checking account Charlie had set up.

Suddenly the memories of the day she and Charlie had spent in Bozeman came flooding back. Memories of Charlie opening joint bank accounts and making sure the new checks would be mailed to her parent's address. He had planned to change the address for bank statements when they moved into their new apartment. She remembered Charlie explaining earnestly that everything he had was now hers. As she stared at the checks with both their names on them, it occurred to her that she had no idea how much money was in those accounts. She picked up the phone to find out.

Once she had answered all the security questions, a conversation with one of the bank officers assured her that the bank statements which had been returned from the fraternity house would be sent to her right away. She was glad she was sitting down when he told her the account balances. Between what she had in her own savings account, the life insurance proceeds, and Charlie's accounts, she had over a hundred thousand dollars. It was as if Charlie was watching out for her, and for their unborn child.

SIX

Karly Barbara Whitcomb came into the world early in October, arriving with a mellow disposition, her mother's heart-shaped face and dark hair and her dad's chocolate brown eyes and dimples. Kate started attending college the following January and by the time her daughter was eighteen months old; Kate had accumulated enough credits to be a sophomore and had decided it was time to enroll as a full time student. She contemplated whether to continue going to school in Billings, or transfer to Montana State University in Bozeman. She discussed it with Genny via e-mail and phone calls, finally deciding the time had come to move out on her own.

"Come and spend a few days with us." Genny had urged, and in the middle of May, Kate packed a bag for herself, three bags for Karly, and headed for Bozeman.

"This is it, baby girl, the first step to being on our own, and we are going to be just fine." Kate said bravely, as she checked on Karly in the rear view mirror. At that moment, the toddler was trying to untie her shoes and paying absolutely no attention to her mother.

Genny insisted on keeping Karly while Kate spent a morning completing enrollment paperwork, paying fees, and talking to an advisor about her classes. Then she browsed the bookstores and familiarized herself with the buildings where her classes would be held.

"The biggest thing on my list is finding a place to live!" Kate sighed.

"I want you to meet my friend Amanda." Genny replied. "In fact, we are invited to her house for lunch tomorrow." She refused to divulge any details about Amanda other than the fact that she was also a single parent, so Kate was quite curious by the time they knocked on the door of a modest ranch style house in a newer subdivision not too far from the campus. Clumps of brightly colored tulips and daffodils bloomed gaily in the flowerbeds on either side of the porch, and there was an older model white van with a car seat, parked in front of the two stall garage.

Amanda met them at the door wearing faded blue jeans, a white MSU sweatshirt and a shy smile. At five foot nine, she stood two inches taller than Kate and Genny. She was slender with short, naturally curly blond hair, a sprinkle of freckles across her nose, and green eyes. She ushered them through the entry and down a short hallway to a large kitchen where light streamed through sliding glass doors leading onto a deck at the edge of a fenced back yard. The room had creamy walls, oak cabinets, wood floors, and a curved built in breakfast nook upholstered in a medium sage that matched the curtains.

The child staring wide-eyed at them from her place at the table, was a miniature of her mother with green eyes, freckles, and blond curls. Kate helped Karly crawl up onto the bench that curved around the oak table and Amanda introduced the two toddlers, mentioning that Madison was one month older than Karly. Karly immediately started jabbering while she nibbled at a toddler lunch of cheese sticks, goldfish crackers, grapes, and strawberries. Madison didn't make a sound, but her eyes were bright with interest as she ate her own lunch and watched every move Karly made.

Amanda served spinach and Swiss cheese quiche and a fresh fruit salad with croissants to the grown up women. The three chatted amiably while keeping an eye on the children. When the lunch things were cleared away and the children were down for a nap, Madison in her room and Karly in another bedroom, Amanda asked Kate about her plans for attending college.

"I've signed all the papers, talked to an advisor and pre-regis-tered for classes in the fall." Kate smiled. "I left the toughest part for last -- finding a place to live. I've never lived anywhere but with my parents, so that should be interesting! I want to find a place now so Karly and I can get settled before classes start in September, and I need to look for a good daycare provider."

"I might be able to help you with all of that." Amanda sug-gested, tentatively. Kate raised her eyebrows in surprise.

"Really? How?"

"Genny wanted us to meet because I'm looking for a roommate to share expenses and child care...." Kate stared at her and then shifted her gaze to Genny who had a 'cat who ate the canary' grin. She looked back at Amanda and grinned.

"I am definitely interested!" She exclaimed. "What did you have in mind?" By the time the two little girls woke from their nap, Amanda and Kate had worked out the financial details and set a date for Kate to move in.

◆ ◆ ◆

"That was quick!" Barb exclaimed when she heard that Kate planned to move to Bozeman in the next three weeks.

"I know! Everything just fell into place, thanks to Genny!" Kate agreed. "I hit it off right away with Amanda and the rent she is ask-ing is way less than what an apartment would cost! I think I'll have enough money to be a full-time student for the three years it should take to get my degree, and still have some money left."

"It's a three bedroom house?" Barb asked.

"Yes. We're going to put the two little girls in the master bed-room because it is big enough for their cribs and everything else toddlers seem to need. It has two closets and room for their toys, and there is a master bathroom with a tub. Each of us will have one of the other bedrooms. They are ten by twelve with a bathroom between them. The rest of the house is already furnished, so I won't have to buy furniture. Oh, and Amanda has been using the dining room as an office, and she said I can put a desk in there so I have study space."

"What's the rest of the house like?" Barb asked. She was already missing Kate and Karly but also pleased to see Kate so enthusiastic about the next phase of her life.

"The living room has an oak entertainment center with a television set and video equipment. There is a mostly green couch and love seat, a tan recliner, end tables and lamps. It was all really plain, but totally functional. The kitchen has a built in breakfast nook and sliding glass doors into the back yard, which is fenced. It has a sand-box and a small patio area. Oh, and there is also a two car garage, so I can park inside. It's perfect!"

"Tell me about Amanda and her little girl."

"Amanda is a little taller than me and has short, naturally curly blond hair, freckles, and green eyes. Madison looks just like her — she's adorable. She just stared while Karly jabbered at her. She prob-ably didn't know what to think!" Kate paused. "I asked Genny how Amanda ended up as a single mother, but she said that's Amanda's story to tell whenever she's ready. Genny hates gossip, you know, but she's been friends with Amanda for a couple of years, and I trust her judgment." Kate paused and again and then said, thoughtfully. "Sometimes Amanda gets a really sad look in her eyes, Mom." Barb didn't say anything, but she was thinking that sometimes Kate got a really sad look in her eyes too.

◆ ◆ ◆

It was a surprise to Amanda when, expecting Kate and Karly, she opened the door and several members of Kate's family trouped in. Kate introduced everyone as she explained their plan. Kate's two grandmothers, Vera and Carol carried tote bags filled with children's books, art supplies, and games. Her grandfathers, Ron and Mike brought in sacks of groceries which they deposited on the kitchen counter.

"Vera and I will take care of meals and coffee breaks." Carol explained.

"And keep the little ones occupied," Vera added, cheerfully, "while the rest of you paint."

"Uh, okay." Amanda blinked. Within just a few minutes, the men were moving furniture from the bedrooms to the living and dining rooms while Barb, Kate and Amanda started taping around windows and doors. By mid-morning, when Vera announced a coffee break, they were ready to start painting.

"How do you like your Chevy van?" Mike asked Amanda while sipping his coffee. "It's a seventy-eight isn't it?"

"Yes, and even though it's getting old, I love it. At least, most of the time, I do." Amanda replied. At Mike's quizzical look, she elaborated. "Right now it must be due for a tune-up or something. It's getting hard to start and sometimes makes odd noises."

"I could take a look." Mike said, his eyes lighting up. "I assure you I am a better mechanic than a painter! With any luck, I can stay busy until the painting is done!" Everyone laughed, and then Kate encouraged Amanda to hand over her keys and Mike went to get his tools out of his pickup.

Kent retrieved the paint trays, rollers and brushes they brought with them from home and then took a can of pale peach to Kate's new room, while Ron started in Amanda's room with something called mellow moonbeam. Ron thought mellow moonbeam looked like off-white, but he wasn't a decorator.

Barb and Kate took the can labeled 'princess pink' to the children's room. Amanda followed them, distracted by the situation with her van, hoping that Mike could fix it, while at the same time wondering if she was wise to trust him with her only transportation.

She remembered buying the van from one of her high school friends when his parents bought him a new pickup for graduation. Originally, it was a good price and she needed transportation. Then her life fell apart and the van had turned out to be a multi-purpose vehicle; she had lived in it for the three weeks it took her to find an apartment after her parents kicked her out of their house. Now it was her personal vehicle and she also used it for her cleaning business. She couldn't really afford to replace it. With an effort, she pulled her mind back to the task at hand.

"I wondered about so much pink," Barb was saying," but with the white trim, white mini-blinds and closet doors, and hardwood floors, it isn't overpowering, at all."

"In Karly's opinion, you couldn't have too much pink, and I'll bet Madison feels the same way!" Kate laughed. Amanda noticed that Kate's family seemed to laugh a lot. By lunchtime, all three bedrooms had their first coat of paint and Mike had installed a new starter in Amanda's van, changed the oil and given it a tune-up.

"Purrs like a kitten!" He assured her as they sat at the picnic table in the back yard. Carol and Vera put a platter of ham and turkey sandwiches, a tray of fresh vegetables and a macaroni salad on the picnic table and handed out paper plates, silverware and beverages. Karly and Madison, who had already eaten, sat in the sandbox filling and emptying buckets and jabbering like old friends, Madison having apparently found her voice at last.

"You don't happen to have any other little maintenance jobs around here, do you?" Mike asked hopefully as he finished his ham sandwich and reached for another, turkey this time. "Besides painting, I mean."

"The gate between the back yard and the driveway needs a new latch and there is a loose board on the deck." Carol told him, before Amanda could respond. "I hope you don't mind, dear, but in all honesty, he is extremely messy with paint. And he whines." This last pronouncement was delivered in a stage whisper and accompanied by a wink. Amanda chuckled involuntarily. After a moment's thought, she added a dripping bathroom faucet and a loose door knob on the hall closet to Mike's list. He finished his handy-man chores by mid-afternoon, at about the same time the painters finished the second coat on all three rooms and the toddlers awoke from their naps. Amanda marveled that the two grandmas had convinced the children to take their naps on make-shift beds of folded blankets on the floor of the office. Normally, Madison was pretty particular about where she would sleep. But then, normally, she didn't have all this activity and someone her own size to play with.

Everyone enjoyed peanut butter cookies still warm from the oven at their afternoon coffee break, and then Mike put Karly's crib and Kate's bed together and everyone helped move the furniture into the freshly painted rooms, and Kate's desk and a set of shelves into the dining room.

When the furniture had been moved and the boxes of Kate's other belongings placed in her room, they enjoyed spaghetti, breadsticks and a tossed salad in the kitchen, where the refrigerator and the sliding glass doors were adorned with art work done by the children that afternoon.

"Are you a college student too?" Kent asked.

"No." Amanda replied with a hesitant smile. "I take adult education classes when I'm interested in a particular subject, but otherwise I'm not much of a student."

"What kinds of subjects are you interested in?" Vera wanted to know.

"I took classes in child development so I could be a better parent, and basic bookkeeping to learn how to keep track of expenses for my cleaning business." She wasn't sure why she told them all of that when she usually went out of her way to avoid explaining herself or any part of her life to anyone.

"Do you clean businesses or homes?" Barb asked curiously.

"Right now I just clean businesses because I can do it after Madison is in bed. My neighbor comes over to babysit and I work from eight p.m. til one in the morning. Once she's in school, I'm hoping to expand and maybe even hire employees." It was the first time Amanda had spoken to anyone about that part of her business plan, but Kate's family accepted her comments without judgment and seemed to follow her logic. Talk soon moved on to other subjects. When the dishes were done and the kitchen tidied, Kate's family picked up their things and in a flurry of good-bye hugs, they were gone.

SEVEN

"Wow." Amanda said, standing in the middle of the living room looking dazed. When Kate raised her eyebrows, she gestured down the hall towards the bedrooms. "Your family…three rooms…my van…household repairs…" She shook her head and dropped onto the couch. "Just, wow."

"I guess they can be a little overwhelming," Kate began, uncertainly, "They mean well."

"Oh! I think they are wonderful!" Amanda assured her. "I've just never seen anything like it. My family…." Her voice trailed off and she just shook her head.

"You family isn't like that?" Kate prompted.

"Not even close!" Amanda asserted emphatically. Kate, not knowing quite what to say, said nothing. Amanda studied her in silence for a few minutes before she spoke again. "So how much did Genny tell you about me?" She asked, finally.

"She told me the two of us had a lot in common because we were both young, single mothers, and she thought we might hit it off."

"That's it?" Amanda asked in surprise.

"That's it." Kate shrugged. "Then you had us over for lunch and we did hit it off."

"Are you serious? Genny didn't tell you anything about my background?" Amanda was incredulous.

"Genny doesn't gossip. Ever. When I asked if she could tell me anything else, she said everybody should have the privilege of telling their own story."

"So you moved in here without knowing anything else about me?" Amanda asked, astounded.

"Well, I know you are Genny's friend, and I trust her judgment, so yeah." Kate said, simply.

"Wow again." Amanda said. She was silent for several moments and then she shook her head.

"What?" Kate asked.

"Genny didn't tell me anything about you either, except that you were a single mom moving to Bozeman to go to school. You told me a little, so I know your husband died, but, I guess we should talk, huh?"

"I guess so." Kate agreed, and to get it over with, she went first, explaining about meeting Charlie, their marriage, the accident, and Karly. When she finished, she sat back expectantly and waited for Amanda to tell her story. She could tell that Amanda didn't like to talk about her past. The silence stretched for several moments and then Amanda began.

"I met Dan when he spent a month training a new manager at the hotel where I worked. He was six years older than me, tall and blond. We dated while he was in Three Forks, and then we had a long distance relationship for over a year. I thought I knew him." She paused, remembering how they had talked on the phone every night and spent most weekends together. Her eyes burned, remembering how happy she had been. She blinked back the threat of tears, cleared her throat and took a deep breath before she went on.

"When I found out I was pregnant, he asked me to marry me, and I said yes. We'd been talking about getting married anyway, but he said he wanted to wait until he started his new job at the first of the year, and I wanted to wait til after the baby came so I would look nice in my wedding dress. You know, for the pictures." She made a face. "I'm not vain or anything, of course."

"Everyone wants to look nice in their wedding pictures." Kate said softly.

"So we bought this house and started getting furniture and settling in. He went to all except two of my pre-natal checkups, helped get the nursery ready, and was in the delivery room when Madison was born. He was so proud and I thought he was going to be a wonderful father." Her voice trailed off. Kate sat quietly and after a moment, Amanda continued her story.

"Madison was three months old when he just didn't show up as expected one Thursday night. I didn't know what to do. It was the worst three days of my life."

"Oh, Amanda. What happened?"

"On Monday, Genny came over with the newspaper where she'd seen a notice about his death. He died of an aneurism." Amanda said tonelessly staring at her clenched fists. "I remember thinking I was glad I'd introduced him to Ben and Genny because otherwise I might never have known. I don't get the paper, and we hadn't made many other friends yet because he was gone so much and we were focused on each other and getting ready for the baby."

"I'm so sorry!"

"According to the paper, he was from Spokane, and he was already married." Amanda said tonelessly.

"Married?" Kate repeated.

"Married. And I never suspected a thing!" She shook her head in self-disgust and plowed on, wanting to get it all out. "I ended up with this house because he bought mortgage protection insurance." Kate stared at her, trying to make sense of the situation she described.

"He had to have been in the middle of a divorce." Kate finally said, thoughtfully. "It's the only thing that makes sense – his actions indicate that he was committed to you and Madison."

"Ben and Genny said the same thing. But he wasn't exactly honest with me, was he? We've all heard of men with professions like salesman and driving trucks, who get away with bigamy for years before anyone finds out." Amanda said, wearily. Kate couldn't refute that statement and the two young women sat in silence for several moments, before Kate tried to change the subject.

"Where do your parents live now?"

"In Three Forks where they've always lived, but I haven't seen them or talked to them since they kicked me out of their house. My dad said I was a disgrace to the family because I was pregnant and not married."

"Kicked you out? But, where did you go?"

"Dan was working out of town, so I put all my stuff in my van and lived in it." At Kate's shocked look, she added. "It was no big deal. I took showers at the 'Y' and ate a lot of sandwiches. One of the girls at work needed a roommate and I moved in with her until Dan got back. I didn't want to tell him over the phone, you know?"

"I just can't imagine…." Kate's voice trailed off. The idea that parents wouldn't want their own child and grandchild was completely foreign to Kate and she had no words. Nor could she imagine being homeless.

"To be honest, I'm not sure my parents ever wanted me all that much. I was one of those accidental pregnancies, late in life." Amanda shrugged as if it didn't matter. "As for Dan's parents, I don't know anything about them, but I doubt they would be interested in his love child, so…I'm on my own." Amanda shrugged again.

"Well, I guess we have that in common." Kate commented.

"Karly isn't a love child – you and Charlie were married. And your family is supportive of you!" Amanda protested.

"But Charlie's mother hates me. Charlie was convinced she would cause us nothing but problems, so we got married without telling his parents or even inviting them to the wedding."

"Were you ever going to tell them?" Amanda asked.

"Yeah, after Charlie graduated, but then he was killed, and as far as I know, they don't know we got married and they don't know about Karly. My mom believes I have a moral obligation to tell Amelia and Huck that they are grandparents. Mom wasn't there when Amelia kicked Dad and me out of Charlie's funeral. No child needs a grandmother like that!"

"Dan's name is on Madison's birth certificate, but last year I went to an attorney and changed her name to match mine." Amanda said, softly.

"I thought about taking my maiden name back, I really did." Kate said. "But I decided that wouldn't be the right way to honor Charlie's memory. So I kept his name, and I wear my wedding ring."

"I bet you still miss him."

"I miss him like crazy. I keep thinking time will help…" She shrugged. "My first priority now is Karly, and one of the reasons I wanted to move away from Billings was to put a little more distance between us and Charlie's mother, just in case."

"I've been worrying about how to explain Dan to Madison when she asks." Amanda said glumly.

"I have some pictures and the obituary in a little scrapbook for Karly. I'm not looking forward to it. I'm sure it won't be easy." Kate replied.

SEVEN

Within a few weeks, Kate and Amanda had established routines and responsibilities, and discovered that they got along quite well. Amanda was a little surprised by the level of interaction between Kate and the girls. She held impromptu picnics in the back yard or at one of the nearby city parks, she played board games and card games, helped with art projects, built forts in the living room, and sometimes she even played in the sandbox. At first Madison watched most of these activities from the sidelines, but soon she was joining right in, becoming more verbal and less shy as the days slipped by. Amanda wanted to be a better parent so Madison would have a better childhood than the one she'd had. Between the painting party and her observations of Kate's parenting, she thought that she could learn a lot from Kate and her family, and she began to join in the activities Kate planned.

◆ ◆ ◆

Amanda tried not to envy the frequent phone calls Kate shared with members of her family. She talked to her parents several times a week and to her sister several times a month, but she also regularly talked to both her grandmothers, who nearly always passed the phone to her grandfathers during their chats. On a Sunday afternoon early in August, the two young women were sitting on the patio supervising their children at play in the sandbox when they heard the phone ring.

"It's probably for you." Amanda smiled. "I'll watch the girls." Kate waved her thanks as she went into the kitchen to answer the phone. When she returned, she had a question.

"Do you mind if my family comes next weekend?"

"Of course not, I'd love to see them." Amanda replied promptly. "What's the occasion?"

"My birthday." Kate replied. "That was Grandma Vera. She said they haven't wanted to bother us while we got settled, but if we don't have anything else going on, they will bring dinner and cake and everything we need and do a party for me."

"Isn't that sweet?" Amanda exclaimed. "It sounds fun."

"When is your birthday?" Kate asked curiously. Amanda hesitated, looking uncomfortable.

"Um. It was last week." She said, finally. Kate stared at her.

"Why didn't you say something?"

"It isn't that big a deal." Amanda shrugged.

"Oh that's where you are wrong, my friend! Birthdays are a huge deal!" Kate exclaimed. She stood up and moved back towards the kitchen.

"What are you doing?" Amanda asked suspiciously.

"I'm calling Grandma back and telling her to make that a party for two!" Kate grinned.

And what a party it was. As they had done on painting day, Kate's parents and grandparents arrived with tote bags and sacks of groceries. They brought burgers and hot dogs to grill, buns and condiments, a potato salad, a fruit plate, and two cakes; the chocolate one had coconut pecan frosting and the angel food was to be served with raspberries and whipped cream. They also brought red, yellow and blue crepe paper, a bag of balloons and a birthday banner.

"All the party decorations are 'Back to School', but we thought the little girls would enjoy that!" Grandma Vera announced. While the women taped up crepe paper streamers, the men blew up balloons and tied them into clusters with pieces of red ribbon. The original idea was to attach them to the 'Happy Birthday' banner, but Karly and Madison had so much fun playing with them that they just let that happen. The tote bags also held party hats, games and prizes.

Everyone played Pin the Tail on the Donkey, London Bridge, and Duck, Duck, Goose while the meat sizzled on the grill. The prizes were pre-school flash cards for colors, shapes, numbers and letters.

"Not exactly adult games, but the girls loved it!" Barb chuckled as they settled down to eat. The paper plates and matching napkins were decorated with letters of the alphabet, books, and pencils. Afterwards the two Grandpas went out to the pickup and brought in gift bags for Kate and Amanda.

"Oh!" Amanda said in surprise, "I wasn't expecting…"

"Open it dear, it isn't anything fancy." Grandma Carol assured her. But Amanda, who could not remember ever having a birthday party, thought it was pretty fancy indeed. From the grandparents, there was a hand sewn velour robe with matching slippers; Kate's in lavender and Amanda's in pale green. Kate's parents gave each of them a card with a fifty dollar bill inside, and the admonition to buy something special. Kate jumped up to give everyone a thank you hug, while Amanda sat on the couch with her gifts on her lap fighting back tears. Vera and Carol sat down on either side of her, one patting her hand and one patting her shoulder.

"Thank you both so much." Amanda whispered. "I don't know what to say."

"You are very welcome, Amanda." Vera said softly. "You are one of ours now."

"We've adopted you dear, like it or not." Carol added so only Amanda could hear. And then it was time for cake, or where the little girls were concerned, bowls of raspberries with whipped cream. Amanda managed to thank everyone more properly when they left for their drive back to Billings.

"Your family is amazing!" Amanda exclaimed. "Did you tell them about my parents?"

"Not exactly." Kate said. "I'm trying to take a page out of Genny's book and refrain from gossip. So when they asked about your family I just said that you weren't close. And you already knew that I told them you didn't usually celebrate your birthday."

"Well, thank you for sharing your party with me -- it was fun." Amanda smiled.

"Glad you liked it – fair warning -- they will probably be back for Madison's second birthday next month." Kate was right. There were telephone consultations about who was going to do what, as Kate's family didn't want to overshadow what Amanda had planned. Amanda prepared Madison's favorite meal of macaroni and cheese with a veggie tray and a fruit plate. There was strawberry ice cream and chocolate cupcakes with pink frosting and sprinkles for dessert. Kent and Barb brought a meat and cheese tray and buns for the adults.

The great-grandmas arrived with gift bags for each of the girls. Each one contained a pink and white princess dress, white ballet slippers, and a sparkly princess tiara. Everyone participated in a rousing game of Pin the Tiara on the Princess. Afterwards, still giggling, the girls glued faux jewels and decals on small wooden jewelry boxes already adorned with their names. After dinner, they pasted stickers mostly where they were supposed to go on the pages of their new princess sticker books.

"This is what we've been doing for Karly." Barb explained as she handed Amanda an envelope containing money. "You can use it for something she needs, or put it in a savings account."

"I have a college fund for her. She certainly doesn't need anything else after such a wonderful party!" Amanda assured her. "I can't thank you enough!"

A similar scenario unfolded in mid-October for Karly's second birthday, but with a ballerina theme, which included pink leotards and tutus, white tights and sparkly pink ballet slippers. They cleared a space in the living room so that everyone could dance with more enthusiasm than skill, created necklaces and bracelets with beads on elastic string, and enjoyed spaghetti with tiny little meatballs. They had chocolate ice cream and confetti cupcakes for dessert.

"My goodness, I think I am partied out!" Amanda exclaimed as she sprawled on the couch. Kate's family had gone and the girls were finally bathed, settled down, and tucked into bed. Kate shook her head.

"Nope!" Kate laughed. "This is just the beginning. My family believes that life has enough problems so we celebrate at every opportunity! Halloween is right around the corner, then Thanksgiving and Christmas. It's party season!"

Sure enough, ten days later, a package from Billings came in the mail addressed to Karly and Madison. Kate opened a large envelope from Barb & Kent while Amanda set the box on the floor and called the girls to explore its contents. The two hand sewn costumes in the box looked like footed pajamas. The first one, in soft white fleece had a large bushy pom-pom for a tail and a matching hat with floppy bunny ears. The second one, also in soft fleece, had tiger stripes, a longer tail, and a striped hat with pointed tiger ears. With squeals of delight, and some help from their moms, Karly and Madison put on their new costumes and cavorted around the living room giggling. When some of the excitement had worn off, Kate retrieved the envelope and gave them the picture books, one about bunnies and the other about tigers.

"Mom and Grandma always made my costumes for Halloween." Kate remembered. "Guess they haven't lost their touch!" Amanda kept her eyes on the girls and did not share the information that the only costumes she'd worn were those she invented for herself, using items she found at the thrift store. That evening, the two mothers encouraged their daughters to draw pictures to send as a thank-you.

EIGHT

Amanda accepted an invitation to Billings to spend Thanksgiving with Kate's family. There she met Kate's sister and her family and was glad to connect faces with the names of people she had heard so much about. Julia was five foot two with a heart-shaped face, blue eyes, and thick dark brown hair like her mother. Her husband Jim towered over her at an even six feet. He was lean and muscular with brown eyes, dark blond hair and an easy smile. At ten and twelve, both of their sons resembled their dad, with blond hair and brown eyes. Scotty was already nearly as tall as his mother and Seth wasn't far behind.

While Kent led the men and his grandsons outside to show them the basketball hoop he had just put up, the two grandmas presented the little girls with a family of pilgrim dolls, including a ten inch father, a nine inch mother, and a six inch brother and sister, all made of sturdy laminated cardboard.

"Oh my goodness!" Kate exclaimed. "Where did you get them? Look at the detail on their faces."

"Grandpa Ron made them at the print shop. He had some advertising graphics that he enlarged and transferred onto white cardboard and then laminated them." Vera explained.

"Then he made bases so they can stand up, and Grandma Carol and I glued velcro to the bodies and made the clothes out of felt so they stick. We had a lot of fun doing it."

"I don't think paper dolls are very popular anymore," Barb commented, "But I remember playing with them for hours." The girls didn't seem to care if paper dolls were currently popular or not; playing with the pilgrim family was their favorite activity throughout the entire weekend and on Sunday, the little family tucked neatly into a log cabin shaped tote bag for the trip home to Bozeman.

The weekend was filled with laughter, food and football. When it came time to share a personal blessing over dessert, Amanda wanted to say that getting to know Kate and her family had enriched her life, but she couldn't get the words out, so she just said that her blessing was making so many new friends.

The two little girls were asleep in their car seats before Kate left the city limits on Sunday afternoon. With the radio playing softly in the background, Amanda sat quietly in the passenger seat, deep in thought. She had tried to push her apprehensions about Christmas to the back of her mind while she enjoyed Thanksgiving weekend with Kate's family. The memories of Dan's death and the betrayal of discovering he'd been married to someone else were still painful. She hadn't celebrated Christmas the year he died, or last year either, for that matter. She knew it was time to change, but she didn't quite know where to start. Her parents enjoyed neither holidays in general, nor Christmas in particular, so she had no childhood traditions to fall back on.

"Is something wrong?" Kate asked.

"What?" Amanda jolted from her reverie. "No, everything is fine."

"You're so quiet that I thought maybe the weekend was too much family for you." Kate ventured.

"I absolutely adore your family, and the weekend was wonderful!" Amanda assured her. Silence reigned for several moments and then Amanda took a deep breath and forced herself to explain. "My parents didn't celebrate holidays much, so I guess you could say that was my first Thanksgiving."

"Oh." Kate said uncertainly. "Was it for religious reasons? That they didn't celebrate, I mean."

"They aren't particularly religious." Amanda said flatly. "I think they are just negative and, ah, cheap." Kate didn't know what to say. After a few moments, Amanda elaborated a little more. "They said holidays were too commercialized, and that people were pressured to buy things they didn't need like gifts for Christmas, or candy and flowers for Valentine's Day."

"So what did you do on holidays, then?"

"Most holidays were just like ordinary days. On Halloween, I went trick-or-treating with friends. It isn't too hard to put together a costume for a hobo or a gypsy. They usually gave me twenty dollars for Christmas, but we didn't decorate, or bake, or put up a tree or anything, and I haven't celebrated much of anything since Dan died." Amanda shrugged and looked out the window. Kate tried to imagine growing up without celebrating holidays. She couldn't do it.

"I definitely want something different for Madison. I want her to have good memories of holidays." Amanda nodded decisively and having stated her objective out loud, turned towards Kate. "Thanks to your family, I've already learned how to have a painting party, and how to celebrate birthdays, Halloween and Thanksgiving, so tell me how you celebrate Christmas."

"Well, we try not to get too crazy on spending money. We make our decorations and some of our gifts. We go to Christmas Eve Church services and leave snacks out for Santa and the reindeer. We have a special breakfast after we open gifts on Christmas morning, and a nice dinner that evening – stuff like that. Everyone has always come to our house, but that will change this year. Mom and Dad are going to spend the holiday with Julia and Jim and the boys in Miles City. Scotty is in middle school and he wants to play basketball. I guess he'll have practice and stuff. Mom says it's time for her and dad to do the traveling for a change."

"Scotty is the oldest?" The two boys were nearly the same height and looked so much alike that Amanda had trouble telling them apart.

"Yeah, he's twelve, Seth is ten."

"You and Julia are close?"

"We are, even though she is six years older than I am. Mom lost a baby between us. Julia is so mellow that she never seemed to mind me tagging along. She mothered me as much as mom did, I think."

"What about your grandparents? Will they go to Julia's too?" Amanda asked.

"They are going to help with Christmas at the hospital and nursing home. They do that every year, so all that will be different this year is that they won't get up early to come over to unwrap presents. Grandma Vera said that all of life is about change and the important thing is to be flexible and adjust gracefully."

"What are you planning to do?" Amanda asked, holding her breath.

"I planned to stay in Bozeman, if it's okay with you." Kate replied. "Then I wouldn't have to worry about driving if the roads are bad, and I'd like to start establishing my own family traditions for Karly."

"That's perfect!" Amanda assured her and breathed feely again.

◆ ◆ ◆

It turned out to be the best Christmas ever, in Amanda's opinion, though admittedly none of her past Christmases had been anything to shout about so she had little with which to compare. They put up a small tree and spent several evenings teaching the girls to make construction paper chains and paper snowflakes to decorate it. They baked and decorated sugar cookies while carols played on the stereo. They spent a weekend taking pictures of the girls and then made personalized calendars for all the grandparents. For Julia's family they sent a gift box from Hickory Farms with McDonald's gift certificates for the two boys.

They went to the mall several times, had pictures taken with Santa, and after much discussion and debate, decided they weren't quite ready for a real puppy. Amanda was so moved by Christmas Eve candlelight services at a church Kate had been attending regularly that she resolved to rearrange her work schedule so she could start attending Sunday services there too.

On Christmas morning, the two little girls received new clothes and pajamas from Kate's parents and grandparents and art supplies from Julia's family. There were dolls under the tree from their mothers and Santa brought a toy kitchen and a shopping cart for them to share. The grandmothers sent patchwork quilts for Kate and Amanda in colors that complimented their recently painted rooms, Kate's parents gave each of them a hundred dollars, and Grandpa Mike enclosed a handwritten certificate for a free oil change and tune-up for each of their vehicles. Grandpa Ron gave Kate a basket of pens, pencils, sticky notes and assorted notebooks to use for her college classes. For Amanda there was a three-ring binder containing several ideas for cleaning company logos, including sample business cards and invoices, and the names of suppliers for decals and magnetic signs to attach to the windows and doors of her van. A handwritten note explained that when she was ready to expand, he would be happy to help her design a logo and order any office supplies she might need – at the family discount price.

"Look at this!" Amanda exclaimed, handing the binder to Kate. "I made just one comment last spring at the painting party, and he remembered! I adore your family!"

"I adore them too." She said absently while she perused the logos. "Oh! I like that one!" Her finger rested on a sketch of a smiling woman with a mop slung over her shoulder and a bucket in her hand, standing beside a white van. She wore lavender overalls with a lavender baseball cap perched jauntily atop blond curls. Amanda agreed with her and the next week, she ordered office supplies and a magnetic sign.

◆ ◆ ◆

When college classes resumed, Amanda added a few homes to her cleaning schedule, working around Kate's classes so someone would be home with the girls. Their lives settled into a routine broken up by ordinary parenting issues like potty training which the girls took to easily, and special events like the spring weekend they went shopping for big girl beds for Karly and Madison. They chose twin beds and dressers in unfinished pine and spent a weekend giving them two coats of glossy white paint. They wandered through the mall on another day searching for just the right bedding. They found matching pink gingham comforters, but Madison insisted on pink and white striped sheets, while Karly settled on plain pink.

Packages from the great-grandmothers continued to arrive for each holiday containing all manner of treats and surprises. Amanda discovered that Valentine's Day was a good time to make heart-shaped pizza, and St. Patrick's Day was an opportunity to bake green sugar cookies. The great grandmas sent baskets full of art supplies for Easter, but it was too cold and snowy to drive to Billings, so they had a party with Ben and Genny, who shared the news that they were expecting a baby.

As winter gave way to spring, they catered to Kate's love for Montana history and packed picnic lunches for day trips in the surrounding area. They made several trips to Yellowstone Park, poked around in the ghost towns of Virginia City and Nevada City, took short hikes in Hyalite Canyon, and made multiple visits to the Museum of the Rockies.

At the beginning of September, Kate and Amanda hosted a baby shower for Genny. In addition to learning about yet another type of party, Amanda thoroughly enjoyed the opportunity to do something special for Genny. Ben and Genny welcomed their son Brian in October, a week after Karly's third birthday.

Amanda consulted with Grandpa Ron while they were in Billings for Thanksgiving, and ordered more business cards, invoices and envelopes for her expanding cleaning business. In no time at all, the holidays were behind them and they were starting another new year, and the next thing they knew, Kate was scheduled to graduate.

◆ ◆ ◆

"Are you planning to go through the ceremony?" Amanda asked curiously.

"It is kind of a hassle, but I know my parents and grandparents are really proud of me, and it is another excuse for a party, after all." Kate teased.

"You and your family have turned me into a party animal!" Amanda retorted. "I hope you can get a job in Bozeman, so you won't have to move just when the girls are ready to start school."

"I don't want to move either!" Kate assured her. Two weeks later, both women were thrilled when Kate accepted a job in the administration office of Bozeman Deaconess Hospital where she had worked part-time as an intern while she completed her degree in business. That fall, when Karly and Madison started kindergarten, Kate helped Amanda set up a payroll system so she could hire college students for her expanding cleaning business. The days flew by, quickly becoming weeks which turned into months and then morphed into years.

◆ ◆ ◆

One weekend Amanda and Kate invited Genny and Ben and their two boys over for a barbeque. The adults were visiting at the picnic table on the deck after dinner while the children played freeze tag in the yard. Marcus, who was the youngest at four, was making a valiant effort to keep up with his eight year old brother, Brian, and the girls who were eleven. He was so focused on running that he kept forgetting to freeze when he was tagged, and that made everyone laugh, though Karly didn't seem to be laughing as much as the other three.

"What's going on with Karly?" Ben asked, abruptly. He was startled at how much she reminded him of Charlie. He'd always known when something was bothering his friend, and Charlie's daughter had that same look.

"You noticed too?" Kate asked in surprise. "She's been really quiet this past week, but I asked her, a couple of times, actually, and she said she was just tired."

"Mind if I talk to her?" Ben asked.

"Of course not!" Kate assured him. A few minutes later, Kate offered to make popcorn and suggested putting in a movie. When everyone else moved indoors, Ben asked Karly for a moment of her time, and she joined him at the picnic table, looking apprehensive.

"So what's wrong, princess?" He said when they were seated.

"Nothing." Karly replied without meeting his eyes.

"That's what you told your mom, but I don't think it's nothing. Whenever I ask Genny if something is wrong, and she says 'nothing' I know that it is definitely something." Ben said. Karly looked down at the table and remained silent, but one corner of her mouth quirked up reluctantly in a fleeting smile.

"Karly?" Ben waited until she looked up. "Your dad was my best friend. When something was bothering him, he got a sad look in his eyes. You have his eyes, and I see that same sad look in your eyes right now." Karly twisted her fingers together, but remained stubbornly silent.

"If your dad were here, could you tell him what is wrong?" Ben persisted.

"If I had a dad nothing would be wrong." Karly blurted and immediately looked as if she wanted to take the words back.

"Maybe it's something you could talk to your Uncle Ben about." Ben said gently. Karly continued to twist her fingers together while Ben waited. Finally she spoke in a low voice.

"I joined the literary club at school, and it was a lot of fun. Then they decided to have a dinner for dads and daughters. I'm the only one without a dad. It's just so stupid! I thought about quitting, but Mom doesn't like quitting, so she would want to know why and..." Her words came out in a rush and then she stopped abruptly, fighting tears.

"I would be honored to fill in for your dad if you want to take me instead." Ben suggested.

"You would?" Karly asked, cautiously.

"I definitely would!" Ben assured her.

"Okay. That would work." Karly said, looking relieved. "Thanks."

"And I want you to remember that anytime you need someone to fill in for your dad, I'm your guy! Promise?" Ben added.

"Okay, promise." She met his eyes. "Um, I guess you're going to tell Mom?"

"No." Ben held her gaze. "You need to do that." Karly groaned as they stood and went through the sliding glass doors into the kitchen.

NINE

The following evening, Karly finally worked up her nerve and told her mother about the literary club banquet and Ben's offer to accompany her. Kate thought she had done a pretty good job of talking to her daughter about Charlie, but as she thought more about it, she realized that Karly hadn't mentioned him in over a year. Not since shortly after her tenth birthday, when she had asked for a copy of their wedding picture for her room. They had made a trip to the mall to find just the right frame, and the picture was still on her nightstand.

"I don't understand why you couldn't just tell me." Kate said. "We've talked about your dad before."

"It's just so unfair that he died! And talking about him always makes you sad, and a stupid dinner just wasn't worth it." Karly blurted.

"Sadness is part of life, honey. I think I'll always miss him and be sad that he died so young, but I don't mind talking about him or looking at the pictures." The two of them went through the pictures again, both the professional wedding pictures and the photo album that Genny had compiled. As Karly turned the last page of the album from Genny, a scrap of newspaper fell out.

"What's this?"

"Oh! That's the obituary that was printed in the paper. I forgot it was in there."

"Charles Whitcomb IV?" Karly asked as she scanned the clipping. "Really?" Kate realized that because she had only ever referred to him as 'Charlie' or 'your dad', Karly had never heard his full name. For the first time, she talked to her daughter about the rest of her father's family and the reasons why Karly had never met them.

"So they don't know about me? At all?"

"I don't think so." Kate admitted. "After Amelia, your, um, grandmother, kicked Grandpa and me out of the funeral, I didn't want to have you anywhere near her."

"Good job, Mom, protecting me from the evil queen!" Karly exclaimed. "I wonder what the rest of the family is like."

"Most of them are lawyers in the family law firm. I got the impression that when Charlie decided to become an accountant, his mother wasn't very happy about it. He said his dad stood by him though. I only met Huck, your grandfather, once. He seemed nice enough." Kate said, "But he was married to Amelia, the um, evil queen, so...."

"I get it Mom. And I'm happy with the grandparents and great grandparents who are nice people. It's just weird to realize I don't know the other half of my family tree, you know?"

"I suppose if you are still curious, you can look them up one day." Kate ventured.

"Maybe." Karly said, doubtfully.

◆ ◆ ◆

Karly's freak-out over not having a dad when she needed one made Madison start to wonder about her own family. She knew her dad had died when she was a few months old, but beyond that her mother had said very little about him and she had never thought to ask. Now she wanted more details, and thinking about her dad led her to wonder about her grandparents and great-grandparents. Her mother had never mentioned them either.

Madison loved Grandpa Kent and Grandma Barb, and 'The Greats', as she and Karly referred to Carol and Mike, Vera and Ron, and she knew they loved her. She also knew that though they considered her one of their own; technically, they belonged to Karly's family tree rather than hers.

Normally, when something bothered her, she talked to her mother. This time she didn't feel comfortable doing that. She mulled everything over in her mind for two weeks, wondering what to do, before she remembered that Karly had discovered new things about her dad by looking at a photo album. Immediately she went in search of the photo album her mother kept in the living room. Plucking it off the shelf, she leafed through it carefully, starting with the most recent pictures. Her new school picture was in there as were snapshots of some of their summer outings. Moving from the back of the album to the front, as if turning back the hands of time, she leafed through pictures of holidays and picnics and birthday parties. She frowned when she reached the pictures of her second birthday party at the front of the album, wondering where her baby pictures were. As she replaced the album on the shelf, her hand brushed against a thin white spiral bound book with no title that she had never noticed before. She pulled it off the shelf, opened it, and found her baby pictures. There was a tall, handsome blond man that she assumed was her dad in several of the photos. She wondered why she had never seen pictures of him before. She also found her birth certificate and a newspaper clipping of her dad's obituary. She read everything carefully, and then she looked through the rest of the books on that shelf and found her mother's high school yearbook, and read that too.

◆ ◆ ◆

"Madison?" Amanda was framed in the doorway of the room she shared with Karly.

"What?" Madison asked without looking up from the book she was reading.

"You've been awfully quiet these past few weeks. I wondered if you, uh, wanted to talk about your dad." It seemed logical to Amanda that Madison might be having a dad-issue, given that Karly had recently had one. Madison huffed out an irritated breath.

"What about him? He's dead." She said flatly.

"He didn't die on purpose, honey, and he loved you very much."

"And did he love you, Mom?" Madison asked.

"Yes he did." Amanda replied keeping her voice steady with an effort as she wondered where this conversation was going.

"Really? Then why didn't he marry you? Oh wait! Maybe because he was already married!"

"How do you know that?" Amanda asked, her stomach plummeting.

"I found a copy of my birth certificate in my baby book. Funny I'd never seen my baby book before, or pictures of my own father! But, whatever." She closed her book with a snap and glared at her mother. "His name was on the birth certificate, and my last name was Reed, but now my last name is Fitzgerald. And the obituary said he was married to someone who wasn't you when he died." Madison was torn between anger and hurt and the words tumbled out in a rush. When she fell silent, Amanda sank down onto the bed and hugged a pillow to her chest while she tried to explain.

"I didn't think eleven was old enough for this story, but since you know part of it, let me tell you the rest."

"Go for it, Mom!" Madison said sarcastically. Haltingly, Amanda explained how she and Dan met, fell in love, and planned to marry. She stressed that the Dan she'd known was a good person and that she had loved him with all her heart. She explained that he had gone to the pre-natal checkups and been present when Madison was born, and how he bought insurance to make sure the house they were living in would belong to them if anything happened to him. All Madison could focus on was that Dan had been married to someone else, and that she didn't have his surname. Amanda tried to explain why that had happened.

"When you were born, we gave you Dan's name, Madison, because we were planning to marry and live happily ever after and have more children. I'm the one who had your name legally changed when you were a year old. I thought it would make things easier. If you are upset about that, you should be upset with me."

"Well what about him being married to someone else? How could you have a baby with a married man, Mom?"

"I didn't know." Amanda said, softly. "I don't know why he started a relationship with me when he wasn't really available and I don't know why he didn't tell me. For a long time, I made myself crazy trying to figure it all out, and then one day I realized that I will probably never know the answers to those questions, so I have to let it go."

"Really? You just 'let it go'?" Madison asked incredulously.

"Not exactly." Amanda said quietly. "I let it go every time I think about it. Sometimes that's once a week, and sometimes its several times a day. This week it will probably be more often than that." She shrugged.

"And you think I should let it go too?" Madison asked with a little less sarcasm.

"You had no control over any of it, so yes; I think you should believe that your dad loved you and that I love you and get on with your life."

"I'll try." Madison said, without meeting her mother's eyes. She still had questions about their family tree, but she was suddenly exhausted and didn't want to talk about it anymore.

◆ ◆ ◆

Karly arrived home from her literary club meeting after school to a very quiet house. The moms weren't home yet, but usually

Madison was somewhere in evidence. Shrugging, she carried her backpack down the hall to the room they shared intending to put her school things away. Flicking the light on as she opened the door, she was startled to find Madison slouched on her bed, staring straight ahead with blank eyes, the cordless phone clutched tightly in her hand.

"Madison?" There was no response until Karly touched her shoulder, and then she turned dazedly, blinking in confusion as if waking from a deep sleep.

"Madison, what's wrong?"

"What? Oh. Nothing." Madison looked around distractedly as if trying to remember where she was and what she was doing there. Her breathing was choppy and the freckles across her nose stood out in stark relief against skin as pale as milk.

"Madison!" Karly put her hands on her hips and glared down at the girl who was more sister than friend. "You tell me, right this minute, what's wrong, or I'm calling your mom!" Madison put the phone down, scrubbed both hands over her face and gave Karly a disgusted look.

"You'd do that?"

"Oh yeah! In a heartbeat! Because you look awful!"

"I'm fine."

"Uh, huh. You are not fine!"

"Okay, I'm not fine." Madison said, wearily, as if she were eighty instead of eleven.

"Well?" Karly waited impatiently for an explanation. Truth be told, she was scared more than angry.

"I think I just talked to my grandmother." It was the last thing Karly expected to hear, and she just stood motionless for several moments with her mouth slightly open in shock, staring.

"Uh, I didn't know you had a grandmother." The comment sounded stupid, at least to her. She searched her memory but could not remember every hearing anything about Madison having grandparents. Most of the time, she forgot that her grandparents weren't Madison's blood relatives. She lifted her hands off her hips and raised them in a shrug, waiting for an explanation. "Well?"

"Well, it was a false alarm. I thought I had grandparents, but I guess I don't after all." She stared at her feet.

"Start from the beginning." Karly demanded.

"Remember I told you about finding my baby book and the pictures of my dad?" She began. Karly nodded. "Well I also found my mom's yearbook from high school. And guess what? She went to school in Three Forks. She never told me that!" Madison sounded hurt. "So I figured if she went to school there, maybe she still had relatives there. I looked in the phone book and found one listing for Fitzgerald. So I called."

"And?"

"And a woman answered. I explained that I was Amanda Fitzgerald's daughter and I wondered if she was a relative of mine." She fell silent, breathing too fast and twisting her fingers together so hard they turned white.

"What did she say?" Karly prompted her quietly. Madison sat silent for so long that Karly wasn't sure she would answer. When she finally spoke, it was in a flat emotionless voice Karly had never heard before, and hoped never to hear again.

"She said," Madison closed her eyes and took a shuddering breath, "Amanda is a slut and we will not be grandparents to any of her bastards." Madison turned to meet Karly's shocked brown eyes and asked in an anguished whisper. "What kind of person says something like that about their own daughter?" The tears she'd been trying to hold back spilled down her cheeks.

"Oh Madison!" Karly exclaimed. "I'm so sorry." She sat down on the bed and wrapped her arm around Madison's shoulders in wordless support. No matter how she tried, she couldn't quite wrap her mind around what she'd just heard. It was just so....wrong. When

Madison regained control, she begged Karly to keep quiet about what she'd done.

"Promise me you won't say anything. I don't want Mom to know that I called."

"I don't like keeping secrets from our moms." Karly hedged. "They'll know something is wrong and if we don't tell them what it really is, we'll have to lie about it."

"Please! I get why she never told me about them, and I don't want her to know that I called. Ever! It will just make her sad. We can't say anything – we just can't!" She pleaded. "I'll figure out what to tell them and you won't have to lie, I promise!" Somewhat reluctantly, Karly agreed to keep Madison's secret.

Madison told her mother that she had a really bad headache and felt sick to her stomach, and since that was in fact true, she didn't feel too guilty about the rest of it. She went to bed early, but didn't sleep well and was pale and exhausted the next day, and for several days after that.

Amanda and Kate insisted that she rest and drink plenty of fluids and were both happy that no one else in their household came down with whatever nasty virus they thought she suffered through.

The two girls discussed this latest thing they seemed to have in common – evil grandmothers -- and decided they were lucky to have mothers who would go to any lengths to protect them. Within a few weeks, thanks to the resilience of youth, Madison was able to put her ill-advised phone call behind her and regain her equilibrium.

◆ ◆ ◆

"Mom?" Madison leaned against the door of the kitchen where her mother was cleaning the oven.

"Hmm?" Amanda asked absently as she used a paper towel to wipe oven cleaner and baked on grime turned to slime from the bottom of the oven. "What is it?"

"Well, um, Karly and I want to paint our room."

"Tired of pink?" Amanda asked, glancing at her daughter with a smile. "Kate and I were wondering if that would ever happen. What color did you have in mind?"

"We found one called faded denim. It will go with the white trim and our white furniture. We want to take down the curtains and just leave the white mini-blinds."

"You two have it all planned, huh?"

"What do you think? Is it okay?"

"It sounds fine to me, we can get some paint tomorrow and you girls can paint this weekend."

"Great! Oh, and do you have any old blue jeans we could have?"

"What do you need old jeans for?"

"We've been talking to Grandma Barb and the Greats, and they are going to help us make patchwork quilts when we visit them next month." The first time the two girls had spent a week in Billings was the summer they were seven. Kate had a big audit at work during the same week that three of Amanda's clients had big events planned and needed extra cleaning done. Barb and Kent were delighted to have the girls come for a visit and the girls had so much fun that going to Billings became the way they kicked off their summer vacation every year after that. The first year they took swimming lessons and attended Vacation Bible School. When they were eight, they went to a ballet day camp. At nine they were both horse-crazy and Kent surprised them with a week of riding lessons. As they had done when Kate and Julia were growing up, Kent and Barb also shared area history with the girls. They visited museums and attended concerts. They hiked the 'Rims' and learned about their geological formation over millions of years. They toured the Little Bighorn Battlefield, the Pictograph Caves, Pompey's Pillar, and drove the scenic Beartooth Highway. They knew that the nick-name of Magic City was because Billings had grown so rapidly that it seemed to appear like magic. And they knew that it was originally a railroad town named for Fredrick H. Billings, who had been president of the Northern Pacific Railroad. This year, it appeared they would be getting sewing lessons.

Madison and Karly spent the next weekend giving their room two coats of denim colored paint, and another weekend daubing darker and lighter shades of blue paint onto the walls with a sponge. Both were convinced the result of their experiment made the walls look exactly like faded blue jeans.

A few weeks later when school was out, they were off to Billings. The Greats had been hoping the girls would show an interest in sewing and were excited about the opportunity to teach basic sewing techniques while they helped make patchwork quilts. The Greats, Grandma Barb and the girls cut up old jeans into eight inch squares and then combed through the closets where Vera and Carol kept what they called their "stash" for pieces of plain or printed red material which they also cut into squares. When all the squares were in piles according to color, they sewed the squares into long strips.

While they worked, Barb told them stories about the history of quilt making, explaining that pioneer women used bits of worn clothing and scraps of fabric to make bed coverings to keep them warm. She described how isolated those women were and how they used quilting bees as opportunities to socialize with other women. She also talked about how they used their creativity to turn some of those scraps of fabric into works of art, and she had several books from the library with pictures of quilts in them.

When they finished sewing the blocks into strips, all of Karly's strips were alternating squares of denim interspersed with red prints and solids. Madison called it haphazard, but Karly insisted it was whimsical. Madison's strips were denim with a solid red square on each end, alternating denim and solid red squares, and alternating denim and red print squares.

Both girls laid their strips out on the table to see what arrangement they preferred before sewing the strips together into quilt tops that were similar in color, but unique to each girl's personality. The Greats helped them calculate how many yards of fabric they needed for the quilt backs, and how much batting they needed for the middle, and then they made a trip to the fabric store. Karly made her selections quickly, but Madison was mesmerized by the vast array of patterns and colors, and could have spent several days wandering amongst the bolts of fabric. Vera and Carol traded grins as they gently nudged her towards the cash register, recognizing the symptoms of someone newly infected with the sewing bug.

The finished quilts were backed in red and tied with red yarn. There were enough squares left to make a pair of big square floor pillows, and at Vera's suggestion they used the scraps of red fabric to make valances for their two windows and accent pillows for their beds.

◆ ◆ ◆

Two of Amanda's best customers were having Christmas parties over the weekend, so she and her employees had cleaned both of their houses that day, and she was pleasantly tired. Business was booming, she had a good crew of employees, and she was happy to be adding to her savings account. Her house was over fifteen years old, and even though she was conscientious about maintenance, she knew it was only a matter of time before the roof or the furnace would need to be replaced. And of course she also had an education fund for Madison to build up.

Amanda was surprised and a little worried to find Kate, not in the kitchen as she would have expected on a night when it was her turn to cook, but slumped on the couch staring blindly at a muted news program on the television screen.

"Is something wrong?"

"Why can't people just leave me alone?" Kate said irritably. "I am perfectly happy with my life just the way it is!"

"Okay…" Amanda said, not quite sure what that meant.

"Sorry, not you." Kate grimaced. "What I mean is the hospital Christmas party is next week, and today I had three people – three! – tell me that it is high time I started dating. I'm not sure if it is just because I will create an odd number at the party by coming alone, or if they really spend their time worrying about whether or not I'm part of a couple! It is just so annoying!"

"I know what you mean." Amanda agreed. "Do you ever think about dating and, you know, finding someone?"

"No, I don't." Kate replied promptly. "I am not opposed to the idea of falling in love again, but I'm not actively looking either. Karly is my priority right now. Her and my job."

"That's how I feel too. I'm trying to make a living and raise Madison." Amanda agreed. "But for some reason other people feel the need to stick their noses into my business and give me advice on how to live my life."

"Exactly! It is nobody else's business." Kate huffed.

"Last month, one of my college employees came right out and asked me if we were gay." Amanda said conversationally.

"You're kidding!"

"Nope. I suppose we give people the wrong idea by living together and not dating much." Kate looked startled for a few seconds and then chuckled.

"Let's be honest. I have had a handful of dates in the last ten years, so I'm the one who doesn't date much. You don't date at all." She sobered. "Well, if I cared what people think, I guess I would be concerned. But I don't, so I'm not." She hesitated and then asked. "Did the question upset you?" Amanda shook her head.

"I thought it was a little rude, but then college kids pretty much say what's on their minds, and maybe that's a good thing." She replied. "I try to keep an open mind and not be offended."

"Do you ever think about finding someone?" Kate asked, suddenly curious.

"Nope." Amanda replied. "Madison is my priority, just like Karly is yours. They are just starting middle school and that's a critical time for kids, so I want to be paying attention. Not to mention that I just wouldn't want to risk it. The first time, I picked someone who was already married. I don't think I'm a very good judge of character."

"You most certainly are a good judge of character! Look at your track record with employees. You have a knack for hiring reliable people who have integrity, personal accountability and a good work ethic." Kate insisted.

"Yeah, well, I don't think hiring someone to run a vacuum and clean the bathrooms is quite the same as choosing someone to share your life with." Amanda retorted dryly. "So what's for dinner?"

"I ordered pizza." Kate replied, just as the doorbell pealed.

◆ ◆ ◆

"I hate middle school!" Karly exclaimed as she dropped her backpack on the floor and sat dejectedly on the edge of her bed.

"Yeah, me too!" Madison agreed. "I don't see why all of a sudden everyone cares that we don't have dads. Nobody cared last year!" She tossed her backpack onto her bed and paced restlessly around the room.

"Do you think they just figured it out?" Karly wondered aloud.

"I don't know." Madison huffed. "But why bug us? Other kids don't have dads!"

"Oh, other kids have dads." Karly corrected her. "They are just divorced instead of dead." She stared dejectedly at the floor.

"Whatever." Madison sat on the edge of her bed facing Karly. "I'm tired of everyone whispering and staring at us or asking rude questions. What are we going to do about it?"

"Well, we aren't going to tell the moms, that's for sure." Karly sighed. "And I don't think this is something Ben can help us with. Do you have any ideas?"

"Not really. Unless," Madison paused, considering. "I suppose we could just tell them our story the next time someone asks a rude question."

"Get it over with, you mean? And maybe they'll quit bugging us?" Karly asked. Madison nodded.

"It's worth a try." Karly agreed, and they worked out what they would say and how they would say it. Then they waited. Sure enough within a few days, someone asked.

"Why do you live together if you aren't related?" The question came from a girl named Louise. She was short with thick blond hair worn loose around her shoulders. She had pale blue eyes behind wire rimmed glasses, a sharp nose and a pointed chin. They assumed she had attended another elementary school, since they didn't recognize her. Not that it mattered; the students from their old school were just as nosy.

"Well," Madison replied, with a glance at Karly who gave her a slight nod. "Our dads are dead." Ignoring the collective gasp she continued. "Mine died when I was just a few months old, so I don't remember him at all."

"Mine died before I was born, so I never met him." Karly contributed. Everyone at the table looked from one to the other as if seated at a tennis match.

"It was hard for my mom to work and take care of me." Madison said. "So she decided to look for a roommate."

"She met my mom when we were not quite two." Karly said. "And we've been together ever since."

"We might not be related, but we are closer than most sisters." Madison said firmly.

"And our moms are best friends." Karly agreed.

"We are really proud of our moms for figuring out a way to support themselves and each other." Madison finished.

"So, do any of you want to talk about the personal stuff that is going on in your families?" Karly looked around the table, but no one replied and several refused to meet her gaze. "From now on, if anyone asks us a rude question, they can expect a rude question right back." As they had hoped, nobody asked them any more questions about their parentage or their living arrangements and they were able to get on with being middle school students.

◆ ◆ ◆

Madison joined art club, library club, and the swim team. Making their bedroom quilts had introduced her to sewing, and by the time they finished middle school, she had a sewing machine and a fabric stash of her own and was designing and sewing her own clothes. Sometimes she offered suggestions for Karly's wardrobe, which in her opinion, was sorely in need of variety.

Karly smiled at Madison's suggestions for her wardrobe, but insisted she liked to be comfortable, and so she usually wore faded jeans and tee-shirts. She sang in the school chorus and several smaller vocal groups, got a part in the school play, and started guitar lessons. She joined the library club and participated in whatever sport was in season.

◆ ◆ ◆

Just as several elementary schools had funneled into one middle school, three middle schools sent their students to one high school, and the process of navigating new surroundings and meeting new people began again. One afternoon while waiting for Karly to retrieve her books from her locker, Madison recognized the voice of their nemesis behind her.

"Well, what do we have here?" It was Bridget Burns, self appointed tormenter of freshman in general, and for some reason, Karly and Madison in particular. Bridget was petite with waist-length blond hair, blue eyes and pearly white teeth. She always wore brand name clothes including shoes all the girls envied and she would have been quite pretty but for her perpetual scowl and the huge chip on her shoulder. The two girls had no idea why she had zeroed in on them the first week of school, but she had gone out of her way to pester them ever since. Now it was January, and since ignoring Bridget hadn't worked, they had spent a large amount of time over the holidays devising a new strategy. It looked like today was the day they would see if it worked.

"Here we go." Madison whispered as she turned around.

"Show time!" Karly whispered in reply, stowing one last book in her bag before closing her locker.

"Hello, Bridget." Madison said with exaggerated politeness. "Did you want something specific, or were you just trying to cause trouble?"

"I bet she is just trying to cause trouble, as usual." Karly said as she turned to stand shoulder to shoulder with Madison.

"I am doing an article for the school paper," Bridget smirked. She stood with her pen poised over the notepad she held in her other hand. "I wanted to know if you two are lesbians like your mothers." She flashed a malicious smile. A crowd had gathered, silent and watchful. During the first month in their new school, Karly and Madison had figured out that Bridget didn't have friends so much as she had people who were afraid of her.

"I can never remember which is which." Karly turned to Madison, "Explain the difference between libel and slander to me again?"

"Libel and slander are types of defamatory statements. Libel is a written defamatory statement, and slander is a spoken or oral defamatory statement." Madison replied promptly, as if quoting from a dictionary.

"Do you think she knows what the word 'defamatory' means?" Karly asked in a stage whisper as she angled her chin towards Bridget.

"Probably not." Madison replied, also in a stage whisper. She shook her head sadly, looked at the ceiling as if deep in thought, and then, as if the idea had just occurred to her, she asked. "Do you think I should explain?"

"Oh yes, please do." Karly nodded politely.

"A defamatory statement is one that hurts someone's reputation." Madison recited.

"So, just to be clear," Karly said, solemnly, speaking loudly enough to be heard by the ever-growing crowd. "What Bridget just said was slander. If she actually writes it down and it gets published in the school paper, then it would be libel?"

"Exactly." Madison nodded. Bridget looked back and forth between the two girls, as if their conversation was the pendulum of a grandfather clock. For once, she seemed to be at a loss for words.

"Interesting." Karly mused. "Can victims of libel or slander sue for damages?"

"That's ridiculous!" Bridget protested. "You can't sue me!"

"Yes, of course! Lots of people sue for defamation of character." Madison replied as if Bridget hadn't spoken. "If you meet the requirements for a civil action, then you can sue whoever has written or said something bad about you. And if you win the lawsuit, damages are awarded by the court."

"Interesting!" Karly said again. "What are the requirements for a civil action?"

"First you have to prove that the statement was false. Then you have to show that the statement harmed you." Madison replied.

"We have a whole crowd of witnesses to what she just said standing right here. It might be hard to prove we are not gay, but on the other hand, it would be just as hard for her to prove that we are." Karly mused.

"So if it became a question of who was more believable; good kids like you and me, or Bridget, the school troublemaker, you think we'd win?" Madison asked.

"Yeah, I think we'd have a good chance." Karly gazed speculatively at the crowd of silent students before continuing.

"And it would be a piece of cake to prove that what she said harmed us. I mean, I already feel distraught, don't you? Here we are in a new school just trying to fit in and we are being bullied and picked on."

"I'm so upset I think I might need therapy." Madison agreed.

"And good therapy is so expensive." Karly shook her head, sadly.

"I'm sure the court would make Bridget's parents pay." Madison assured her. "I mean, since it would be her fault we needed therapy in the first place, and neither of our mothers could afford it, being single parents and all..." The crowd had gone from silent to snickering and many were now murmuring their agreement.

"I'll testify for you." Offered a boy neither of them knew and before they could respond, there was a chorus of 'yeah' and 'me too' from several other on-lookers. Bridget stomped her foot in frustration and stalked off in a rage muttering under her breath. As the crowd dispersed, there were several who flashed thumbs up gestures. The boy who had offered to testify said admiringly, "Nice work!"

"Thanks." Karly replied. She waited, but he just stood there smiling at them. She and Madison were five six, so she judged this young man to be about five ten, slender with dark blond hair still bleached from the summer sun. His skin was tanned and he had hazel eyes, thick eyelashes, and a lopsided grin.

"I'm Seth." He said. "This is Mitch. Mind if we walk out with you?" Until Seth had gestured towards him in introduction, neither girl had noticed Mitch standing in the shadows with an athletic bag slung casually over one shoulder. Slightly taller than Seth, with olive skin, dark eyes and dark curly hair, Mitch lifted his hand and smiled in acknowledgement of the introduction. He had dimples.

"Bridget is in our class." Seth began as the foursome started down the hall. "We're juniors, and she's been a bully since we were in kindergarten. You two handled her better than anyone I've ever seen."

"I'd like to know what her problem is." Madison said thoughtfully.

"We all would." Seth agreed. "But enough about her. We have practice now, but we'd like to, uh, talk to you some more. Maybe we could, uh, grab a soda after school tomorrow?" Karly raised her eyebrows at Madison who shrugged.

"Sure, I guess so." Karly replied.

"See you then!" Seth called over his shoulder as he and Mitch turned left and headed down the hallway towards the gym. It wasn't until they were alone again that the girls realized Mitch had said not a single word.

TEN

Amanda and Kate were seated at the kitchen table on a Sunday afternoon. In their first weeks after Kate moved in, Sunday afternoon was a time they scheduled to discuss the logistics of child care, household chores and any problems that came up. Fourteen years later, the habit of the Sunday afternoon chat remained, even if they had nothing of importance to discuss. Both of them looked up when the girls appeared wearing identical serious expressions.

"Mom." Madison began. "Could you hire Karly and me to clean for you?"

"Why?"

"We could get some valuable work experience while we earn a little extra spending money." Madison's green eyes were serious as she presented her case. Amanda studied her sixteen year old daughter. They were nearly the same height now. Amanda kept her naturally curly blond hair short and it curled around her face. Madison wore hers long, the weight of her tresses stretching the curls into waves.

"You already babysit for extra spending money."

"Yeah, but babysitting isn't a regular job that you can plan on. We want, you know, a salary." Amanda considered that as she mentally compared the young woman in front of her to herself at the same age, when she had lied about her age to get a job cleaning for an older woman in their neighborhood. Her parents hadn't noticed she was gone more than usual, or that she had extra spending money.

She was so very grateful for the close relationship she enjoyed with her daughter. Her attention returned to the girls when Kate spoke.

"Karly?"

"I'd like to earn some extra money too, Mom. Now that we're in high school, there might be, ah, other expenses."

"Such as?"

"Oh, hanging at the mall with friends and maybe buying a new pair of shoes, or something?" Karly's heart-shaped face and dark brown hair were like her own, but looking into those warm chocolate brown eyes always reminded Kate of Charlie. He would be so proud of their daughter. Sometimes Kate still missed him so much it made her heart ache. She blinked the past away and tuned back in to the present.

"I think you would be wonderful employees," Amanda began, "But I just hired two new people, and I would have to let them go if I hired you. They are both working their way through college, so that doesn't seem like a very nice thing to do." The girls slumped in disappointment.

"I guess you're right." Madison grumbled. "Could we be first in line next time you hire someone, though?"

"Don't give up so easily, girls." Kate admonished. "Sometimes there are other ways to get what you want, if you negotiate." All three of them turned to look at her, and she smiled. "For instance, I would happily pay to have someone else do my share of the cleaning around here."

"Great idea, Kate!" Amanda grinned. "So would I. And if someone else is doing it, this place could use some fall cleaning, especially the windows, so would you two be interested in working right here?"

"What would the pay be?" Madison asked.

"And the hours?" Karly asked

"Both very good questions!" Amanda approved. "We will pay minimum wage, which is the salary all my employees start with, and do an evaluation after three months to see if you deserve a raise. The two of you can work out a schedule for a total of ten hours per week, working together or separately. We will look at your proposal and adjust it if necessary, according to our schedules. That way you won't be cleaning the oven at the same time dinner is cooking."

"Okay." Madison said. "But once we get the fall cleaning done, and I'm assuming you'll have a list of chores for that, the regular cleaning probably won't take ten hours per week."

"Oh these girls learn fast, don't they?" Kate commented. "It seems to me that there are also outdoor chores that need doing. Right now there are leaves to rake, soon there will be snow to shovel, and the lawn will need to be mowed regularly all summer. You could even clean and organize the garage, right Amanda?"

"Oh yes, please! Clean and organize the garage!" They all laughed, because there was no doubt the garage was a mess. When the laughter died down, Amanda continued. "I would also be willing to take you with me sometimes when I clean offices in the evenings, so you can learn the difference between what needs to be done in a home and what needs to be done in an office." Amanda personally cleaned the offices of her original clients, not only because she appreciated them giving her a chance when she first started her business, but also because she enjoyed the quiet routine of cleaning by herself. Lately, however, she had been thinking that she should train someone else so she would have a backup plan in place for her clients, in case she got sick or needed time off.

"That sounds perfect! When can we start?" The two moms agreed to draw up a prioritized list of chores so they could start right away. When the girls had gone back to their room, Amanda looked at Kate and sighed.

"They met boys, didn't they?"

"That would be my guess." Kate agreed. "It was bound to happen sooner or later. We should be glad it didn't happen in middle school. They are great kids – don't worry, they'll be fine."

And they were fine. Karly and Seth dated for two years, usually in a foursome with Mitch and Madison. When the two boys went off to college, Karly had other dates, but Madison didn't seem interested in dating, preferring to work on her sketches or turn the designs she created into clothing all the girls envied.

◆ ◆ ◆

Karly and Madison decided to have an open house to celebrate their high school graduation. In addition to the local friends who might stop by, they were expecting Kate's parents, the Greats, Julia and Jim, Ben and Genny and their sons Brian and Marcus who were now fifteen and eleven.

"We have good news, and other news." Karly said as they were deciding on the menu for the event. Kate and Amanda exchanged a look and then turned expectantly to the girls.

"What kind of news is other news?" Kate asked, suspiciously.

"Well, we aren't sure if you'll think it is good or bad, so it's just - other." Karly grinned.

"The good news is that we are both going to college." Madison informed them.

"And the other news is that we aren't moving out." Karly said.

"We've decided to go to school here." Madison said. "So if you were looking forward to having an empty nest..." Both girls grinned.

"Get over it." Karly finished.

"I thought we talked about you two moving to a new place, having new experiences, and meeting new people." Amanda said when she recovered the power of speech.

"Well, we did. But other than moving to a new place – which we can always do at a later date, we'll be doing everything on the list." Madison explained.

"Yeah, and for a lot less money." Karly added.

"You both have college funds." Kate reminded them.

"True, and scholarships, plus we could get jobs. But you have taught us to be frugal, right? MSU is a great school, and if we stay here each of us has a room that is bigger than we would have in a dorm, a roommate we know we'll get along with, jobs with flexible hours that keep us in spending money and new shoes, and…. kitchen privileges!" Neither Kate nor Amanda could argue with that.

Karly decided to major in education, aspiring to become an English teacher like her Grandma Barb. She felt like she was born to teach and had already honed her leadership skills with experience as a teacher's aide and a camp counselor.

Madison went into nursing. Quite a few people, including her mother, wondered why she didn't choose fashion design. She had thought about that and discussed it with Karly, but in the end she knew that she didn't have the temperament for the cutthroat fashion industry, so she decided that sewing and designing clothes would be a great hobby. She became interested in the medical profession when she signed up for a basic first aid class and CPR as part of lifeguard training.

◆ ◆ ◆

With the girls immersed in their freshman year of college and Amanda focused on expanding her business, Kate found herself a bit at loose ends. She considered attending graduate school or developing a new hobby, but nothing really got her fired up. Then one day, as she was leaving the grocery store, a stranger asked her for directions to the library.

The woman was lean and fit in black pants, a gray fleece pullover, and tennis shoes. She had short brown hair that curled around the edges of a baseball cap pulled low over intelligent gray eyes.

Her face was tanned and there were laugh lines around her eyes and mouth. She could have been any age between thirty five and fifty. Kate explained how to get to the library and then continued on to her car. As she pulled out of the parking lot, she caught another glimpse of the woman, standing beside a bicycle while she fastened the strap of a helmet under her chin. Attached to the bike was a trailer; the enclosed kind Kate had seen people use to transport a child or two in comfort and safety. But instead of a child, the trailer held what appeared to be personal belongings.

The image of the woman, her bicycle, and the trailer stayed with Kate, popping into her mind at odd times during the day and sometimes into her dreams at night. Slowly the idea of taking an extended bike trip took root in her mind. The more she thought about it, the more she wanted to do it. Kate being Kate, she came up with a plan. She made a list of things to do and equipment she would need, outlined a fitness program, and constructed a time-line so that she would be ready when Karly graduated from college. Then she unearthed her old ten-speed bike from the garage and took it to the bike shop for a tune-up. When it was ready, she began riding it regularly to get in shape.

ELEVEN

On what should have been an ordinary, quiet evening of work, Amanda parked her van, unloaded her supplies and carried them into the clinic to clean Dr. Grant's office. When she unlocked the door and stepped inside, she nearly ran into a tall, dark haired man with broad shoulders and blue eyes.

"Oh! Excuse me, I wasn't expecting…" her voice trailed off, while her heart raced. She attributed her accelerated pulse to the shock of encountering someone in the office after hours, and she assumed his speechless stare was because he hadn't expected to see her either. "I'm the cleaning lady." She explained, once she found her voice.

"I'm the son. Of the dentist, I mean." He offered his hand. "I'm Dave Grant."

"Do you want me to come back later to clean?" Amanda asked, gently disengaging her hand from his when he didn't seem inclined to let go.

"No, you go ahead with your routine. I just came to pick up Dad's glasses. He left them on his desk and he can't read the paper without them." He smiled at her. "But I would like to know your name, if you don't mind."

"Amanda." He raised an eyebrow at her. "Fitzgerald. Amanda Fitzgerald." She stammered, feeling her cheeks flush.

"Nice meeting you, Amanda Fitzgerald." With a wave and a smile, he opened the door and let himself out. That should have been the end of it, but the next time she went to clean for Dr. Grant, Dave was waiting for her and this time he invited her for a cup of coffee when she finished cleaning. She refused as politely as she could, explaining that she usually didn't finish until after midnight and that was too late for coffee. It surprised her that she felt bad about saying no. On the rare occasions when men asked her out, she was always able to brush them off firmly and politely without a second thought.

A few days later, Dave called and said he hoped she would be more comfortable getting to know him over the phone. He shared information from his own life, and asked her general questions about herself. She answered his questions because the alternative was to be extremely rude. She told herself that she didn't want to be rude to the son of one of her favorite clients, but the phone chat left her feeling a little off balance. Dave called again the next night, and the next. They discovered that they had similar taste in music and movies and had read some of the same books. She learned that he had just finished twenty years in the Army, had a degree in computer science, and was in the process of starting a cyber-security business. He had returned to Bozeman because his parents and his brother lived there, and he was planning to build a house. She was not as forthcoming with details of her own life, but eventually she shared some of her past with him. The following week he sent her a small bouquet of daisies, with a note that said he enjoyed talking to her. She wasn't sure how to handle the fact that she enjoyed talking to him too.

The next time he asked her out for coffee, she accepted and sat across from him in a booth, nervously twisting her hands in her lap while she tried to explain that she wasn't interested in dating. He listened thoughtfully, sent her a single yellow rose the next day with a note that said he'd like to be her friend, and went back to calling her on the phone. They never seemed to lack for conversation, and against her better judgment, Amanda found herself looking forward to their chats.

◆ ◆ ◆

"You did what?" Amanda asked in surprise. She was unloading the dishwasher when Kate got home from work.

"I got a job at Monroe's Steak House, just on weekends." Kate replied. "I start Friday night."

"That's tomorrow."

"I know. I sure hope I haven't forgotten how to be a waitress."

"Why, though?"

"Well, I'll need a new bike and a trailer, and some other supplies if I'm going to do that bike tour I've been thinking about. I'll also need to take time off." Kate shrugged. "All of that will take money."

"You're really going to do it then? Do you know when?" Amanda asked.

"Not until after the girls graduate from college. I figure it'll take me that long to get in shape and get the equipment and plan the route. There's a lot to do. A project like this is kind of like a party – the planning is half the fun." Kate shrugged. "So tell me what's going on with you? I've noticed the flowers and phone calls, but I haven't met him."Amanda sighed and told Kate all about meeting Dave and the mixed feelings she had about him.

"I don't know what to do!" She finished. "He keeps calling and he's easy to talk to and everything, but I don't want to have a relationship right now -- with anyone."

"News flash, Amanda. You are smack dab in the middle of a relationship, whether you admit it or not." Kate said bluntly.

"We aren't dating!" Amanda protested. "We had coffee one time!"

"But you talk to him on the phone nearly every day. That's a relationship. If you like him, what's the problem?" Kate asked. "Personally, I'd love to see you fall in love again."

"I just don't want to make another big mistake." Amanda said miserably.

"This is different, though. You know his parents, for one thing." Kate gave her a sympathetic pat on the shoulder, but didn't say anything more. It would be hypocritical of her to be giving advice when she wasn't sure she wanted to risk loving – and losing – again either.

Amanda continued to refuse dates that involved spending actual time together, but she couldn't quite bring herself to stop taking phone calls from Dave.

◆ ◆ ◆

As the girls started their sophomore year in college, Kate joined a fitness club so she could continue to train for her bike trip regardless of the weather, added yoga and weight training to her routine, and enrolled in a bike maintenance and repair course offered by the adult education association. She came home discouraged after the first class.

"There is so much to learn." She lamented to Amanda. "I'm going to need a tool kit, and spare parts!"

"You'll be fine. Anything new is overwhelming at first, right?"

"I guess." Kate agreed reluctantly. "And at least I know how to use basic tools." She hesitated. "One of the guys asked me out!"

"Is that bad?" Amanda teased.

"I don't know. It took me by surprise, I guess. I mean, I took the class to learn about fixing my bike and suddenly this guy is asking me for a date."

"What did you say?"

"I said I had to work, which is true, because I do." Kate said defensively.

"Are you kidding?" Amanda raised her eyebrows. "You think I should give Dave a chance, but…"

"Well," Kate said defensively. "I'm just focused on this project right now. And besides, there was absolutely no chemistry."

◆ ◆ ◆

Kate answered the chimes of the doorbell on a Saturday afternoon late in September and encountered two policemen standing on the front steps. She was instantly transported back in time to the day she had learned that Charlie was dead. Policemen at the door never brought good news, and the question of who in her family had died ricocheted around in her head, bouncing off the inside of her skull and screaming to get out. Was it Karly? One of her parents? Her sister? She couldn't ask, because she couldn't breathe, and there were spots in front of her eyes.

"Amanda Fitzgerald?" One of policeman asked.

"No, I'm…I'm Kate." She stammered, as she sagged against the door, while the voice in her head began to chant, 'Not Madison! Not Madison! Please, not Madison!' Kate clung to the doorknob as she struggled to draw breath, knowing this would kill Amanda. As if summoned by Kate's distress, Amanda came through the doorway from the kitchen, halting abruptly when she saw the two officers standing in the entry.

"Are you Amanda Fitzgerald?" She stood frozen watching the officer's lips move, unable to hear a word he said above the roaring in her head. The officer who had spoken moved to her side, took her gently by the elbow and led her to the couch, while his partner did the same for Kate, who was still hanging onto the doorknob, her anguished gaze on the friend she loved like a sister. Once both women were seated on the couch, the officer spoke again.

"Ma'am? Are you Amanda, the daughter of Herb and Alice Fitzgerald?" She wondered vaguely why he was asking about her parents, but she managed to nod.

"Yes." Her voice was a raspy whisper.

"I'm sorry to inform you that your parents are both deceased." He waited patiently while she assimilated his words, finally understanding that it wasn't Madison who was dead. Instead, it was her parents.

"What happened?" Amanda asked when she could form words and push them past the lump in her throat.

"There will be an atopsy, but the initial indication is that their furnace malfunctioned and filled the house with carbon monoxide. They died in their sleep." The officer replied. When the officers left, Amanda turned to Kate.

"I was afraid it was Madison! Now I feel guilty because I'm just so glad it wasn't!"

"Me too." Kate agreed. "I am sorry about your parents, Amanda."

"I wanted to reconcile with them, you know. I wanted to introduce them to their granddaughter. I always thought I'd have more time." Before either of them could say anything else, Madison and Karly burst through the door in a panic, questions erupting from both simultaneously.

"What happened?" Karly demanded.

"We saw the police!" Madison gasped.

"Everything is okay." Amanda assured them, quickly.

"We thought… one of you…" Karly said, relieved that the moms were okay, but still in a blind panic about the other people in her family.

"Yeah, I know. We thought it was…" Kate put her hand over a heart that was still beating too fast and shuddered. "It was awful!"

"So who….?" Karly braced herself as they sank onto the couch. As if she had ESP, Kate realized where her daughter's mind had gone and hastened to explain.

"Amanda's parents." She said quietly.

"Oh." Karly said. She exchanged a look with Madison that neither mother picked up on. Kate's eyes were closed while she took a calming breath, her hand still pressed to her breast. Amanda sat hunched forward with her hands clasped tight in her lap, looking at the floor as she steeled herself to explain this to her daughter.

"Mom?" Madison asked tentatively.

"I never told you about my parents, your grandparents, that they lived in Three Forks." She choked out. "You have every right to be upset."

"Well, why didn't you?" Madison asked reasonably. "You must have had a good reason." Amanda squared her shoulders and explained what her childhood had been like and how her parents had kicked her out when she told them she was pregnant.

"I've been trying to reconcile with them by sending letters every few months, but, well, they never wrote back."

"Well, no wonder you didn't tell me about them. It doesn't sound like they wanted a kid, so they probably didn't want a grandkid either." Madison said. "I'm sorry they died Mom, but I guess if I'd been in your shoes, I wouldn't have told me either."

TWELVE

Amanda spent the next few days making funeral arrangements. The service was held on Saturday in the funeral home chapel. Kate and the two girls were there, of course, and Amanda was surprised and touched that Kate's parents and grandparents came from Billings. Having them sitting with her in the section reserved for family was unexpectedly soothing.

Amanda recognized other mourners, including several of her parents' neighbors, a handful of people her father had worked with on the county road crew, and a few of her old high school teachers. The parents of two of her high school friends were there, too. They had always made her feel more than welcome in their homes, probably well aware that her home life left something to be desired. And then there was Miss Phillips, ruler of the public library for as long as anyone could remember. She was thin and frail and not very tall, with snow white hair pinned in an untidy bun on top of her head. She had a face full of wrinkles, intelligent dark eyes, and a wide mouth over a slightly protruding chin. She wore a long dark purple corduroy skirt and a matching cardigan over a silky lilac blouse with a big loopy bow at the neckline. Her shoes were sensible black oxfords with rubber soles and she leaned on a wooden cane that looked like it had been hand carved from a piece of driftwood.

Amanda knew that her mother had been a voracious reader, and that she had spent a lot of time at the library. Even so, when Miss Phillips had left word at the funeral home that she would take care of the reception details, Amanda had been at a loss for words. Her note assured Amanda that the Library Ladies would want to pay tribute to her mother in their own way, and that she was not to worry. There were twelve of them, most of the same vintage as Miss Phillips, many also wearing long skirts and cardigans. They arrived with platters of finger sandwiches and deviled eggs, a large fruit salad and three sheet cakes. Under their supervision, the reception proceeded like a well-choreographed dance.

Amanda didn't notice that Dave had come to the services until he appeared at the end of the reception line, grasped both her hands in his and asked if she needed anything. When she thanked him and said she was fine, he nodded and sat down at a table with Miss Phillips. Amanda kept darting glances in their direction because the two of them appeared deeply involved in an interesting conversation.

◆ ◆ ◆

The following day, Amanda drove to Three Forks to begin cleaning out her parent's home and found Dave waiting for her, dressed in old jeans and a sweatshirt, with a pair of work gloves sticking out of his back pocket.

"I came to help." He said simply. Amanda shook her head, but as she opened her mouth to protest, Dave added. "Let me help you, Amanda, please." She hesitated briefly and then nodded, reluctantly admitting to herself that she was grateful for his presence. She had a feeling that cleaning out her childhood home would be harder emotionally than it would be physically.

They started in the kitchen, boxing the contents of the pantry to donate, and then clearing out and cleaning the refrigerator. They worked in silence for an hour or so before Amanda's curiosity got the better of her and she asked if he and Miss Phillips knew each other.

"No. She was just sitting alone, so I joined her." He replied. "She apparently knew your mom pretty well. Told me she felt sorry for both your parent; saw them as tragic heroes." Startled, Amanda stared at him for a moment before rolling her eyes.

"Of course she did – she's an old spinster librarian! Honestly!" Amanda scoffed. "She's probably read every book in that building." She paused, but curiosity got the better of her again.

"So what all did she have to say about them being tragic heroes?"

"She said your dad worked hard, hardly ever smiled, and wanted your mom to stay at home." Dave replied. Amanda nodded but said nothing, so he continued. "She said your mom was raised in an orphanage and got married mostly for convenience."

"Why did she think that?"

"Apparently your mother told her that. She also said they never planned to have children and didn't really know what to do with you when you came along."

"That sounds about right." Amanda commented, trying to keep the bitterness out of her voice. She hadn't known about the orphanage, but she guessed it made sense. Neither of her parents had ever mentioned having a family.

"Miss Phillips thought they were both emotionally unavailable."

"They were." Amanda agreed, and then she went back to work, suddenly wondering if she, too, was emotionally unavailable. It was an unsettling idea.

◆ ◆ ◆

The only things Amanda decided to keep from her parents' house were pictures and a set of china, creamy white with a classic silver line around the edge. She was pretty sure the china had never been used because she didn't remember ever seeing it before, and the entire set seemed to be in the original packaging.

She packed up the contents of the battered pine desk and dented metal file cabinet and took them home, then spent several evenings with Kate helping to sort and organize everything so she could pay the final bills.

Once the personal items were removed, it took another week to organize and price everything that was left for a combination estate and rummage sale. After the sale, she cleaned the house from top to bottom, listed it with a local real estate agent and hoped for the best.

The house sold within six weeks and when all the loose ends were tied up and the final bills were paid, she added eighteen thousand dollars to her savings account, and tried to let go of the regrets she still had about her relationship with her parents. She also admitted to herself that she missed working with Dave every day.

◆ ◆ ◆

"Kate?" Amanda asked. "Do you think I'm emotionally unavailable?" Kate laid down her pen and put the catalog of bikes and biking equipment aside.

"No." Kate said. "Why?" Amanda explained about Dave talking to Miss Phillips and her opinion that Amanda's parents had been emotionally unavailable. She had been unable to get that conversation out of her head, and after worrying it to death, had done some research.

"I did some reading, and I think Miss Phillips was right about my parents. And I might be emotionally unavailable too."

"I don't think so, Amanda. You have great relationships with Madison, me, Karly, my family, quite a few friends, all of your clients and your employees." Kate exclaimed. "That isn't emotionally unavailable!"

"What about Dave?" Amanda asked, tentatively. Kate grinned.

"Well, with Dave, you are just taking your time because of a bad experience when you were younger. Once you figure out Dave can be trusted with your heart, you'll be fine."

"You think he can be trusted with my heart?"

"Yeah I do, and I think you are already in love with him. That's just my opinion, of course." Kate smiled and went back to perusing the catalog she had picked up at the bike shop. She was finally going to order a new bike and trailer.

The more she thought about it, the more Amanda realized that Kate was right. It was time to stop pretending she wasn't in a relationship with Dave. She certainly didn't want to be the kind of people her parents had been. She resolved to stop pushing Dave away and admit that she wanted him in her life. As always, when she made a decision, she acted on it. When next she talked to Dave, she shared her epiphany with him. Dave said he knew, if he was just patient long enough, that she would realize they were perfect for each other. Almost overnight, Amanda's family increased to include Dave's parents, his brother, and Dave's friends. At Kate's suggestion, she invited him to Billings for Thanksgiving. He proposed on New Year's Eve and soon Amanda was busy planning for a June wedding.

◆ ◆ ◆

Rough day?" Kate asked looking up from the lawn where she had just erected her new three man dome tent. Amanda slumped onto the bench and leaned back against the picnic table.

"Nice tent. Is it hard to put up?"

"Nope. Pops right up in a couple of minutes. Lightweight, water repellant, big enough for me and my stuff, and has a storage sack. The fluorescent green is a bonus." Kate replied with a grin. When

Amanda didn't respond, she sobered. "So, are you going to tell me why you look so stressed?"

"I've been shopping for a dress."

"By yourself?" Kate shook her head disparagingly, as she took the tent down and folded it for storage. "You didn't know that women are required to shop for wedding dresses in groups? Or at the very least, in pairs? I'm pretty sure that's a rule!"

"I'm not really a group shopper." Amanda said, ruefully, making a face. "Or a shopper at all, apparently. I just can't find anything I would consider wearing."

"Reminds me of when I married Charlie," Kate mused, coming to sit beside her on the picnic bench. "I was looking for simple elegance I could afford and everything I found was elaborate and way too expensive. It was frustrating."

"What did you do?"

"I was running out of time and beginning to panic so I asked my grandmothers to make my dress. Then Grandma Carol said she still had hers. She showed it to me, I loved it and it fit perfectly. Problem solved."

"That won't work in this case. Maybe we should just elope." Amanda said, glumly. "Then a dress wouldn't be such a big deal."

"Of course you shouldn't elope!" Kate exclaimed. "You'll get through this, I promise. Now, why don't close your eyes, take a deep breath and describe the kind of dress you want."

"I think it's easier to tell you what I don't want." Amanda sighed, glaring at her toes. "I don't want strapless and I don't want a big full skirt, or beads, or a train, or anything very fancy." Neither of them had noticed Madison standing by the screen door until she spoke.

"Honestly, Mom, you didn't follow Kate's directions to take a deep breath and close your eyes!" She shook her head in mock disgust. Crossing the deck she handed Amanda a sketch pad. "Take a look at this and see what you think." Amanda looked down at a drawing of a floor length gown with cap sleeves, a modest v-neck, a fitted bodice and a skirt that fell in soft folds.

"Madison! Where did -- did you design this?" Amanda was stunned. "This is exactly what I've been looking for, without even knowing I was looking for it."

"I can sew that for you." Madison grinned. "It'll take about a week. And I think it should be ivory or champagne instead of white, to go better with your coloring."

"That would be perfect!" Amanda said, gazing at her daughter in mingled amazement and respect. The wedding gown Madison created for her mother was as pretty as the picture she'd drawn, and once the wedding dress dilemma was solved, Madison also designed and sewed the bridesmaid dresses; deep lilac for Kate and pale lavender for herself and Karly.

◆ ◆ ◆

By the middle of March, the flowers, cake, invitations and arrangements for the ceremony and the reception were coming together nicely. Still, Amanda seemed stressed out about something and Dave thought he knew what it was.

"Let's take my parents to Billings on Saturday and introduce them to Barb and Kent." He suggested. Amanda looked startled, and Dave continued. "Mom wants to meet your adopted family, and talk to Barb about their dresses. And I thought you might want to talk to Kent, in person, about giving you away."

"Giving me away?" Amanda repeated.

"Well yes. He'll want to do that." Dave asserted, nodding his head.

"How do you know?"

"I know because, when I met him at Thanksgiving, he gave me the 'dad talk'." Dave replied.

"Dad talk?" Amanda frowned. "What in the world is that?"

"That's when the dad asks the boyfriend what his intentions are and threatens him with bodily harm if he doesn't treat his little girl right." Dave said promptly. "He meant it too."

"But, technically, I'm not his little girl." Amanda objected. "And anyway, don't you think I'm a little old for that?"

"I don't think Kent sees it that way, Sweetheart." Dave pointed out gently. "I think Kate's whole family adopted you years ago and they see you as one of their own. Kent's feelings will be hurt if he doesn't get to give you away." Amanda thought about that for a few minutes in silence.

"What did you say, you know, when Kent gave you the dad talk?" Amanda asked.

"I said I knew you were special the first time I bumped into you, and it took a year for you to agree to let me be your boyfriend. I told him I wanted to marry you as soon as you were open to the idea." Dave replied promptly. "So, should we do a road trip to Billings to introduce the parents?"

"I guess we should." Amanda replied absently, still focused on the idea that Kent thought of her as his little girl.

◆ ◆ ◆

Barb and Kent and both sets of their parents were old friends with Eric and Joanna Grant within five minutes of shaking hands. The men gathered around the burgers on the grill while the women discussed dresses as they prepared a salad and a fruit plate in the kitchen. Joanna had a picture of her dress, a floaty a-line in dark mauve that would really set off her white hair and blue eyes. Barb brought out the dress she planned to wear, a simple sheath in deep rose. Amanda showed them pictures of the corsages she liked; a mix of pink rosebuds, lavender and white carnations tied with purple ribbon, and said all the boutonnieres would be lavender carnations.

As they returned to Bozeman that evening, Amanda was more relaxed than she had been in weeks, and Dave knew that he had been right that Kent had been expecting to be asked to give Amanda away, and that Amanda had been worried about that aspect of the ceremony.

THIRTEEN

Kate had taken several weekend bike trips in May, travelling distances of between eighteen and thirty-five miles to Hyalite Canyon, Bozeman Hot Springs, and Three Forks Campground. Having gained some confidence in her ability to pack correctly and set up camp, she was ready to venture further, so she had signed up for a more challenging two day bike ride through western Montana. The sponsor provided food, a baggage shuttle and overnight arrangements so the riders could concentrate on enjoying the cycling. Kate saw it as an opportunity to see how she would manage the distance, without having to worry about towing her trailer, setting up camp or fixing a meal. Some rides were actually races, but this one was supposed to be a recreational and social event. Hopeful that it would turn out that way, she loaded her bike into the rack and drove to Missoula on Friday after work. On Saturday morning, she joined the other cyclists as they rode alongside the Blackfoot and Clearwater Rivers to Seeley Lake where they stopped for lunch. The scenery was spectacular, and Kate was pleasantly surprised that she was in good enough shape to ride comfortably. After lunch they rode on to Bigfork where they had dinner and stayed overnight. The shower felt great, and the hot tub felt even better. Kate was pleased with her performance. She sat with a group of eight women from a bicycle club in Hamilton who said they did this particular ride every year. Kate wasn't shy about asking questions, and all of them were happy to offer advice when they heard she was planning a trip around the state the following summer.

"You'll love it!" A petite, suntanned woman whose name tag identified her as Marianne advised. "If you think of it as a series of day trips, it will keep you enjoying the moment, instead of worrying about how far you have left to go." There were nods of agreement around the table.

"You'll meet the most fascinating people!" Phyllis chimed in. She was tall, with auburn hair pulled back in a pony tail, a sprinkle of freckles across her nose, and twinkling green eyes.

"Most long-distance cyclists fall into two groups. Either they just graduated from high school and are taking a break before college, or their kids are the ones who just graduated and they are the ones taking a break."

"That's true." Pam chimed in. "Last year, I took six weeks to go down the coast after my youngest went off to college. I still e-mail with a couple of women I met along the way. One of them was newly divorced then, and just met a really nice guy through her bicycling club."

"Was it hard to be gone that long?" Kate asked.

"Not at all. It was hard to arrange time off, but I would have loved a longer trip. Too bad I have to work for a living!" Pam grinned, her blue eyes twinkling. "I used my vacation days and took some time without pay, and it was so worth it!"

"Was it expensive, if you don't mind my asking?" Kate asked tentatively.

"I roughed it, and spent a couple thousand dollars." Pam replied. "Lots of campgrounds have showers and laundry areas, so I camped. If you stay in motels, it would be more, of course."

On Sunday, riding beside Flathead Lake and then south along the Mission Mountains, they returned to Missoula. Kate was euphoric over her achievement of two hundred and twenty-six miles in two days, and glad she had made the trip. She knew she was at one of life's crossroads, and that everything in her life was about to change. First would be Amanda's wedding and then the girls would be graduating from college, and go off on their own. Kate wasn't unhappy with her job, exactly, but she was bored with it, and she felt like she needed a change. Well, she grinned to herself, a bike trip would give her plenty of time to think about what she wanted to do next. Her goal was to have enough savings to finance a three month bike trip and three months to adjust to whatever she decided to do next.

◆ ◆ ◆

Madison and Karly, lovely in their dresses of pale lavender, were nearing the front of the church. Kate had just started down the aisle wearing her gown of deep lilac. All three of them carried white wicker baskets brimming with purple and white lilacs interspersed with pink roses.

"Amanda." Kent put one finger under her chin and gently tilted her face until his hazel eyes looked into her green ones. "You are a beautiful woman inside and out, and as dear to me as Julia and Kate. I want you to know that I'm proud to be escorting you down the aisle to marry Dave. Are you ready?" Amanda looked into his kind face, blinked back tears, and nodded. She could feel the love and support from Kent and all of Kate's family surrounding her. Twenty years later, she finally accepted those words from her first ever birthday party when Vera had whispered 'You are one of ours now' and Carol had added, 'we've adopted you dear, like it or not.' Feeling like a princess in the gown Madison had designed for her, she floated down the aisle on Kent's arm where her prince awaited, his brother and two teenaged nephews beside him, all in black tuxedos with pale lavender shirts and lavender carnation boutonnieres.

It was a simple ceremony with scripture readings and traditional wedding music. There wasn't a dry eye in the church when Dave and Amanda read vows they had written themselves and then lit a unity candle as Karly played her guitar and sang an old love song called "Welcome to my World".

◆ ◆ ◆

Madison was surprised to see Mitch at her mother's wedding reception. She had helped address the envelopes, so she knew he had not been sent an invitation and couldn't figure out why he was there. Making her way through the crowd to say hello, Madison couldn't help but notice that Mitch was the definition of tall, dark and handsome in his charcoal suit, crisp white shirt and charcoal striped tie. She hadn't seen him since high school when the two of them had tagged along with Karly and Seth without ever really becoming an official couple themselves. Surprisingly, Mitch had written to her from college and Madison had answered his letters, at first merely to be polite, but as he kept writing, she discovered that they had a lot in common. She had enjoyed being his pen pal and considered him a friend; a long distance friend.

There was a woman at his side, short and slightly plump, dressed in a pale blue dress with long sleeves and a cowl neckline. As Madison got closer she was surprised at how relieved she was to see a cloud of snow white curls around a lined face. Not a girlfriend, then.

"I'd like you to meet Grace Peterson. I'm her date this evening" Mitch smiled. "I'm also her chauffeur and her favorite grandson." Grace patted his arm affectionately, her blue eyes twinkling as she explained that she was one of Amanda's first clients when she expanded her cleaning business from offices to private homes.

It was an odd feeling to suddenly be attracted to someone she'd previously thought of as a friend and pen pal. In fact, it made her nervous. Mitch didn't seem nervous, though, and by the end of the evening, he had asked to see her the next day. Given her reaction to him, she wasn't sure that was such a great idea. She knew from his letters that he had just graduated from Colorado State. As they chatted at the wedding reception, he mentioned that he would spend the summer in Bozeman to help his grandmother get her house ready to sell so she could move into an assisted living facility. While he was taking care of minor repairs, he also planned to look for a job. It seemed to Madison that he just needed someone to hang out with for a few weeks. They had been friends in high school, and pen pals since then, so she didn't know why the idea of hanging out with Mitch made her nervous. As she found herself agreeing to a burger and a movie, she tried to ignore the feeling she was headed for a broken heart at the end of the summer. Why she thought that, she had no idea, since she'd never had a broken heart before.

◆ ◆ ◆

Kate enjoyed her weekend bike trip through the Swan River Valley so much that she signed up for something called the Century Ride, put on in mid-July by the Helena Bicycle Club. There were three choices offered for a day trip; one hundred kilometers/sixty-two miles, eighty miles, or one hundred miles. Since she hadn't had trouble with the ride in June, she opted for the hundred mile ride. It was billed as a gentle meandering trip along the Missouri River, retracing part of the path Louis and Clark had taken. With her bike in the rack and her camping gear in the trunk, she drove to Cascade after work on Friday and found a spot in a campground beside the Missouri River. The next day, she pedaled along the scenic journey from Cascade to Wolf Creek and an extra ten mile scenic ride before heading on to the end of the Recreation road at Spring Creek and back to Cascade. It was everything it was advertised, and more. Kate was exhilarated by the ride itself, drank in the scenery, and thoroughly enjoyed the opportunity to chat with other riders at the meal afterwards. It seemed like most everyone else knew each other, so Kate was asked lots of questions. She explained her plan for a bike trip around Montana the next summer, and asked for advice.

"Stick to the basics, is my opinion." This came from a silver haired man who could have been sixty, eighty or any age in-between. He was in great shape, with clear gray eyes behind silver wire-rimmed glasses, a neatly trimmed mustache and goatee, and a broad smile. "You need a quality bike and trailer, a good helmet and a cell phone."

"And keep that phone charged!" added the petite silver haired woman at his side. "It's your life-line in an emergency." The pair introduced themselves as Paul and Ginger Bates from Helena, and told her they were avid cyclers.

"You have to be ruthless about leaving things at home." Ginger said. "Every ounce will seem like a pound at the end of a long day. And be sure to buy the good stuff -- durable, lightweight things that are comfortable to wear and easy to clean."

"And you only need one good pair of biking shoes and maybe a pair of sandals or flip-flops to wear around campground showers." Paul grinned at his wife, and she rolled her eyes at him before explaining that on their first trip she packed an extra pair of shoes, and never wore them.

"And I'm never going to hear the end of it!" She lamented. "They weighed two pounds! Doesn't sound like a lot, but every pound adds up, believe me!" A woman named Joanne advised her to always stock up on water and food in unfamiliar areas so as not to be taken by surprise in small towns with one store that closed early, and Aaron cautioned her to keep track of her surroundings so she would know where the nearest shelter was in case of a thunderstorm.

"What made you decide to do a bike trip?" Ginger asked, curiously.

"My daughter will be graduating from college. I've always been interested in Montana history and I thought traveling around the state by bike would be fun."

"Speaking of history…" The speaker, a man named Will, was muscular with blond hair and brown eyes. Kate thought she remembered that he was from somewhere around Kalispell. "Did any of you see that article about the Coram Rock?" Nobody seemed to know what he was talking about, so he explained.

"There was an article in the paper awhile ago. Back in 1959, someone found a rock near Coram, which is a little town on highway two between Hungry Horse and West Glacier. There was an inscription on that rock."

"What kind of inscription?" Ginger wanted to know.

"J. Smith Died July 17, 1801." There was silence as the significance of the date registered among the history buffs.

"But the Louisiana Purchase wasn't made until 1803." Paul Bates commented with a frown creasing his forehead. "And Lewis and Clark weren't even here – in Montana -- until eighteen oh five or six. They were supposed to be the first non-natives in the area."

"Exactly!" Will replied. "But that's not all. The article mentioned the Herron Rock which was discovered west of Kalispell, with a date of 1744. And the Hershman Grave, which was discovered north of Polson in the 1970's and has a date of 1717."

"So that means people were probably living here long before Lewis and Clark showed up." Ginger commented. "Maybe our history books need to be re-written." A lively discussion followed about how to establish authenticity for carved rocks. There was some speculation concerning who might have been in the area so long before it was a territory, much less a state. Kate hated to see the evening end.

FOURTEEN

"You and Mitch, huh?" Karly commented. They had just finished mowing the grass and were relaxing on the deck with glasses of iced tea.

"He's just here to help his Grandma while he looks for a job." Madison shrugged, trying to be nonchalant.

"I always thought you two were perfect for each other, even back in high school." Karly said, eyeing her friend speculatively.

"Get serious!" Madison retorted. "We only spent time together because you and Seth dragged us along wherever you went. Mitch hardly ever even talked to me!"

"He didn't say much to anybody as I remember, but he really liked you. I could tell." Karly nodded her head wisely. "He used to watch you when you didn't notice." Madison gave her a skeptical look.

"I think he still likes you." Karly grinned, but Madison wasn't convinced. She thought it was more likely that Mitch was hanging out with her because he was in the neighborhood and they were old friends. Unfortunately, she liked everything about him except that he sometimes ordered pineapple on his pizza. The more time she spent with him, the more she liked him. In fact, somewhere along the way; she had given him her heart and it was not making her happy.

By mid-August Mitch's Grandma Grace had moved into her new apartment and the closing date had been set on the sale of her house. Madison knew that Mitch would be moving when he got a job, and he was sure to get a job soon. The thought of him leaving was making her crazy.

"I got a job offer that I'm thinking of accepting." Mitch ventured, casually.

"Oh. Well. Congratulations!" Madison forced a smile, trying to be glad for him while the pizza they were sharing turned to cardboard in her mouth. "Uh, when will you be moving?"

"That depends on you." Mitch said seriously, his eyes locked on hers.

"Excuse me?" Madison stared at him, bewildered. "How could you moving to accept a new job depend on me?" Mitch reached across the table and took her hand. Her fingers were like ice.

"Madison, from the day we met, I knew you were special, but I also knew that we were way too young to get serious, so I've been waiting for the timing to be right, and hoping like hell that you didn't fall in love with someone else while I was gone." He paused. Madison continued to stare at him, speechless.

"The job offer is here in Bozeman. If there's a chance for us then I'll take it and stay here." Still Madison said nothing, so he took a deep breath and pressed on. "If you don't want to build something permanent with me…"

"No!" Madison gasped, her icy fingers twisted against his palm.

"You don't want a relationship with me?" He forced the words out because he had to know, even though he knew that hearing her say she didn't want him would shred his heart.

"No. I mean yes." Madison closed her eyes briefly, opened them, focused on him and started again. "What I mean is that no, I don't want you to go. Yes I want to build a relationship with you." She smiled weakly and added. "Very much!"

"Glad we got that settled without me having a heart attack." Mitch said dryly, as the band around his chest eased and he could breathe again. "For a minute there, I thought you were going to break my heart!"

"And I was afraid you were going to break mine by leaving!" Madison retorted. Mitch accepted the job in the University accounting office, and Madison enrolled in classes for her junior year.

◆ ◆ ◆

When Amanda and Dave returned from their honeymoon, they moved the rest of Amanda's things into the new house he had just finished building. It felt odd to Kate, having Amanda's bedroom empty and her toiletries removed from the bathroom. The girls still did all the housework and yard work though now they did it in lieu of paying rent, but mostly they were only there to sleep. Kate was glad she had her bike trip to focus on, because most of the time, she felt like she lived alone. She wasn't sure she liked it.

In October, she took part in a one day Bike tour from West Yellowstone to Old Faithful and back. The summer crowds were gone, the aspens had turned to gold, and the elk were bugling. It was a great way to wind up the summer biking season.

Throughout the winter, Kate picked up extra shifts to build up her trip fund, continued with her gym membership to stay in shape, and started compiling a list of specific places she wanted to visit.

Mitch proposed to Madison on Valentine's Day and they set a date for June of the following year. Madison wanted to graduate before the she got married.

◆ ◆ ◆

Karly met the man of her dreams in Helena at the end of her junior year. She split the blame, or more accurately the credit, equally between her mom and Madison. Madison was busy with her classes and spending all her spare time with Mitch, leaving

Karly at loose ends. Kate was training for her bike tour, making Karly feel like a slacker in comparison, so when some of her friends suggested entering the Governor's cup half marathon to be held in June, Karly saw it as the perfect project and an opportunity to get back in shape.

The training gave her something to focus on and the race went pretty well, in Karly's opinion. She finished it, at least, and could still function afterwards. She was relaxing at the post-race social when their eyes met across a crowded lawn. He was not quite six feet tall, lean and tan with high cheekbones and dark brown hair streaked with red and gold highlights from exposure to the sun. His gray eyes were locked on hers as he moved towards her with purposeful strides. He stopped in front of her and extended his hand.

"My name is Adam."

"I'm Karly." She replied, accepting his handshake. Adam kept her hand in his and led her to a picnic table away from the crowd. Once they were seated, he suggested they get acquainted. He told her he worked in his dad's construction company in Helena.

"Right now I split my time between the office and the field. I worked on the crew all through high school and college, and I would happily have continued to do that," he explained with a smile. "But Dad thought I should get a degree in business. Mom always handled the office stuff for him, but he said I couldn't count on marrying someone who understood bookkeeping. Do you have bookkeeping experience?" Karly laughed and shook her head.

"I'm a teacher, or I will be when I finish school."

"Doesn't matter, I want to hear all about you." So Karly told him about herself and before they knew it the sun had gone down and the air turned chilly. It was the first either of them noticed that the crowd had thinned. Adam caught Karly's hand again and they walked to a nearby diner where they ordered pie with ice cream and coffee and continued to talk. It was late when he walked her back to her car and asked for her phone number.

That weekend was the beginning of a short distance relation-ship (Helena being only ninety miles from Bozeman) that lasted for the remainder of the summer. By the time Kate was ready to start her senior year, Adam had proposed and they were planning to marry after she graduated.

◆ ◆ ◆

"Karly?"

"Hmm?" Karly looked up from packing some of her classroom supplies for student teaching and saw Madison hesitating in the doorway of their room. She frowned. "Is something wrong?"

"Uh, no." Madison moved into the room and stood nervously beside the bed. "Mitch and I were just wondering," she hesitated and then finished in a rush "if you and Adam would be interested in having a double wedding." Karly's eyes widened and then she leapt to her feet and enveloped Madison in a hug.

"Yes! Yes! Yes!" She chanted happily, dancing around the room. "That would be perfect!"

"Don't you think you should discuss it with Adam?" Madison asked, laughing at Karly's happy dance.

"Well," Karly admitted with a grin. "We already talked about it and I was actually trying to think of a way to suggest it to you, but I was afraid it would interfere with the plans you've already made."

"Great minds, huh?" Madison teased. "We might as well get married the same way we've done everything else in our lives so far, right? Together!"

"I agree!' Karly said with a grin and then sobered. "It's going to be weird going our separate ways, though, don't you think?'

"I know. But we'll stay in touch." Madison said firmly. "Bozeman and Helena aren't that far apart, as you already know, plus we can call and text and e-mail."

"True! Do you think a double wedding will be hard to plan?" Karly asked, changing the subject.

"I've already done some checking," Madison said. "Everything I've arranged so far will work for the two of us, so I think it will be easy enough."

"Well, if nothing else, it will save all the relatives a second trip to Bozeman!" Karly laughed. "So let's talk about the basics. What are you doing for a dress?"

"I haven't decided if I want to design something or wear the dress I made for Mom. How about you?"

"I think I'll take the easy way out and wear the dress Mom wore. It was originally Grandma Carol's. I like the style, and I love the idea of wearing a family dress." Karly responded.

"And you don't like to shop." Madison pointed out.

"That too."

"I'm just glad to hear you aren't planning to wear jeans!" Madison teased. Karly rolled her eyes. "So, moving on to my next question, are you going to ask Ben to give you away?"

"I already did. He's been there for me every time I needed a dad, so it felt like the right thing to do. He said he would be honored, and I could tell he was pleased. What about you? Do you want me to ask Ben to escort both of us? I'm sure he would."

"I asked Dave." Madison said, softly. "He's only been my step-dad for a short time, but I've always liked him, and when I asked if he'd mind, he said he'd love to, and honestly, I thought he was going to cry."

And so the best friends who were closer than sisters tied the knot in a double ceremony on the fifteenth of June. Since they had the same group of relatives and a lot of the same friends, the reception wasn't much larger for two than it would have been for one. They had one minister, two cakes, two photographers, and twice as many flowers.

◆ ◆ ◆

Mitch and Madison planned a trip to Catalina Island for their honeymoon. When they returned, they were planning to rent the house Madison had lived in all her life from Amanda. While Karly was student teaching, they had already moved all of Karly and Madison's furniture into Amanda's old room in order to redecorate the master bedroom with oak furniture, fresh paint and new curtains and bedding. The space in the dining room previously occupied by desks, file cabinets and shelves now held an antique oak pedestal table and eight chairs with a matching china hutch. The furniture was a wedding gift from Mitch's grandmother. She chuckled while she explained that she decided not to sell them as soon as she saw Mitch and Madison together at Amanda's wedding.

Karly and Adam had a cruise planned for their honeymoon and then would make their home in Helena where Karly planned to substitute teach if she didn't get a full-time teaching job. When she finished student teaching, Karly moved her things to the house in Helena that she and Adam had decided to purchase.

FIFTEEN

On the Monday after the wedding, the house was eerily silent as Kate wandered through the rooms, to make sure she hadn't forgotten anything. She had spent Sunday finalizing her preparations. There were no perishables left in the refrigerator and the garbage was empty. Her parents were on their way back to Billings with her belongings in the back of their pickup, and would store the boxes in their garage. Her car was parked in the garage where Karly would pick it up when she and Adam returned from their honeymoon.

The bike trailer was packed and ready, with everything organized for easy access. The tent and sleeping bag were tucked into their own storage bags. Her clothing was packed in a medium sized athletic bag along with her i-pad. There was an empty backpack for use if she went on a hike. A small tote bag contained a mess kit and tableware, a long handled fork, a paring knife, a butane firelighter (in lieu of matches), a roll of heavy duty aluminum foil, a box of plastic storage bags, and some basic seasonings. Another tote bag contained toiletries, washcloths, towels and a pair of flip-flops for trips to campground showers. Bike supplies including a tool kit, a patch kit, a spare tire tube and a pump were stored together in a small duffle bag. There was a cooler for extra water and food. At the moment it contained a gallon of water, a jar of peanut butter, a plastic container full of butter, a bottle of honey and a loaf of bread. There was a peanut butter and honey sandwich, 2 hard boiled eggs, pretzels, and an apple that she planned to have for lunch, and a container of leftover home-made beef stew and two dinner rolls that she planned to eat that evening. She had a water bottle, chocolate protein powder, granola bars, energy bars and homemade trail mix, as well as a first aid kit, sunglasses, sunscreen, cell phone, and her wallet.

It was time to go! Her system thrummed with excitement as she buckled her helmet, pulled on her gloves, and mounted her bike to embark on what she hoped would be a wonderful adventure. She pedaled west out of Bozeman on Highway 84, turned onto highway 287 at Norris and traveled through Ennis and Virginia City. The sun was warm on her back, the rolling hills were still green and dotted with shrubs and trees, and there was just a slight breeze. It was a very pleasant ride. She paused mid-day to eat her lunch, but did not stop to explore since she had already been to each town many times during her years in Bozeman.

Kate arrived at the campground near the town of Twin Bridges late in the afternoon, pitched her tent and made use of the shower facilities. Then she warmed her beef stew over the campfire. She was pleasantly tired after biking nearly a hundred miles and went right to sleep. She awoke refreshed, consumed a protein shake and a granola bar for breakfast, and was ready to explore.

Kate knew that Twin Bridges was home to less than four hundred inhabitants, and that the Ruby, Beaverhead and Big Hole rivers converged nearby to form the Jefferson River, creating a fly-fishing paradise. That was an interesting fact, and she would certainly make note of it in the journal she was keeping on her i-pad, but she had not come for the fly-fishing; she had come to see the round barn and the orphanage.

Kate left her trailer beside the tent at the campground and rode her bike a mile and a half north of town to see the Doncaster Round Barn. It was a one-of-a kind three story wood framed structure, shaped like a wedding cake with each floor smaller than the one beneath it. One of the lesser known Copper Kings, a man named

Noah Armstrong, built it for his race horses. Noah was originally from Kentucky and loved everything to do with horses and horseracing. He apparently put more thought into building a barn for his horses than most people put into the houses they live in themselves. The barn was round and contained a twenty foot wide track around the outer wall so that horses could be exercised indoors during the winter. Besides the indoor track, the enormous ground floor also contained box stalls, a tack room, living quarters for jockeys and stablemen, offices, and a veterinarian room. The second floor was large enough to store fifty tons of hay and twelve thousand bushels of grain. There was a freight elevator for transporting feed and other supplies to the second floor, and the hay and grain could be dispensed to each of the horse stalls on the ground floor using chutes. The third floor held a large storage tank filled with water that came from a well under the barn. It was pumped to the storage tank using wind power from the windmill on top of the barn and then dispersed through a gravity based plumbing system. Water could be delivered anywhere in the barn, including to each individual horse stall. It was, all in all, a very fancy, ingeniously designed place in its day.

Unfortunately, there was only one race horse born on the property who ever achieved a level of fame. His name was Spokane and he won several races, including the 1889 Kentucky Derby. By today's racing standards, he would have been the equivalent of a Triple Crown winner.

Armstrong sold the property in 1900 and it went through several owners before being abandoned to sit empty and deteriorating for many years. Renovations were presently underway by the latest owner who planned to transform the structure into a community event venue for weddings, reunions, conferences and the like. It was certainly a gorgeous setting, and Kate was glad she had taken the time to see it.

She returned to her camp and fixed a peanut butter sandwich for lunch. As she ate, she thought about the next item on her agenda, the old Twin Bridges orphanage, and her reasons for wanting to see it. She'd read about the place in the newspaper in 1977, when she was a freshman in high school searching for a topic for a history paper. She hadn't realized that there were orphanages still in existence, but the subject intrigued her and she decided her paper would be about orphanages -- or children's homes as they were often called.

She quickly discovered the existence of two other children's homes in Montana, both affiliated with the Catholic Church. St. Joseph's in Helena was built in 1892 by the Sisters of Charity and operated until 1965. In Great Falls, the Sisters of Providence founded the St. Thomas home in 1908. It was a place for orphans, but it was also a school, a boarding home for children living in rural areas and a safe environment for children whose parents were facing tough times. In the mid-sixties, when the needs of the community changed, St. Thomas evolved into a child care service in support of working parents.

Kate had been surprised to learn that her Grandma Carol's next door neighbor, Mabel Larson, had actually grown up in the Twin Bridges orphanage. Mabel was happy to be interviewed, although Kate got the impression she glossed over many parts of her experiences. Mabel said that she and her younger sister and brother weren't truly orphans. She had been seven when her mother died in childbirth and her father could not deal with his grief over the loss of his wife and infant, make a living, and also care for his children, so he left them at the orphanage. There were other children living there in the same situation, and some of them received letters and visits from parents who couldn't care for them full-time, but Mabel and her brother and sister never saw or heard from their dad again, and had no idea what happened to him. Mabel was philosophical about the ten years she spent in the orphanage.

"They were strict, and everyone worked, of course, but learning to work is a good thing. It was a place where we learned life skills."

Mabel explained with a shrug, "We had a roof over our heads, clothes to wear and food to eat. It could have been worse."

The State Orphan's Home was established in 1893, changing its name to the Montana Children's Center in 1959. When the state legislature cut funding for state-run orphanages in the seventies, the facility closed. Between two hundred and three hundred children usually lived there, though during the depression there were as many as four hundred. They wore homemade uniforms and were housed in dorms according to their age and sex. The orphanage had its own elementary school and hospital. Thanks to generous support from private donors including Butte's copper kings, the facility also had an auditorium with a raised stage and projector room and an indoor swimming pool.

The whole place had fallen into disrepair after nearly thirty years of abandonment, but new owners were in the process of repairing and restoring the twenty-six buildings, in hopes it could be used for a new purpose. Kate hoped that worked out, but after exploring the site for several hours, she thought it would be a very big job.

Kate had dinner in a café, still thinking about orphanages and the children who had lived there. Society didn't seem to have the answers to the question of how to help children in need. It was obvious that orphanages had their dark side, and so did foster care. Apparently Mabel had been able to deal with the issues of being raised in an institution, but Amanda's mother had not been so lucky. Kate admired and respected Amanda for her determination to create a loving environment for Madison. She found it fascinating that some people managed to survive and even triumph over the hardships of their lives. Not for the first time, she wondered if she would have been as strong as Mabel and Amanda had been. She had been so blessed to have the support of a loving family and the financial resources Charlie left for her.

◆ ◆ ◆

The next morning after breakfast, she headed towards Whitehall. It was another beautiful day perfect for biking with moderate temperatures and a slight breeze. About ten miles down the road, she passed through Silver Star, touted as the third oldest town in Montana. Legend had it that Edward, Prince of Wales, and the Son of Queen Victoria, spent three days in the Silver Star Hotel in 1878. Kate assumed that was in the town's glory days when mining was big. Today, though the town boasted a post office and several craft and gift shops, population was only about sixty -- including the out-lying residents.

She ventured off the highway at Parrot Castle Road and after about two miles, came to Renova Hot Springs. It was a far cry from Fairmont or Chico that was for sure. There were two spots on a side channel of the Jefferson River where hot water seeped to the surface. Someone had arranged rocks around the seeps in several spots to form pools. The river flowed over the rock walls into the pools to mix with the thermal water. It was a primitive set-up, and the local couple who were there told Kate that the river level determined whether the springs were submerged with river water and therefore too cold, mixed just right, or too hot. Today, they assured her, the temperature was just right. Had it been the end of her ride, she might have been tempted to have a soak, but she thanked them for their information and headed back to the highway and on to Whitehall.

Kate thought it was interesting how each town, regardless of its size, had found a way to capitalize on its location or history, or famous people who had visited or lived there. Whitehall, for example, was fifteen miles from Montana's first state park, Lewis and Clark Caverns. Kate and Amanda had taken the girls there when they were in elementary school. The Whitehall Chamber of Commerce advertised their town as being not more than sixty miles from three major airports, four colleges, five ski resorts, three hot springs, and several rivers and lakes. Newscaster Chet Huntley, who was also one of the developers of the Big Sky Resort, graduated from Whitehall High School in 1929. In addition to its location and famous resident, the town boasted spectacular murals commemorating the journey of Lewis and Clark. They were done by local artist Kit Mather, who incorporated journal entries into the pictures depicting events from the Lewis and Clark Expedition. Kate biked leisurely around town to enjoy them, then purchased bananas, apples and bottled water at the local grocery store and went to the city park to enjoy her lunch and add to the journal she was keeping on her tablet. Originally, she planned to pack a spiral notebook and a pen, but the girls rolled their eyes and made fun of her for being a technological dinosaur. They had been thrilled when she purchased a cell phone and had helped her learn to use some of the apps and taught her to text. She remembered other cyclists telling her to keep the phone charged and made a mental note to do that at the next opportunity.

As she made notes about her trip so far, she had to admit that typing was easier than writing by hand, and the pictures she was taking along the way would make a nice addition if she decided to print the journal one day. It had taken all morning to travel less than thirty miles, and she remembered the advice to avoid worrying about making miles by thinking of each day as an adventure of its own.

After lunch she rode west from Whitehall and after about four miles, turned right onto Pipestone Road. She wanted to hear the Ringing Rocks of Montana. The road was gravel, but it looked like it had been graded recently and though it was steep and winding, she geared down and kept pedaling. When the road got too rough, she decided to hike the last mile or so. The view from the top was spectacular, and she was glad she had made the effort.

Kate had read that pipestone was a type of red rock the Native Americans had carved into pipes. The rocks in the unique geological formation chimed melodically when tapped lightly with a hammer (or a small rock), but if removed from the pile, they would no longer ring. Kate thought that was odd, since obviously the Native Americans had removed the rock in order to carve it. Theoretically, the ringing of the stones was the composition of the rocks themselves and the way they have eroded. There were thousands of rocks with slightly different pitches and timbres. She tapped in several places and was amazed at the sounds.

Kate hiked back to her bike and retraced her route until she could access the interstate. It was only another twenty miles to Butte, but the road climbed over Homestake Pass and by the time she arrived at the KOA Campground, she was ready to set up camp and have a shower.

◆ ◆ ◆

On Thursday Kate took the trolley ride. It was convenient because it boarded next door to the campground at the Chamber of Commerce and it was a great way to get an overview of Butte's historical district. The only place it stopped was at the Berkeley Pit viewing area. Kate paid attention, knowing her dad would ask her about it. He was a history buff too, but he liked the battles and historical structures, while Kate was more interested in unusual places and the lives of the people. Berkeley Pit was the largest truck operated open-pit copper mine in America, and an engineering marvel. Unfortunately, it was also one of the largest Superfund sites. Kate wondered if there was a life lesson there. Perhaps there was a downside to every upside, or maybe it wasn't always a good thing to be the biggest.

The first place Kate went on her own that afternoon was to the Copper King Mansion, built by William Andrews Clark. According to historians, he was the first, the last and the richest of the copper kings of Butte. Everything Kate had researched about Clark indicated that although he was a brilliant businessman, he was also something of a scoundrel.

It was said that Clark adored his wife and six children, and apparently, he also adored Butte. Though he owned mansions in New York, Santa Barbara, Washington, D.C. and Paris, France; his mansion in Butte was the family home. The thirty-four room Victorian certainly illustrated the opulent lifestyle of a multimillionaire. There were stained glass windows, parquet floors in a variety of exotic woods, hand carved stairways and mantelpieces, antique furniture and artwork, and a huge ballroom on the top floor. Kate thoroughly enjoyed the guided tour of the mansion that Clark built.

In addition to multiple mansions, Clark owned multiple businesses, and donated to multiple philanthropic organizations. He built Columbia Gardens, Montana's first and only amusement park, intending it to be a gift to the city – a place for families. For over sixty years, it was a place for people to have fun and create memories. It had a dance pavilion, a picnic area, a carousel, flower gardens, a roller coaster and a variety of carnival games. The park operated at a loss the entire time Clark owned it. When he died, The Anaconda Company purchased the park from his estate and continued to operate it – at a loss – until it closed in September of 1973. With plans still up in the air about whether to re-open or relocate the park, it was destroyed by a fire in November of that year.

◆ ◆ ◆

Kate decided to have a pasty for dinner that evening, and there were plenty of pasty shops to choose from. The traditional miner's lunch consisted of pastry dough wrapped around beef, potatoes, and onion and baked until crisp and golden. It originated as a miner's noonday meal – taken in his tin lunch pail down into the underworld of the mine. With coal blackened fingers, he could eat his pasty down to the crimped edges of crust, referred to as the handle, and then discard the rest. There was nothing fancy about it, but it was a satisfying meal similar to the campfire meals she herself prepared, and Kate enjoyed it.

On Friday morning, Kate visited the Mai Wah museum to see the collection of artifacts and exhibits documenting the lives of Chinese miners who came to Butte to work the copper mines. When the mines closed, many chose to stay, and opened small businesses that didn't require a lot of capital or reliance on an employer. Some became tailors, gardeners, vegetable growers, or herbal doctors. Others opened laundries or noodle parlors. Kate learned that Butte had Montana's largest Chinese community.

That afternoon, she toured the Dumas Brothel Museum. There were forty-two rooms; nearly all of them intact as they were originally designed, with everything from opulent suites and posh parlors to bare bones cribs, which is what the tiny rooms with space for only a bed were called. Tunnels connected the entire Red Light District to the business corridor, allowing clients and working girls alike to escape the area in the event of a police raid. The brothel was built in 1890 and sexual services were sold there over a period of ninety-two years making it the longest running active brothel in the world.

It was mind boggling for Kate to learn that the year the brothel closed, 1982, was the same year she married Charlie. She wondered what had happened to the women who worked there, realizing that some of them would be about her age.

After touring the brothel, Kate enjoyed another of Butte's delicacies for lunch; a sandwich from Pork Chop John's. Burklund started selling his pork chop sandwiches from the back of a wagon on the corner of Mercury and Main Streets in 1924. Eight years later, he opened a restaurant on Mercury Street consisting of a counter with ten stools and a walk-up window. That original store became a landmark and is still the flagship retail location and home office. Kate went there to have her lunch, sitting at the counter on one of those ten stools.

The sandwich was a boneless pork sirloin, lightly breaded and deep fried, served on a bun with a choice of toppings. Kate had hers with the traditional mustard, dill pickles and onion, and a side of fries. Afterwards she took a walking tour to burn up some of the calories she had consumed while she learned about the architecture and the history of some of Butte's most notable buildings.

Saturday, Kate took a bus tour to Our Lady of the Rockies. It was built in the likeness of Mary, Mother of Jesus and dedicated to women everywhere, especially mothers. Like many big projects, it had small beginnings. A local man's wife had cancer and he promised the Virgin Mary that if she recovered, he would build a five foot statue of her in his yard. She did recover, and he began the process, assisted by fellow workers who gradually changed the size and scope of the project. Many people in Butte donated time, materials, labor and skills to the project, and with their help, the end result was a ninety foot statue that stood high above the city and was lit at the base so it was visible for miles, especially at night. In fact, Kate could see it from her campsite as she went for a swim and then wrote in her journal that evening.

◆ ◆ ◆

Kate almost hadn't noticed the Mountain View United Methodist Church while on her walking tour. The brick building at the corner of Quartz and Montana blended right in with the historic buildings on the hill. She decided to attend church there, and on Sunday morning, she slipped quietly through the doors and sat in one of the back pews just as someone began to play the pipe organ. The music seemed to flow right into the center of her soul. After the service there was a coffee hour, and Kate stayed to visit with the congregation, all of whom were elderly and very curious about their visitor. Over coffee and cookies, she explained about her bike tour and her interest in history, and they filled her in on the history of their church.

It was constructed in 1899, financed by the wealthy, and designed to imitate a nineteenth century European opera house, which accounted for the amazing acoustics, the balconies, the beautiful stained glass, and the oak adornments. That was an era when the church was the center of the neighborhood, with several hundred active members and a myriad of programs including Sunday school, choir, and women's groups. Now the aging congregation was dwindling and it was obvious that the day was fast approaching when the facility would become too expensive for them to maintain and operate. Kate fervently hoped the grand old building would be able to re-invent itself to serve another purpose.

SIXTEEN

On Monday morning, Kate left Butte and rode her bicycle to Philipsburg, a distance of slightly over fifty miles. The town was located in the Sapphire Mountain Range, which stretched south from Missoula for about eighty-five miles on the eastern side of the Bitterroot Valley. The mountains weren't very high, really, at least not compared to other peaks in Montana, but Kate thought they were interesting for two reasons.

First of all, Mount Sentinel, the northernmost point of the Sapphires, was the "hill" where the University of Montana M was located. She and Amanda had brought their girls to Missoula when they were in middle school and they had all hiked up to that M.

Secondly, the Mountain Range got its name because sapphires were mined there, and she had been interested in sapphires since Charlie gave her the Whitcomb engagement ring. Kate had worn it and her wedding ring until Karly was ten. In an effort to move on with her life Kate moved the rings from her finger to a chain around her neck. In preparation for her bike trip, she had taken the chain off and tucked the rings into her jewelry box for safekeeping. She had been startled at how often she reached to touch them as if they were a talisman of sorts. It made her uncomfortable, and she didn't think she would wear them again once she got home.

She shook off her memories when she got to Philipsburg. The town boasted a main street that was four blocks long and lined with beautifully restored historic buildings. The old blacksmith shop had become the storefront for Gem Mountain. The building next door which had been the site of the very first Ford dealership in the state was now one of three places in town where you could buy a bucket or bag of sapphire gravel and use a wash screen to poke through it looking for your very own sapphires. Sure it was a touristy thing to do, but Kate wanted to do it anyway. It was a lot of fun, and she found a small sapphire to keep as a souvenir.

She decided to stay in a motel so she could attend a performance in the Opera House Theatre, which claimed to be the oldest continually operating theatre in Montana. The night's performance was a comedy and quite enjoyable, as was sleeping in a bed. With her tablet and phone re-charged, she sent e-mail to her parents, Amanda, Ben and Genny, Karly and Madison updating them on her trip and reminding them that she was heading towards Glacier Park where internet and cell coverage were non-existent.

The following morning, she took a side trip to Granite Ghost Town State Park, another silent testament to the boom and bust cycle of mining. Once the home for three thousand miners, all that was left were the ruins of the mine superintendent's house and the old miner's union hall. She ate her sandwich and an apple for lunch and then biked to Missoula where she camped at a Campground just off of Interstate 90. She headed towards Polson the next day, stopping to eat lunch and spend a couple of hours wandering through the St. Ignatius Mission.

The Mission was built in the early 1890's of bricks made from local clay and filled with gorgeous murals and woodwork. Next door was a museum and gift shop, and the original log home that served as a residence for the first nuns.

Polson was her next stop, at the tip of Flathead Lake, which Kate knew was the largest freshwater lake west of the Mississippi. She gave a mental salute to her parents, especially her dad, for the historical trivia that filled her memory. For instance, she remembered that Flathead Lake enjoyed a mild climate that made it possible to grow apple, pear and plum trees, but the region was most famous for its cherry orchards. And she knew that there were sightings of the so-called Flathead Lake Monster for over a hundred years. In 1955, a 181-pound white sturgeon was caught; whether it was the monster or not, it was certainly a monster of a fish. It was preserved and on display at the Polson- Flathead Historical Museum and she stopped to see it and other displays relating to state and local history.

While enjoying her breakfast of a protein shake and a granola bar the next morning, she debated which side of the lake to travel, deciding on the west side so she could make a stop at Wild Horse Island. When she got to Big Arm, she debated again between rent-ing a canoe or a kayak to paddle the two miles to the island and tak-ing a tour, since Wild Horse Island was only accessible by boat. On the one hand, paddling or rowing would give her a nice upper-body workout, but on the other hand being part of a tour group would leave her free to take pictures and socialize with other members of the group. She opted for a tour, and enjoyed the afternoon with two women about her age, a family of four, and a knowledgeable guide. He gave them an overview from the boat, and then they spent a couple of hours hiking around the island. Kate had almost as much fun watching the couple with the two elementary age boys as she did touring the island. They morphed from explorers to pirates and back again, scrambling up the trail with enthusiasm. Kate and the two women, both of them teachers, hiked around the island. They were lucky enough to see five wild horses – one paint and four black - as well as big horn sheep, mule deer, a bald eagle and a falcon.

There was plenty of daylight left for Kate to bike to Dayton and set up camp. The next day she visited the Mission Mountain Winery. Although only about twenty years old, wineries were a new industry in Montana, and this one was the first bonded winery in the State. It was family owned, and Kate recognized the label, having noticed it in the grocery store. She had never been to a winery before, and the tour and the tasting were educational and fun, even though she wasn't much of a wine drinker.

She spent the night at a campground beside the river in Columbia Falls and then took the North Fork Road to Polebridge the next day. There wasn't a lot to this little town, located just twenty-two miles from the Canadian border. There were a few houses, the Northern Lights Saloon and the Polebridge Mercantile. The Mercantile had a variety of merchandise and baked goods for sale, and offered cabins for rent. The rental cabins were rustic, meaning there was no running water or bathrooms. The town itself was without cell service, or the traditional kind of electricity; all the power came from noisy diesel generators and a handful of solar panels. It was, all in all, an interesting place to visit.

According to the National Register of Historic Places marker outside the saloon, The Mercantile was established by Bill Adair in 1914, just four years after Glacier became a national park. The saloon, which was only open during the summer, served a limited selection of highly priced alcoholic beverages and soft drinks stored in propane powered coolers, and offered a limited menu. The food was prepared on a wood stove located in a lean-to behind the building. And the only bathroom was an outhouse.

The North Fork Road continued past Polebridge for another twenty-two miles to a spot that was, at one time, a border crossing into Canada. That crossing closed in 1944, and Kate opted not to make the trip. The reason she had come to Polebridge was because it provided access to Bowman Lake, in a part of Glacier Park that many tourists don't visit. Located just seven miles away, it was one of the most beautiful and serene spots she had pitched a tent. She saw several dear and an elk with a calf drinking from the lake. In the middle of the night she heard a wolf howl and was glad she had not, so far at least, encountered wolves – or bears.

The following day, she biked into Apgar and found a campsite to use as a base while she explored Glacier Park. Her spot was across the road from the campground host. According to the license plates on the motor home, they were from Florida. She assumed it was a couple, though she only saw a man. She guessed him to be about her dad's age, medium in height and stocky in build. He wore cargo shorts and a faded gray sweatshirt with what looked like a sports logo splashed across the front.

When her tent was set up, Kate stowed everything except the cooler inside it and then mounted her bike to go grocery shopping at the general store in West Glacier. She bought ice for the cooler and then chose a t-bone steak to grill for her evening meal and a chicken breast for the next day. She bought potatoes, carrots, and an onion to steam in foil packets, and lettuce, cucumber, green pepper and tomatoes for a salad. A loaf of bread, more peanut butter, a bottle of Italian salad dressing, tea bags, eggs, butter, apples, bananas and several bundles of firewood completed her list. With the trailer loaded, she returned to her campsite and had finished putting her groceries away when she had a visitor.

"It looks like you'll be staying for a few days at least." It was the campground host from across the road. He shook hands with a firm grip and said his name was Tony. He wore a baseball cap pulled low over pale blue eyes and had a friendly smile.

"It's my first time here, and there's a lot to see." Kate replied introducing herself as she returned his handshake.

"I wonder if I could ask you for a favor." He said as he glanced over his shoulder at the motor home in the space across the road. Before Kate could respond he rushed on. "My wife sprained her ankle and, well, she's going a little bit crazy sitting around with her leg propped up on a pillow...."

"And you think she might like some company?" Kate asked with a smile. Tony nodded.

"Sure, I can do that." She agreed, and when she had stacked her firewood and laid the fire to cook her evening meal, she walked across the road and knocked on the door of the motor home. Tony ushered her in and introduced her to his wife Sylvia. She was slightly plump with salt and pepper hair and a dimple in her left cheek that flashed whenever she smiled, which was often. She sat at the table, with her foot propped on the bench under the window on her left. She gestured to the bench opposite her and Kate took a seat. While Tony poured each of them a glass of iced tea and placed a plate of cookies on the table, Kate glanced around. The motor home was large with a bedroom at one end. There was what looked like closet and storage space on one side of the short hallway, and a door that Kate guessed led to a tiny bathroom on the other. The galley kitchen had double sinks and an oven, and the dining area bumped out to seat eight quite comfortably around the table. To the right of the entry, in another bumped out expansion was a sitting area with a television and two glider chairs with ottomans, a side table and a pole lamp between them. When they were provided with refreshments, Tony excused himself and went outside.

"This is amazing!" Kate said, admiringly. "But wouldn't you be more comfortable sitting in a glider chair with your foot up on an ottoman, rather than on these benches?"

"I sit there in the mornings and evenings, but I can't see outside from there, so…"

Sylvia's bright blue eyes twinkled. "Now, tell me your story."

"My story?" Kate repeated, disconcerted.

"Yes, dear. I'm a people person. Tony and I spend our summers as campground hosts so I can meet and greet and be nosy with people I'll never see again. It's usually great therapy all around, but I've been cooped up in this motor home for three days now! That's my story. Your turn!" Kate couldn't help but laugh. And then she gave Sylvia a condensed version of her life and explained about her bike trip.

"Is it just empty nest, or are you also feeling left out because your friend and both of the girls just got married?" Sylvia asked bluntly. Kate had been contemplating exactly that question for many miles and hadn't yet arrived at an answer. Somehow she didn't mind talking with Sylvia about it, maybe because she probably wouldn't see her again.

"I'm happy for Amanda and the girls, and I don't believe I envy them." She replied thoughtfully. "After Charlie died, I think I started just doing the next thing, and now I don't know what the next thing is."

"It sounds like you were married, and widowed within a very short time, so you might have emotional baggage to work through." Sylvia mused. "Sometimes when major life events come one right after the other, we end up stuffing our emotions and then we have to deal with them later."

"Are you a psychiatrist, then?" Kate teased.

"Psychologist, actually, retired." Sylvia admitted with a rueful smile. "I don't have a practice anymore, but I still tend to pry! Sorry!"

"I don't mind and you could be right. I'll have to think about it." Kate said, lightly. They talked of other things and then Kate took her leave.

◆ ◆ ◆

To begin her exploration of Glacier Park, Kate splurged on a Red Bus Tour from Apgar. It went over the continental divide to Many Glacier and back. The vintage 1930's Red Buses were thought to be the oldest fleet of touring vehicles in the world. Recently refurbished by Ford Motor Company, the Red Buses no longer had crank starters, but the area on the bottom of the grill where the crank start used to be was still visible if you looked closely. They no longer had standard transmissions either, but the drivers would probably always be called Jammers, from the days when they jammed the gears while navigating the steep grades on the Going-to-the-Sun Road. The buses were practical rather than luxurious with four rows of benches, each seating four across. The seating may have been a bit primitive, but the roll-back tops were perfect for full views of the mountains, and the drivers were full of information about the park.

The Many Glacier Hotel stretched for quite a distance along the shores of Swiftcurrent Lake. With a stone foundation and architectural details reminiscent of a Swiss Chalet, the four story structure was part of the series of hotels and back country chalets built by James J. Hill and his son Louis in an effort to make Glacier Park a destination resort reached by the Great Northern Railroad. It was finished in 1915 and Kate was amazed to learn that the huge structure took only a year to build. She and the rest of the tour had lunch in the dining room overlooking the lake and had time to browse through the gift shop before climbing back into the Red Bus.

When she returned to her campsite from the bus tour, Tony invited her to visit Sylvia again, and to bring her cords and recharge her electronics. This time it was Kate who broached the subject what was going on in her life.

"Do you think I avoid personal relationships because Charlie died?"

"What do you think?" Sylvia replied. Kate considered the question.

"I thought I was focused on other things, or hadn't met anyone interesting. That's what we, Amanda and I, told ourselves...but..." her voice trailed off and she shrugged. "I haven't dated much."

"But Amanda met someone, and now she's married."

"Yes." Suddenly Kate grinned. "And it's a good thing Dave was persistent and creative! She refused to date him for nearly a year, so he called her every day and sent her flowers now and then!"

"But she still had to decide whether to take the risk, didn't she?" Sylvia asked, and Kate agreed.

"If I decide to take the risk, there's another thing I'll have to do." Kate muttered.'

"What's that dear?" Sylvia inquired.

"Learn how to date." Kate sighed. At Sylvia's raised eyebrows, she elaborated. "I only had a couple of dates before I met Charlie, you see."

"Charlie was your first love, then." Sylvia said sympathetically. Kate nodded.

"I don't know where to start." She admitted. "I had a handful of dates while Karly was growing up, but most of them were awkward and uncomfortable."

"Start by just being aware of how your react when you meet people." Sylvia suggested. "Take inventory of your feelings and notice how you respond. Then you can decide what to do next."

◆ ◆ ◆

Kate spent a whole day at Lake McDonald Lodge. Everything about the lodge was big. On one wall of the lobby, there was a stone fireplace large enough to stand in. The lobby itself soared up three stories, exposing massive timber beams and trusses. The walls were decorated with skins and taxidermy mounts of native birds and animals. Balconies looked down from the second and third stories where the rooms were located; rooms that remain true to the era in which the lodge was built with no television, air conditioning or elevators, and bathrooms located down the hall. There was a large dining room and a small lounge, both with views of the lake.

The main structure was built during the same time period when the Great Northern Railroad was building other hotels and chalets as part of a trend by railroads to build destination resorts. Like those other hotels and chalets, this hotel was built to look like a Swiss Chalet with a stone foundation, brown wood siding and white jig-saw patterned window frames. The difference was that this lodge was built by a local land speculator named John Lewis, and was called the Lewis Glacier Hotel Lodge.

Originally, visitors boarded a boat in Apgar and arrived by water, but after construction of the Going to the Sun Road visitors were able to arrive by car at what had been up to that time, the rear entrance. John Lewis sold the lodge to The Glacier Park Hotel Company in 1930, and the name was changed to Lake McDonald Lodge in 1957.

Within walking distance of the lodge were two other lodging options. One featured three suites, and the other contained eight hostel-style rooms with shared bathrooms. Kate had lunch at Jammer Joe's Grill and Pizzeria, wandered through the general store and took the two hour scenic boat cruise before biking back to the Apgar campground.

She spent the rest of the week riding her bike around the park. The days were warm and sunny, but it was cool in the shade of the forest as she pedaled her bike through Fish Creek, Sprague Creek and Avalanche campgrounds, and browsed in the gift shops in Apgar and West Glacier. She spent a lot of time thinking, and had many opportunities to follow Sylvia's advice, because there were people everywhere; all of them friendly, and at least half of them men.

On Sunday, Tony invited Kate for dinner to celebrate Sylvia's ankle being back to normal. Kate took her tablet to share some of the pictures she'd taken so far on her trip, and then the three of them enjoyed a delicious roast beef dinner and huckleberry pie. Afterwards Kate and Sylvia sat at the campfire while Tony made his evening walk-through of the campground.

"Have you met any interesting people this week?" Sylvia asked.

"Men, you mean?" Kate laughed. "Yes I have, and I've been doing as you suggested and paying attention to how I respond."

"Well?"

"I act naturally with women and kids, and older men, but I get, um, reserved with men who are about my age, and, um, appear to be single."

"Very good, Kate! Noticing your behavior is a wonderful first step."

"It is?" Kate asked doubtfully.

"Oh yes. All you have left to do is decide when, or if, you want to take that risk we were talking about."

"Which is easier said than done!" Kate commented.

"Of course it is, dear. Everything is easier said than done." Sylvia agreed.

♦ ♦ ♦

The following week, Kate rode the shuttle to Logan Pass on two different days. It felt strange to be able to look around without worrying about traffic. Snow banks lingered in the shady areas and on the mountain peaks. Waterfalls were visible across the valley and beside the road. Blackened trees from the most recent forest fire towered over new growth.

She hiked from Logan Pass to Hidden Lake one day, encountering mountain goats, ptarmigan and marmots on the trail. They seemed quite accustomed to people, eyeing her as curiously as she eyed them, and sauntering off the path in their own good time. Later in the week, she hiked from Logan Pass along the Highline Trail to Granite Park Chalet. She saw more mountain goats, and another hiker with binoculars pointed out a bear and a cub on the hillside across the valley.

There were about a dozen people eating their lunches at the chalet. Kate visited with a group of college students who were trying to imagine what it had been like to arrive by horseback, have a meal waiting, and sleep in the rustic wooden bunks overnight. They decided it would have been an adventure, especially for wealthy people accustomed to luxury.

Having seen Granite Park Chalet, Kate wanted to see Sperry Chalet too, but this time she opted to travel by horseback. The trail was one switchback after another through the trees, dusty and littered with horse manure, which attracted flies, so she was glad she had not opted to hike. Once they got above the trees, the views were spectacular. Like Granite Park, Sperry was built from native stone, which was probably one of the reasons they had survived when the other chalets had not. Sheets, blankets and towels were provided, but the accommodations were rustic, meaning that they were without lights, heat or water. Kate had heard that the meals were repeated every few days and was glad she got in on the holiday style turkey dinner the first evening. The next day after a breakfast of bacon and eggs, she hiked the four mile trail to see Sperry Glacier. She enjoyed her sack lunch before returning to the chalet for another amazing meal; some kind of chicken dish, accompanied by freshly baked rolls.

She finished her week with an all day fifteen mile river raft trip down the Middle Fork of the Flathead. She had never been simultaneously so cold, so wet, so scared, and so exhilarated. It was a good way to end her stay. She'd been in Glacier Park for two weeks, and it was time to move on. Tony and Sylvia invited her for a fish fry with rice and steamed vegetables on her last night at the campground.

"I owe you big time for the therapy sessions." Kate told her, only half joking, as they finished their dessert of warm cherry cobbler with ice cream.

"Nonsense, dear, I'm a firm believer that everything happens for a reason. I like feeling that I can help people, even though I'm an old retired lady."

"You are not old." Kate scoffed. Sylvia smiled and enveloped Kate in a hug.

"Let me know how things go, won't you?" She whispered, and Kate promised that she would.

SEVENTEEN

Kate biked from West Glacier over Marias Pass on highway 2, thinking about Sylvia's belief that everything happened for a reason. She had never understood the reason for Charlie's death, but as the years passed, she knew that she was a different person as a widow and a single mother than she would have been as Charlie's wife; stronger and more independent on the plus side, with emotional issues to deal with as a minus. It was a lot to contemplate.

When she reached East Glacier, she turned left off the highway and rode under the railway overpass and up the hill. The train depot where Amtrak would stop was on her right. Glacier Park guests were usually met by one of the Red Buses and transported across the road and up the hill to the Lodge. There was a broad expanse of lawn and flowers sweeping upwards to the East Glacier Park Lodge set against the backdrop of the Rocky Mountains. Kate marveled at the sheer size of the place as she explored. The three story lobby was two hundred feet long and one hundred feet wide, lined with columns made of Douglas-fir trees forty feet tall and three feet or more in diameter. Giants would be comfortable moving around in here, she thought.

Louis Hill, president of the Great Northern Railroad, successfully lobbied Congress to designate Glacier as a national park, and immediately after that happened in 1910, he began building the Glacier Park Lodge. It was intended to be a signature building, the first in a series of the lodges and backcountry chalets. Hill's plan was for visitors to arrive by train and stay in a luxury hotel before traveling by horseback to campgrounds and back country chalets like Granite Park and Sperry. Hill's competition, The Union Pacific Railroad and the Northern Pacific Railroad had routes in close proximity to Yellowstone National Park, and had already demonstrated an increase in ridership by appealing to the tourist trade there. He planned to do the same in Glacier.

When the lodge was completed in 1913, the sixty one guest rooms were in such great demand that work began immediately on an expansion that would house another hundred guests. The lodge also contained a lounge, a large dining room, and a veranda on the west side with a view towards the mountains. A nine-hole golf course – the first golf course in the state of Montana -- was added to the lodge complex in 1928.

The railroad sold the hotels in 1960, but Amtrak continues to market the park as a destination for its Empire Builder passenger train and many visitors still arrive by train. Glacier Park is among the last resorts with a railroad connection.

◆ ◆ ◆

Kate had not planned to stay in East Glacier, until she discovered Brownie's Hostel and Bakery, purported to be the only Hostel International location in Montana. Intrigued, she inquired within, and discovered that it was also a general store, a café, a gift shop and a deli. The building itself was a log cabin constructed in 1908 to house the workers who were building the Lodge. The building was far from soundproof, as Kate learned when she decided to spend the night there, lured by free WIFI, bicycle storage, a laundromat -- and showers that were located in shared bathrooms. One of the other guests snored loudly, so she didn't get much sleep, but the place had a lot of character, and there were also a lot of characters staying there. Kate enjoyed visiting with the other guests, some of whom were practicing their English, so conversation included gestures and acting, much like a game of charades.

While she was there, she read and responded to e-mail from Karly, Madison, Amanda and Genny. The next day, she stocked up on groceries and water, knowing she was headed towards a primitive campground. She pedaled seventeen miles on highway 49 and turned onto Cut Bank Road. From there it was four miles on a dirt road to the Cut Bank Campground. She set up camp there, prepared her evening meal and a lunch to take with her on her hike the next day. She was on the trail by eight a.m. for the seven and a half mile trek to Triple Divide.

It was a glorious morning with not a cloud in the sky, but it was cool as she hiked through the forest along the North Fork of the Cut Bank Creek. The air temperature warmed up as the trail rose above the tree line and Kate paused several times with the dual purpose of catching her breath from the climb and enjoying the view. She could see the whole valley, including Medicine Grizzly Lake.

At eleven she reached her destination; the almost magical place at the junction of three separate watersheds. From this spot, runoff from the east side flowed into the Gulf of Mexico, from the west it flowed into the Pacific and from the north it flowed into the Hudson Bay. She had read that divides were not always the highest peaks, and that was certainly the case here. Triple Divide was, in fact, surrounded by taller peaks on every side. She savored the view as she ate her lunch, and took quite a few pictures before retracing her steps, reaching her tent in mid-afternoon. Only about half of the fourteen sites were occupied, and mindful that when people make their way to primitive campgrounds, they are looking for quiet and solitude, Kate did not interact with any of them as she built a fire and fixed a ham and cheese omelet for her supper. When the coals died to embers, she treated herself to s'mores for dessert.

◆ ◆ ◆

Kate retraced her route on Cut Bank Road to highway 49 the next day, turning onto Looking Glass Road and following the steep, winding highway until it joined highway eighty-nine. The road was riddled with potholes and there were no guard rails. Kate pulled over at every opportunity to savor the spectacular views and take pictures. She followed highway 89 into Browning where she spent some time at the museum of the Museum of the Plains Indians.

Kate remembered from her history classes that there were seven Indian Reservations in Montana, and she knew a little bit about the Crow Indians because their reservation was close to Billings. The Blackfeet oral history claimed they had been around for over ten thousand years. They were a nomadic people, following herds of buffalo, deer, elk, and antelope throughout the vast area between what is now Edmonton, Alberta and the Yellowstone River.

Kate learned that the Blackfeet have the dubious distinction of being the only Native American Tribe whose interaction with the Lewis and Clark expedition ended in bloodshed. The expedition encountered eight Blackfeet teenagers returning from a horse-capturing mission. Early the next morning, one young man was killed attempting to steal guns from the expedition and another died attempting to steal horses.

From Browning, Kate headed south to Choteau with the expanse of prairie stretching out on her left and the Rockies rising majestically on her right. She spent an entire day in Choteau, a town that had gained national attention a few years earlier when late-night talk show host David Letterman purchased a ranch to use as a vacation home. Historically more important, at least to Kate, Choteau was where the world's first discovery of duck-billed dinosaur embryos occurred in 1978. The paleontologist who identified those bones was Jack Horner, a native Montanan. That history changing discovery led to scientific papers proposing a new theory that some dinosaurs cared for their young and earned Horner a MacArthur genius grant and countless awards over the years. He wrote eight books, advised Steven Spielberg on the 'Jurassic Park' movies and raised nearly eight million dollars for the Museum of the Rockies, which didn't have a single dinosaur exhibit in 1982 when they hired him. Not bad for a guy who dropped out of college because of severe dyslexia, Kate thought.

The next day Kate biked to Great Falls, a town that got its name from the series of five waterfalls along the upper Missouri River. It took the Lewis and Clark expedition thirty one days of hard labor to travel this ten mile stretch, because they had to portage around each of the falls. These days there is a hydroelectric dam on each of those falls, giving Great Falls the nickname of 'Electric City'. Until 1970, Great Falls was the largest city in Montana, but then was passed by Billings and Missoula so that it became the number three spot for population. Skirting along the edge of Great Falls, Kate made a series of turns that put her on the road to Fort Benton where there was a lot of history.

Fort Benton was established as a fur trading post on the Upper Missouri river in 1846, making it one of the oldest settlements in the American West. When the fur trade declined, the American Fur Company sold the fort to the US Army and it was named after Senator Thomas Hart Benton of Missouri. Fort Benton was the uppermost navigable point and one of the most important ports on the Missouri River system. It was the stepping off place for the fur and buffalo trade and the miners headed west in search of gold. Until the construction of the transcontinental railroads, steamboats were instrumental in the development of the west because they carried goods, merchants, gold miners and settlers from St. Louis, Missouri to Fort Benton. Fort Benton was the birthplace of Montana, the starting place for the Whoop-Up Trail and the hometown of a couple of congressmen, a federal judge, a four-star admiral, and Shep.

Shep, the herding dog that eventually became a symbol of loyalty, first appeared at the railway station in Fort Benton in 1936 just as a coffin was being loaded onto an eastbound train. The dog began to meet each incoming train after that, faithful through the scorching heat of the summer and the bitter cold of the winter. Railroad employees noticed and came to realize that the body in the coffin must have been Shep's owner, and those railroad employees looked after Shep until 1942 when, old and stiff and hard of hearing, he died after being run over by a train.

Kate wandered through the museums, along the river walk and across the first bridge to span the Missouri River which was now open only for pedestrian traffic. She admired the bronze statue of Shep in the park across from another landmark, the oldest hotel in Montana.

When The Grand Union Hotel opened in 1882 it was reputed to be the finest hotel between Chicago and Seattle. A century later, it closed its doors and sat empty and neglected for over a decade. It reopened in 1999, restored to its former elegance and enhanced with updated plumbing and modern technology, including cable television and internet access.

◆ ◆ ◆

It was an easy ride of about forty-five miles from Fort Benton to Great Falls the next day where Kate stopped at a campground on the edge of town. She spent the afternoon catching up on laundry and shopping for groceries and bike supplies including a spare tire for her trailer. She had patched it twice already and didn't want to risk being stranded between towns.

The next day as she biked to Lewistown, reviewing what she knew about the geological center of the state as she pedaled. The area was known for its yogo sapphires, which were unique to the area. The cornflower blue stones were originally discovered by men who were looking for gold. Gold was scarce, but they did find what they called blue pebbles. While most everyone else discarded them, one curious miner collected them until he had a cigar box full, and then sent them to Tiffany & Co. in New York for identification. The leading gem expert in America at that time identified them as high quality sapphires. The stones were hard to mine, though, which probably contributed to their value, both then and now.

Thinking about sapphires again pulled Kate's thoughts to the ring Charlie had given her, now safely tucked away in her jewelry box and stored with the rest of her possessions in her parents' garage. At first she had felt naked without it, but now she wondered if she would ever wear it again.

Kate set up her tent at the Kiwanis Club Campground and decided she had enough time to go see the Labyrinth Gardens before she fixed something to eat. It took her less than fifteen minutes to get to the Frank Day Park on her bike. Though she had read about and seen pictures of meditation labyrinths before, Kate had never walked through one. She had put this one on her itinerary after she heard about it from a woman at church.

Kate picked up a brochure to learn about labyrinths in general and this one in particular. Lewistown's Labyrinth Gardens was nine years old, established in 1996 by a small group of gardeners who continued to volunteer their time to weed, prune and care for it. That was quite a commitment, she thought.

It was a seven-circuit labyrinth, meaning there were seven concentric rings around the center. In medieval times, the seven circuits corresponded to the seven visible planets and a walk through the labyrinth was like taking a cosmic journey through the heavens. The seven circuits could also represent the days of the week, the chakras, colors of the rainbow, or musical tones. Some people believe that the geometric shape of a labyrinth produces an energy field that calms the mind and balances the thoughts so that one can allow intuition, or knowingness, to fill the consciousness. Most labyrinth walkers believe that having a pre-determined path leaves them free to focus on contemplation. Some call it prayer and some call it reflection, but whatever its name, the practice has been nourishing souls all around the world for several thousands of years.

Unlike a maze which is designed to be difficult with choices of paths and directions, a labyrinth has only one path and is designed to be easy to navigate. The path of a labyrinth weaves back and forth, in and out, until it ends in a central circular area where walkers can pause to reflect before walking back the way they came, hopefully carrying the wisdom they gathered on the inbound journey. Labyrinths represent both the journey to our spiritual center and back to the world; at the same time they symbolize the physical path we walk as we journey through our lives.

Kate finished reading the brochure and contemplated the labyrinth before her. There were several other people walking, each of them focused inward, and Kate decided to follow their example. After several slow deep breaths in an effort to clear her mind, she started walking. As she cast about for something to focus on, her eye was drawn to the stones that lined the path. The brochure had called them celebration stones, given in remembrance of family and friends, including some who had left this life for the next.

Thinking about loss always drew her thoughts to Charlie. The two of them had dreamed of opening an accounting practice one day and working there together. When Charlie died, Kate continued with her plans to study business because it was a familiar goal. Now she admitted that she was good at it, but she didn't love it. Sitting behind a desk all day working with numbers paid the bills, but it did not feed her soul. Her part-time job as a waitress where she earned extra money for her bike trip had been more satisfying than her day job at the hospital.

Meeting Charlie, loving him and then losing him had caused a chain reaction in her life. He introduced her to Ben and Genny, and knowing them gave her the courage to move to Bozeman. Genny introduced her to Amanda, and because of their friendship,

Karly had grown up with Madison. Kate remembered how she had wavered for several months over whether to stay with her parents or go out on her own and how when Genny invited her to visit and introduced her to Amanda everything suddenly just fell into place and the way ahead seemed obvious. Idly she wondered if that happened often in life. Perhaps she was missing just one thing that would make all the pieces in the puzzle of her life suddenly form a clear picture. For Amanda that one thing had been when she finally opened her heart to Dave.

When she reached the bench in the center of the labyrinth, she sat for awhile thinking about Sylvia's belief that things had a way of working out, and that everything happened for a reason. Perhaps this bike trip was similar to a labyrinth, giving her the time to think about what to do with the rest of her life. As she retraced her steps, she prayed that she would be able to patiently work through these latest challenges in her life, and as she retrieved her bike, realized that she felt lighter somehow, and more relaxed.

Back at her campsite, she cooked chicken and vegetables in a foil packet over the campfire. She had just started to eat when a group of fifteen bicyclists arrived and claimed the camp sites around two vans that were there when Kate arrived that afternoon. She glanced their way several times while she ate her meal. As they set up a buffet line, she realized that the people driving the vans were the support staff for the group. She watched the organized chaos as they filled their plates with spaghetti, salad and garlic bread and sat down at the picnic tables. It kept her mind off the next leg of her trip across the long stretch of sparsely populated prairie about which she knew relatively little.

As she was tidying up, two women about her own age walked over and invited Kate to join them for dessert. She was glad she had accepted when they dished up sponge cake heaped with strawberries and cool whip. It was the best dessert she'd had since Sylvia's huckleberry pie and cherry cobbler. Naturally, everyone in the group wanted to know where Kate was from, where she was going, and why she was traveling alone.

"I grew up in Billings and moved to Bozeman when my daughter was two. She finished college and got married this year." Kate shrugged. "I'm single, I've always had an interest in Montana history, and biking is an interesting way to travel, so here I am."

Clara and Molly, the two who had invited Kate to join them, started the introductions from the group. They were high school friends who became sisters-in-law when they married brothers. They started biking to lose weight about the same time their oldest children were in middle school.

"It's a great way to stay in shape and we are hoping it keeps us sane when the kids go off to college." Clara said and Molly nodded in agreement. It was hard to imagine either of them had had a weight problem. Clara was a blond and Molly a brunette, and like the entire group, they were fit and toned.

Janet had short black hair, dark eyes and olive skin. She was a middle-school teacher whose ex-husband had custody their two kids for a month. Brenda and Liz were a mother-daughter duo who could almost pass for sisters with their blond pony tails and green eyes. They were enjoying some time together before Liz left for college.

Fred and Jerry had driven the vans and were in charge of maintenance, repairs, first aid, and meal preparation. They said they weren't able to bike long distances anymore. They were in their early seventies with similar builds and short gray hair, and they were obviously doing something to stay in shape. Kate was glad that Fred had a mustache and Jerry was clean shaven so she could tell them apart.

The two married couples were Tom and Olivia, Terry and Ann. They were retired teachers who had been friends for many years. Olivia was of medium height while Ann was petite. Both had curly gray hair and had taught third and fourth grade throughout their careers. Terry was a former history teacher, bald with a gray mustache and blue eyes. Tim wore glasses and had shaggy dark hair going white. Salt and pepper, her grandma would have called it. He was a former math teacher.

The last three members of the group were men in their mid-forties who had grown up together in Lewistown. Both Logan, an engineer from Billings and Greg, an attorney in Lewistown, were single. Drew was married and owned an insurance agency in Lewistown. He was accompanied by his fifteen year old son, Andy, visiting from Los Angeles where he lived with his mother.

Everyone in the group had either grown up in the Lewistown area or resided there now, and their informal cycling club met once or twice a year for a road trip. They planned to take about ten days to ride to Mt. Rushmore and back.

"You are welcome to ride with us." Jerry invited.

"Oh, I wouldn't feel right crashing your group!" Kate objected.

"We're all going the same direction. Come with us at least as far as Sidney." Fred assured her with a shrug. "Enjoy having some company, since you've been traveling by yourself."

"And take a break from cooking." Jerry grinned at her. "Feeding one more is no trouble for us." In the end, Kate agreed to travel with their group as far as Sidney, but she insisted on paying towards the cost of her meals. After some discussion, they agreed on sixty dollars and she added her name, e-mail address and cell phone number to the clipboard Jerry handed her, and received a list of contact information for the others in the group.

Kate was immediately comfortable with nearly everyone in the group as they visited around the campfire. Fred and Jerry and the two couples reminded her of her own parents and grandparents, and she identified with the moms in the group, especially Brenda as she faced empty nest.

Kate didn't even notice how much time had passed until someone commented that it was nearly eleven o'clock and time for bed. When she turned away from the fire and faced the inky darkness between the fire and her own campsite, she berated herself for leaving her flashlight in her tent. Almost before she completed the thought, Logan materialized beside her with a battery operated lantern.

"I'll walk with you." He said. Kate gave him a polite smile of thanks, wishing it had been anybody else in the group who offered to escort her to her tent. She felt like Logan had been watching her, and it made her nervous. Neither of them noticed Greg and Drew staring after them in stunned silence.

"Did you see that?" Greg asked in a low voice. "I can't believe it! I was going to offer to walk her to her tent."

"I bet you were, Casanova!" Drew grinned, then immediately sobered. "I haven't seen Logan pay attention to a woman since what's her name."

"Me either." Greg mused with a glance over his shoulder as he and Drew moved in the opposite direction toward their tents. "He couldn't take his eyes off this one though."

"I'd like to see him find someone and be happy." Drew said.

"That's because you got lucky the second time." Greg grinned and cuffed his shoulder. "If you can do it, maybe there's hope for Logan."

"What about you?" Drew ventured. Greg was an outrageous flirt, but he didn't seem inclined to risk his heart. Drew wanted both of his friends to find someone to share their lives with.

"I'm doing just fine, thanks." Greg grinned as he stooped to unzip the flap of his tent. "This thing with Logan is going to be interesting!"

"Don't tease him by flirting with her!" Drew said sternly.

"Would I do that?" Greg asked in mock indignation.

"Of course you would!"

◆ ◆ ◆

"I don't usually start a campfire for breakfast, so I don't have coffee, and I miss it!" Kate exclaimed. "I could get used to eating like this. The food is delicious!" It was the next morning and they were all enjoying french toast, bacon and scrambled eggs.

"What do you eat when you do your own cooking?" It was Logan who asked in a deep voice. She judged him to be nearly six feet tall with high cheekbones and jet black hair. He appeared to have gone several days without shaving. Just like last night, his dark eyes were focused on her. Or maybe it was her imagination. She tried to be matter-of-fact when she answered his question.

"For breakfast, I usually have a chocolate protein shake, a granola bar and a banana if I have one, and a peanut butter and honey sandwich for lunch." Kate replied. "Trail mix and protein bars for snacks, and something easy for supper." As she spoke, she became aware that she was using the cool, detached tone of voice she and Sylvia had discussed.

"What do you consider easy?" Logan asked with a raised eyebrow and a half smile.

"I often do breakfast things at night, like omelets or french toast. Otherwise I make macaroni and cheese and add chili or tuna or diced ham, and I do a lot of campfire meals."

"What are campfire meals?" Kate could feel Logan still watching her intently and was thankful that the question came from Liz. She had no idea why he was watching her.

"They are just meals cooked over the fire in a packet of aluminum foil. I put hamburger or chicken, with onions, potatoes, carrots or whatever, and seasonings of course, all in one packet. Sometimes I use barbeque sauce on the meat, and then I do the veggies in a separate packet with a little butter."

"Have you tried any of the desserts in foil?" Liz's mother Brenda wanted to know. "I saw some recipes on-line, and they looked delicious, but I haven't tried them."

"Apples, cherries or blueberries are all good with cinnamon, butter, sugar, and granola if you have it." Kate agreed. "And if you make a lot for dessert, you can have the leftovers for breakfast." She grinned. "Fruit and granola, what's not to love?" Everyone laughed.

◆ ◆ ◆

Kate found herself near the middle of the group as they started out and just followed along without paying much attention to their route. They'd been pedaling for about ten minutes when she noticed that they were biking southeast towards the Little Snowy Mountains.

"You're frowning, is something wrong?" Logan asked. Kate managed not to jump even though she was somewhat startled to find him so close. She had thought Brenda was riding beside her, which meant she really hadn't been paying attention, because Brenda was a petite blond. She wondered what Logan's reaction would be if she told him she thought he was Brenda, and choked back a laugh.

"Um, I guess I thought we'd be heading east." She replied, distractedly.

"We're going to Bear Gulch to see the pictographs."Logan explained. At her blank look he elaborated. It's the largest collection of Plains Indian rock art ever found. There are thousands of individual pictographs and petroglyphs, some as large as a dinner plate, some as small as the eraser on a pencil, and all sizes in-between."

"I know pictographs are drawings or paintings, but what are petroglyphs?" Kate asked.

"Petroglyphs are etchings." Logan replied.

"I've been to the pictograph caves near Billings. It was fascinating, especially the one of the turtle that is over two thousand years old. There are other paintings of animals and warriors. It's like a documentary of Native American history." She paused. "But I've never heard of this place, and I researched this area before my trip." As she spoke, she realized that she would have missed the opportunity to see them if she hadn't joined this particular group. She was beginning to believe Sylvia was right that everything happened for a reason. She pulled her attention back to what Logan was saying.

"This site isn't a big tourist attraction yet, though it probably will be at some point. It's on a private ranch that's been in the same family since 1919. For years they referred to them as 'Indian pictures' and their family respected them as sacred, but they also assumed similar pictures could be found in other areas." Logan smiled at her and her stomach gave a little lurch. "I've been there several times. I think you'll enjoy it."

They arrived at Bear Gulch mid-morning and everyone paid the fee for the tour. Their tour guide introduced herself and began her talk as they hiked to the site. First she explained that her grandparents had homesteaded the ranch and called it Bear Gulch because Bear Creek ran along the base of the cliff where the pictographs and petroglyphs were found.

"The ranch was in my family for seventy years before I realized the full importance of the site. I grew up knowing it was a sacred place. I gave talks in classrooms at area schools, and if anyone was interested, I brought them to see. I suppose we got a hundred or so people each year."

"What changed?" Drew wanted to know.

"In 1989, I happened to meet some archeologists who specialize in rock art. When they came to see the drawings they were just blown away. The first thing they told me was that we had to preserve this site because it was irreplaceable. They said there was no other place like it." Kate was struck by the coincidental nature of "happening" to meet archeologists who specialized in rock art, as she recalled Sylvia's belief that everything happens for a reason.

"The pictographs and petroglyphs you are about to see depict figures of warriors holding shields and clubs, ochre-red elk and bison, handprints, and other scenes from Native American life. I was told that some of the rock art was done before bows and arrows came into use around 500 A.D. and nearly all of them were done before horses were introduced in the seventeen hundreds." When they arrived at the cliff, their guide fell silent to give them all a chance to examine the drawings and take photographs. The wall was about half a mile long and a hundred feet high and crowded with pictures.

"It's incredible!" Olivia exclaimed to murmurs of agreement.

"Nobody knows exactly what inspired the artists who left their work here." Their tour guide commented. "The area is secluded with dramatic cliffs, and there are several parts of the gulch that produce echoes. It is assumed that the area was used for vision quests and that some of the drawings and engravings tell the stories of those quests." When they had looked their fill and taken pictures, they started back.

"How do you go about protecting the site?" Tom wanted to know. "Seems to me that if its been here all this time, there isn't much you can do."

"Funny you should ask." She smiled. "I suspect they are really talking about documentation rather than protection. After their first trip here, the archeologists published several papers about the site. This summer, they came back with about thirty volunteers, including members of the Oregon and Montana archeological societies. They spent two weeks studying, taking inventory and making copies of over three thousand images. I'm sure that was just the beginning of the process."

"As word gets out, you'll have more and more people coming to see." Greg commented, and Kate remembered that he was an attorney. "That will put a lot of pressure on you and your family."

"That is one of the reasons we started charging admission. We'll need guides, parking, restroom facilities... the list is endless. My family and I believe everyone is called for some purpose, and ours is to protect this site and share it with the public."

"What a treasure!" Brenda breathed. "Bless you and your family for all you've done and are doing to preserve this part of our state's history."

◆ ◆ ◆

After a quick sandwich, they got back on the road with the goal of making it to Mosby to camp that evening. Besides the post office and a campground, there wasn't much to mark the spot. When they arrived just after six o'clock, Jerry and Fred had assembled a taco bar with a choice of sautéed chicken or ground beef. There were corn and flour tortilla shells, two kinds of grated cheese, diced tomatoes, olives, hot sauce and sour cream. Corn chips were accompanied by salsa or guacamole, and there were brownies for dessert. Everyone was starving and they opted to eat before they set up their tents.

Once they gathered around the campfire the talk turned to the day's ride. There was quite a bit of discussion about Bear Gulch and the pictographs, including what a responsibility it would be to discover something like that on your property. As the fire died to embers, Andy asked about a road sign he'd seen before they got to Mosby.

"Is Cat Creek a town? I asked Dad but he didn't know." Andy seemed mature for fifteen, tall and lanky like his dad with red hair and freckles. He was roasting his second marshmallow, in spite of having eaten two brownies after dinner. If she ingested that much sugar, Kate thought, she would never get to sleep.

"The name is familiar, but I don't remember why." Drew explained with a shrug. He still had freckles, but his hair and beard had darkened to auburn. Like Logan, he had been avoiding a razor lately.

"Cat Creek got its name because a cowboy supposedly roped a mountain lion somewhere along the creek that flows into the Musselshell River." Jerry explained.

"I'll bet that was something to see!" Tom's wife Olivia chuckled. "Is it true?"

"It's hard to say if it really happened or is just a tall tale, but that was this area's only claim to fame for quite awhile. Then oil was discovered in 1919." Tom recalled.

"Of course! The Cat Creek Oilfield!" Drew exclaimed.

"It was the first major commercial oil field discovered in Montana. They say that the oil was of such high quality that it could be used in tractors and Model T automobiles just as it came out of the ground, without any refining." Jerry picked up the story. "Predictably the area experienced a boom with that discovery."

"One aspect of the boom was hundreds of people moving here to work in the oilfield or on the pipeline, or to provide supporting goods and services." Fred continued, "So the State of Montana created a new county by carving off the eastern part of Fergus County where Lewistown was the county seat and the western part of Garfield County where Jordan was the county seat. They called it Petroleum County and the town of Winnett became its county seat."

"Conoco started operating the field in the thirties. By the early sixties, production declined, and by the nineties, the oil boom was completely over and the field was essentially shut down as uneconomic, so the town of Cat Creek died." Jerry added.

"After the boom, comes the bust. And another ghost town is born!" Molly commented. "Montana is full of ghost towns that are fascinating and sad all at the same time."

◆ ◆ ◆

They were on the road early the next morning, pushing to make it to Circle, a distance of about one hundred and twenty miles. Everyone was grateful that the day was cloudy and cool, without rain. There wasn't much traffic so they were able to ride hard. They stopped for a half hour to eat turkey sandwiches at midday, and were more than ready for the bubbling pans of lasagna, toasted garlic bread, and big green salads that Jerry and Fred had waiting for them when they arrived at the campground near Circle.

"Circle seems an odd name for a town." Ann commented as she held her plate out for a second helping of lasagna.

"I happen to know how it got its name." Ann's husband Terry said with a smile as he also accepted more lasagna.

"Of course you do, dear." Ann said, rolling her eyes at him. "By all means, enlighten us!" Terry winked at her.

"Originally, it was the brand for a cattle ranch. At that time it was a common practice for ranches to be known by their brand rather than by the name of their owner. Years later, someone started a store and a post office in what had been the ranch house, and it seemed natural to name that post office 'Circle'. When the area became a county, Circle became the county seat." Kate could certainly tell this man had been a teacher, and wouldn't have minded sitting in on his history classes.

"What do they do here?" Olivia asked, curiously.

"The population is about six hundred, so it's a typical small town. They have a vet clinic, schools, a weekly newspaper, medical care, stores, and several churches. In other words, all the usual goods and services small towns need to support themselves and the farmers and ranchers in the surrounding area."

"Just like home, then." Liz nodded in understanding. "My class only had about a hundred kids, but there was always a lot going on, and the same went for the town." There were nods of agreement.

When the sun went down, they settled around the campfire to wait their turn for the two showers in each of the bathrooms. Greg brought out his guitar and started to strum softly, his shaggy blond hair and scruffy beard glinting in the glow of the fire. When he began to sing in a low tenor, Kate and several others in the group joined in, and before long he was taking requests for camp songs and golden oldies. Reluctant to leave the campfire, Kate was one of the last to take a shower. It rained that night, and the soft, rhythmic patter on the roof of the tent lulled Kate to sleep.

EIGHTEEN

While Kate was making new friends, Emma Whitcomb was adjusting to a new home. Life was one change after another, and sometimes the changes weren't easy. Still, she hadn't lived eighty-five years without learning a thing or two. She and Chaz had found their way through changes both large and small over the years. Like when they were first married and discovered that Chaz was a bright-eyed chatty morning person, and Emma, well, wasn't. After a few months of her burning the toast or spilling the coffee, Chaz had said he was perfectly capable of fixing his own breakfast and making a pot of coffee. After that she had a cup of coffee and read the paper while the night fog lifted, and the days started out on a more positive note for both of them. That had been a small change in the grand scheme of things; this change they were dealing with now was big, or at least, bigger.

It wasn't as if they had been forced to move into a nursing home, at least not yet. While neither of them had any major health issues, when you got to your mid-eighties, it was wise to be prepared. Nobody lives forever, after all. Together they made the decision to downsize and move into this assisted living community mostly because they didn't want to be a burden on their children and grandchildren.

Both of their sons were part of the family law firm. Will was the youngest and specialized in tax law. His wife Rachael was a physician's assistant. They were busy with their careers and their sons, one starting college and the other with a year of high school left.

Their older son, Charles III, or Huck as everyone called him, had been through hell after his son was killed just before he was to graduate from college. The whole family had been devastated by the accident that took Charlie's life so young. For the next five years, Huck's wife Amelia really went off the rails, her behavior becoming more and more erratic. When she tried to commit suicide several times, Huck finally placed her in a hospital for treatment. Predictably, she resisted counseling and refused to participate in any activity, including group meals. She alternated between rage and depression, and was on suicide watch the entire five years she was there, before she died peacefully in her sleep. She had been gone fourteen years now. Emma was thankful that Amelia was finally at peace – and so was Huck. It would be nice, she thought, if he found a woman to share the rest of his life with, but of course that was none of her business. Huck's remaining son, George, was part of the family law firm. He was married to Melissa who was a social worker, their two sons were both in high school.

Emma looked around at their new apartment. It was bright and spacious, with enough space for many of her favorite things. Her mother's china hutch nestled against one wall of the dining area, displaying her grandma's china tea set through the glass, and family photographs littered the mantel over the gas fireplace. The apartment had two bedrooms, plenty of storage, and an efficiency kitchen that opened onto the patio through sliding glass doors. They had signed up for weekly cleaning, but opted do their own laundry, and there was a community dining room where they could go for meals if they so desired. At the moment, Chaz was having breakfast there, and she imagined he enjoyed having his morning meal prepared for him and people to visit with, for a change. She put her coffee cup in the dishwasher and went to get ready for the day.

As she styled her hair and applied light make-up, she perused her reflection. White hair, brown eyes framed by silver wire rimmed glasses, full lips, and her fair share of laugh lines which she refused to call wrinkles. She looked like what she was, she thought, comfortably; a grandmother and great-grandmother. She decided to wear coral slacks, a pale cream blouse and sandals.

Chaz was back from the community dining room when she returned to the kitchen. He was a handsome man of medium height with steel gray hair, warm brown eyes behind black wire- rimmed glasses, a square jaw, and dimples. He kissed her cheek and smiled as he handed her an envelope.

"You got a letter." He deposited the rest of the mail on the counter and went to pour himself a cup of coffee. She glanced at the unfamiliar return address, picked up a letter opener to slit the envelope, and removed a folded sheet of pale blue stationery and another envelope, also pale blue. Laying the envelope aside, she scanned spidery handwriting.

"Oh, it's from one of the women I played bridge with last fall." She leaned against the counter to read more carefully. As her eyes moved rapidly across the lines on the paper, her smile faded, her fingers trembled, and the color drained from her face.

Dear Emma,

We play bridge at several tournaments every year, and exchange Christmas cards, so I consider us to be friends. But we are not best friends who have shared every detail of our lives, and so I have dithered for over a month now, and I am still not sure I am doing the right thing by writing to you. I finally asked myself if I would want to know if the situation was reversed. I believe I would. That's assuming you don't already know, and I'm not sure about that either.

Anyway, I make a habit of reading about weddings, and this one especially caught my interest because it was a double ceremony. My dilemma began when I noticed your grandson's name as the late father of one of the brides. I enclose the clipping from the paper, and I sincerely hope I have not caused you any grief.

Your Bridge Buddy,
Margaret

With trembling fingers, Emma lifted the flap of the blue envelope and removed a newspaper clipping. Under a black and white photograph of two couples in gowns and tuxedos, she read:

Best friends Madison Fitzgerald and Karly Whitcomb exchanged wedding vows the same way they grew up -- together.

On June 15, 2005, Madison Amanda Fitzgerald married Mitch Andrew Peterson and Karly Barbara Whitcomb married Adam John Prescott in a double ceremony held at the Bozeman United Methodist Church. Each of the brides served as maid of honor to the other.

Madison designed her own floor-length strapless gown in champagne silk overlaid with lace. She carried a bouquet of pink and white roses and was escorted to the altar by her stepfather, Dave Grant. Mitch was attended by his high school friend Seth Simons. They wore black tuxedos with pale pink shirts and pink rosebud boutonnieres. Parent of the couples are Amanda and Dave Grant, and Michael and Janet Peterson, all of Bozeman.

Karly wore a sleeveless family heirloom gown in pale cream brocade, previously worn by her mother and her great-grandmother. She was escorted down the aisle by her late father's best friend, Ben Sinclair carrying a bouquet of white roses and lavender mums. Adam was attended by his brother, Joel. They wore black tuxedos with pale lavender shirts and lavender mum boutonnieres. Parents of the couple are Charles Whitcomb IV (deceased) and Kate Whitcomb of Bozeman, and Sean and Patsy Watson of Helena.

The reception following the ceremony was held at the home of Dave and Amanda Grant. Following their honeymoon, Mitch and Madison Peterson will make their home in Bozeman, while Adam and Karly Watson will reside in Helena.

"Em? Em, what's the matter?" Emma realized that Chaz had said her name several times as she forced her eyes to focus on his worried face. She struggled to find her voice.

"Charlie," She whispered and couldn't continue past the lump in her throat. She swallowed and tried again. "I think.....Charlie... has... a daughter..." With trembling fingers, she passed him the newspaper clipping, groped for a kitchen chair and collapsed into it while Chaz scanned quickly, zeroing in on the information about Karly's father being the late Charles Whitcomb IV. He stood immobile for a few moments, before pulling his cell phone from the pocket of his khakis. As if the world hadn't just shifted on its axis, he calmly asked the receptionist to let Huck know they would need a few minutes of his time in about half an hour, if he could manage it.

◆ ◆ ◆

Huck cleared his desk while he waited for his parents. It was not unusual for them to stop by, and if they were on their way to lunch, today he would be free to join them. He was glad they were settling into their new place and looked forward to hearing all about it. He smiled a greeting when they arrived, but sobered as Chaz closed the door before the two of them sat down in front of his desk.

"What's up?" He asked, looking from one parent to the other. Wordlessly, his mother handed him the newspaper clipping and they waited while he read it. Stunned, he looked up.

"Where did you get this?" Emma explained about keeping in touch with other bridge players through the occasional note or card, and how one of them had sent her the clipping from the Bozeman paper.

"Did you know that Charlie was married?" Chaz asked, curiously.

"No, I didn't." Huck replied. "Charlie said he was planning to ask Kate to marry him, and I gave him the family ring. That was right before Thanksgiving. He didn't mention it again, and neither did I. We went to Arizona for a few weeks after Christmas, and then the, uh, accident was the tenth of February."

"So you knew Kate, then?" Emma asked.

"Not exactly." Huck shook his head. "We met her once, and Amelia was, well, you know how she was. Rude would be an understatement."

"What do we do now?" Emma asked anxiously, her hands clasped tightly in her lap. "We've missed so much. They are part of our family, and Karly is... our only great-granddaughter!" Her eyes filled with tears. Chaz took her hand in comfort, and they waited for Huck to speak.

"I think we start by getting in touch with Kate. Depending on how that goes..." he trailed off, wondering if Kate would want to hear from Charlie's family, or not. He looked to his father and Chaz nodded in agreement.

"Kate must have had reasons for not contacting us. We'll need to remember that." Chaz commented, seeming to follow Huck's thought processes. He helped Emma to her feet and the two of them moved towards the door. "We'll leave it to you, son. Let us know what you find out." Huck nodded as he picked up his phone, expecting that within minutes, he would find a phone number for Kate and be able to speak with her. But he was wrong. Kate Whitcomb wasn't listed in the Bozeman telephone directory. He sighed. Probably she used a cell phone, he thought. Cell phones were so inconvenient when you were trying to find someone.

◆ ◆ ◆

"George?" Huck hesitated in the doorway of his son's office until George looked up from the file on his desk. "Did you know Charlie was married?" George looked startled and then shook his head.

"Are you sure?" George demanded. "How do you know?" Huck crossed the office with the newspaper clipping, which he had laminated so it wouldn't tear from so much handling, explaining briefly where the clipping had come from as he did so. George scanned the article quickly.

"I'll be damned!" George exclaimed when he had finished. "Charlie had a wife -- and a daughter."

"We need to find them, Kate first, but I haven't been able to locate a phone number. Any ideas?" George drummed his fingers on the desk for a moment, thinking, then pulled out his cell phone and pushed several buttons.

"Bozeman" he said, and then, "Sinclair Insurance Agency." He jotted a number down on his desk blotter. "Fingers crossed." He said to Huck as he entered the number into his phone and waited.

"May I speak to Ben please?" He paused, gave his name and waited again. "Ben! George Whitcomb here…. I'm fine, thanks…. listen, I have a problem I was hoping you could help with." He paused. "Well, one of my grandmother's bridge buddies from Bozeman sent her a newspaper clipping of a double wedding. You were mentioned as escorting one of the brides…Karly, yes." His shoulders relaxed as he listened for a moment and then replied. "Well, the thing is, we, none of us, had any idea that Charlie was married, much less that he had a daughter." He listened again and then nodded. "That would be outstanding, Ben. I really appreciate it!" He closed his phone and relayed the information to Huck that Ben was planning to visit his parents in Billings over the coming weekend, and would be happy to meet with George, Huck, Chaz and Emma to explain what he knew and answer their questions.

◆ ◆ ◆

The four Whitcombs waited anxiously in the conference room of the law office on Saturday morning. There was fresh coffee and a tray of pastries in the middle of the table, but none of them were hungry. Ben arrived right on time and greeted everyone, before sitting down and accepting a cup of coffee.

"I was hoping this day would come." He said, smiling at them. "It wasn't my story to tell, but now that you've asked, I'm happy to tell you what I know." He paused. "I have to be honest and tell you that the reason Charlie married Kate without letting anyone in his family know, was because of his mother." There were grim nods around the table.

"Were you at the wedding?" Emma asked.

"Yes, ma'am, I was the best man." Ben said gently. He showed them a snapshot of Charlie and Kate cutting the cake, and told them a little bit about the wedding.

"Did Charlie know he was going to be a father?" Chaz wanted to know.

"No." Ben replied. "Kate didn't discover she was pregnant until after Charlie's funeral. I think preparing for the baby was the only thing that kept her sane. She and Charlie were very much in love, and his death hit her hard."

"Did Kate's parents support her, then?" Chaz asked.

"She stayed with her parents til Karly was nearly two, and they helped her with Karly while she lived with them. But Charlie provided for their financial needs." Ben replied, and he told them about Charlie moving his money into a joint account the week after the wedding, and making Kate the beneficiary of his life insurance policy.

"So he had a life insurance policy." Chaz commented, nodding in approval.

"I wondered what happened to his bank accounts." Huck mused. "But then I forgot about it. It didn't seem to matter. Nothing seemed to matter during that time."

"How did they end up in Bozeman if Kate's family is here?" Chaz wanted to know.

"Genny and I encouraged her to come to Bozeman so that she could finish college. It wasn't hard because Kate thought she needed to be on her own. She didn't want to become too dependent on her parents."

"Do you think Kate would talk to us?" Emma asked tentatively.

"I'm sure she would. She was never comfortable with keeping the marriage a secret." Ben replied, "But it will be tricky getting ahold of her." He explained about Kate's bike tour.

"She sounds like she was a perfect match for Charlie!" Emma exclaimed. "A free spirit, but practical, too. When do you think she'll be back?"

"Early fall would be my guess." Ben replied. "I can send her an e-mail explaining what has happened, if you like." They agreed that would be a good place to start, and Ben sent the e-mail that evening.

NINETEEN

Kate's last day with the Lewistown bike group dawned cool and cloudy, but thankfully the rain had stopped during the night. Fred and Jerry served pancakes, sausage and eggs for breakfast before they packed up and started for Sidney. Not quite awake yet, she didn't notice Logan sit down across from her until he asked her to pass the syrup.

"You stayed dry in last night's rain?" he asked as he poured syrup over his stack of pancakes.

"Yes I did." She mumbled, focused on her mug of coffee.

"I enjoyed making beautiful music with you at the campfire last night, darlin'." Greg interrupted with a wink as he sat down beside Logan.

"Thanks. I enjoyed it too." Kate replied, smiling at him. His flirty conversation was entertaining and Kate bantered with him in much the same way as she had done with her customers when she was a waitress. She knew he wasn't serious, and in any case, she was wary of people who tossed endearments out so casually. She wondered vaguely why Drew frowned and nudged Greg none too gently with his elbow as he sat down beside him. But Greg just grinned at him and went back to his breakfast, so it was probably nothing serious.

"Maybe you should come with us to Mt. Rushmore." Logan said suddenly. Kate eyed him over the rim of her coffee mug. One thing she was going to miss when she left the group was having coffee ready every morning.

"I've really enjoyed traveling with all of you, but I want to follow the same path the railroad did along the hi-line. I'm planning to go to Culbertson and then west on highway two."

"I just thought I'd throw it out there." Logan said casually, as they finished their breakfast and got ready to go. They stopped at a farm outside of Sidney late that afternoon after a relatively easy ride. Kate was never quite sure who was friends with the owners of the farm, but apparently there were no suitable campgrounds in the area, so they had obtained permission for the group to camp there overnight. There was plenty of fresh water, but the bathrooms were port-a-potties, and Kate was glad it was only an overnight stop. She was also glad she had a plastic wash basin, making it easier to clean up.

Fred and Jerry grilled hamburgers to go with a macaroni salad and a variety of fresh fruit for the evening meal. While they roasted marshmallows for s'mores, someone asked Terry if he knew anything about Sidney.

"Well, let's see." He looked skyward as if wracking his brain. "The town is ten miles from the North Dakota border and was named after a six year old boy because the people in charge thought his name, Sidney, had a nice ring to it."

"It is better than Cat Creek!" Liz giggled. "What else do you know?"

"The area has seen some oil and gas exploration, but the underlying economic stability comes mostly from farming and ranching. The biggest employers in town are the Health Center, the school system…and the sugar beet factory."

"Really?" Liz asked in surprise. "A sugar beet factory?"

"Sugar beets are the biggest cash crop in the area." Terry assured her. While the rest of the group talked about the area, Olivia was busy taking pictures with her phone.

"Sunsets are like snowflakes; none of them are the same!" she exclaimed. It was true, Kate thought, tonight the clouds on the horizon were splashes of pink and yellow. Last night the setting sun had bathed the entire sky in a fiery glow of red, orange and gold, and the night before that the colors had been deep pink, purple and navy blue.

The next morning, Kate said good-bye to the group and thanked them for their company. She didn't mind spending time alone, but it had been fun to socialize for a few days, especially across that long lonely stretch of Montana prairie. She found a laundromat in Sidney and washed her clothes and her sleeping bag, thinking about Logan's parting comment that he'd be in touch. She wondered if he meant it, and if she wanted to hear from him. She always felt a little off-balance when he was around.

She biked the thirty seven miles to Culbertson, population about seven hundred, and checked into a motel before she spent the afternoon exploring the town. She wandered through the Culbertson Museum first. It was like a trip back in time looking at the country church and the one room school. The displays included a barber shop, a doctor's office and a combined general store and post office. Outside, there was an authentic Sioux teepee, a blacksmith shop, a railroad caboose and quite a few antique tractors. She learned that the town sprang up in 1887 with the arrival of the railroad. Next to arrive were horse ranchers who provided horses for the calvary at the military posts along the Missouri River. Finally the homesteaders arrived and cattle ranching and farming were added to the economy.

She remembered to charge her phone and tablet that night and she updated her journal but the internet was down and she couldn't send or receive e-mail.

It was a hundred miles from Culbertson to Fort Peck, and a very nerve-wracking ride because highway two was so narrow. She found lots of recreational sites bordering the shores of Fort Peck Reservoir and selected a nice quiet spot to pitch her tent. The reservoir was the largest in Montana by surface area, even though Flathead Lake held a greater volume of water due to its depth. Kate chuckled to herself.

She had yet to come across a town, small or large, that didn't make a claim to be the first, the oldest, the biggest or the best at something.

She spent the next day exploring. The main lobby of the Fort Peck Interpretive Center was occupied by a life sized model of Peck's Rex, the Tyrannosaurus Rex that was discovered just twenty miles away. She spent several pleasant hours viewing the other dinosaur exhibits as well as learning about the history of Fort Peck Dam.

That evening, she attended the Fort Peck Theater which was originally built to entertain the 50,000 U.S. Army Corps of Engineers and their families during the construction of the dam. After the dam was completed, it evolved into a community theater, drawing patrons from miles around, especially for its summer productions.

◆ ◆ ◆

Kate biked to Malta the next day and camped in a beautiful campground beside the Milk River. The community was another that had been established with the coming of the railroad in 1890. It was said that the town got its name when a Great Northern official spun the globe and stopped it with his finger resting on the Island of Malta in the Mediterranean Sea. The railroad brought a wide variety of people to the area, including fur traders, homesteaders, miners -- and outlaws. In 1901, Kid Curry, who robbed and killed on his own and also in the company of Butch Cassidy, robbed a train west of Malta, making off with about forty thousand dollars.

Kate spent the afternoon in the Phillips County Museum where she met Leonardo, a seventy-seven million year old Brachylophosaurus. Discovered north of Malta in 2000, he was one of the best preserved dinosaurs ever discovered, and one of only four that were mummified. The history of the area was beautifully depicted by exhibits of cowboys, outlaws, and pioneers. The museum also offered multiple resources for tracing genealogy, including cemetery records, homestead maps, and school records.

Kate returned to her campsite to fix her evening meal, update her journal and take advantage of the free internet services. When she checked her e-mail she found messages from Karly, Ben, and, she looked twice to make sure she wasn't seeing things -- Logan.

She held her breath as she opened the message from Ben first hoping nothing was wrong. It was odd to be hearing from him rather than Genny. The message was dated two weeks earlier.

Kate – I heard from Charlie's brother, George, last week. It seems one of his grandma's bridge buddies sent her a clipping of the wedding from the Bozeman paper. They were shocked to learn about your marriage to Charlie and about Karly. I met with George, his dad and grandparents this past weekend, and they asked me to contact you on their behalf. They are hopeful that you will be willing to meet with them. (FYI – Amelia passed on fourteen years ago after spending several years in a psych ward.) I explained about your bike trip and that you weren't due back until fall. Let me know what you want to do when you get this. They are nice people, and extremely upset that they didn't know about you and Karly. Hope you are enjoying your trip. Genny says hi. Ben

Kate stared at her tablet for several minutes, stunned. Because of Amelia's thinly veiled animosity, she had put the thought of having a relationship with the Whitcomb family out of her heart years ago. Even so, the estrangement had bothered her from the moment Charlie suggested it. She wondered if she would have contacted Huck if she had known about Amelia's death. She thought she might have, because fourteen years ago, Karly had been really feeling the absence of her father. She sat lost in her memories for several minutes before she typed her reply.

Ben – I will be happy to meet with Charlie's family when I get back. I'll probably stay with my parents til I figure out what I'm doing next, so I'll be in Billings for awhile. I'll let you know when. Kate

Next she replied to Karly's e-mail about getting settled in their new house and relayed the information from Ben, guessing that Karly would contact him immediately for a more detailed report. Then she sent a note to her parents. Finally, she turned to Logan's note, which was a brief update about the ride to South Dakota. For some reason, after she answered his questions about how her trip was going; she decided she might as well give Logan a few more details about the story of her life. Briefly, she explained about the wedding she and Charlie had kept from Charlie's parents, the seven week marriage, the accident, being a single parent, and the latest development with Charlie's family. She closed with a request for him to tell her his story and hit send. That should scare him away, she thought, and immediately wondered why she wanted to scare him away. Finally, she sent an update to Sylvia of everything that had happened since she left Glacier Park, knowing she would be interested, and hoping she might have some good advice.

◆ ◆ ◆

Kate's next destination was Havre, the largest town on the Montana hi-line. The town was picturesque with the Milk River running through it and the Bear's Paw Mountains to the south. Storm clouds appeared in the afternoon and Kate arrived just a few minutes ahead of a thunderstorm, so she decided to stay in the Budget Inn where she was able to bring her bike and trailer inside to keep them safe and dry. It was a good decision, because the lightning and thunder lasted all night and the heavy rains continued into the next day.

After her usual breakfast of a protein shake and a granola bar she connected to the internet to learn about the history of Havre. As the mid-way point between Seattle and Minneapolis-St. Paul, the town was founded primarily to serve as a major service center for the Great Northern Railroad built by James J. Hill. She made a note to take a look at the statue of Hill at the Amtrak station. His name had come up often in connection to the railroad, Glacier Park, and the history of the state.

The town was originally called Bullhook Bottoms, and Kate was betting everyone was glad that didn't stick. When they incorporated in 1893, they held meetings to decide on a new name. Many of the original settlers were French, and perhaps it was due to their influence that the town was renamed Havre after the city of Le Havre in France.

In other trivia, Kate read that Havre was the birthplace of three Montana Governors, a professional rodeo clown, a major league baseball player, an opera singer, an NFL football player and the bass player for Pearl Jam.

Kate used the morning to catch up on her laundry, and when the rain let up, she went out for lunch and then biked to the northwest corner of town behind the shopping center to see the Wahkpa-Chu'gn buffalo jump and archeological site. Over two thousand years old, it was one of the largest and best preserved sites where Native Americans drove bison over the edge of a cliff to kill them so they could skin them and preserve the meat. Just picturing the carnage and imagining the smells caused Kate to shudder.

On her way back to the motel, Kate stopped at the train station to see the statue of James J. Hill that had been erected to commemorate his role in the history of the state in general and Havre in particular. She learned that the Amtrak route through Montana is called the Empire Builder in his honor. A Great Northern Steam Locomotive was also displayed there, as well as a sculpture representing the friendship between the United States and Canada.

Kate picked up a map the next morning and spent the whole day wandering through the thirty-six block historic district, where she found a wide variety of late nineteenth and early twentieth century architecture displayed in the homes of historic Havre entrepreneurs. Most of the names were not familiar to Kate, but she did recognize Frank Buttrey. She knew he founded a line of department stores which eventually became Buttrey Foods. At one time there were as many as forty-four Buttrey stores operating in Montana, Wyoming and North Dakota.

A lesser known fact about Buttrey was that he founded the first radio station in Montana in 1922. The call letters were KFBB; the K because the station was west of the Mississippi, FB stood for Frank Buttrey and B was for broadcasting.

That afternoon, Kate bought a ticket to visit 'Havre Beneath the Streets' and joined a tour group that included two couples who were probably college age, and another woman who fell into step beside Kate and introduced herself as Tori. Petite with short strawberry blond curls, green eyes and freckles, she exuded friendliness and within a few minutes, Kate felt as if they had known each other for years.

Throughout the downtown area Kate had noticed small grids of purple squares on some of the sidewalks. They turned out to be skylights for the subterranean passages that had been used and inhabited by the city's earliest residents.

According to the tour guide, a large area of Havre's business district burned in January of 1904 and a shortage of building supplies made it impossible to rebuild immediately. Resourceful business owners moved underground into their basements. Eventually, passageways, some of which were originally steam tunnels, connected the underground businesses to one another, and (because racism was rampant) they also served as safe places for the Chinese railroad workers. The passageways reminded Kate of the underground tunnels of the red light district in Butte.

Throughout history, the Havre underground included several businesses, including a brothel, a Chinese laundromat, a saloon, a drugstore, a dentist office, and a drug store. There were also areas used for smuggling alcohol during Prohibition and at least three opium dens. Some of the areas they viewed were original and some were re-created, but all of them were historically accurate — and Kate found them fascinating.

She and Tori chatted comfortably throughout the tour, exclaiming over the restoration and chuckling at some of the comments made by their tour guide. When the tour ended, Tori suggested they have dinner together so they could continue their conversation. She led Kate to her pickup.

"Nice ride." Kate commented as they drove to a nearby restaurant. The pickup was bright red and had a gray leather interior. "My dad has a pickup, but it isn't this fancy!"

"I like it." Tori agreed. "It's my only vehicle, so I wanted it to be comfortable. But I also need cargo space when I go to estate sales, and of course I wanted four-wheel drive for winter. After driving a pickup, I'm not sure I'd want a car again."

Once they were seated and had ordered their food, Tori peppered Kate with questions. She asked about the bike trip. She wanted to know about Kate's job, family, and friends, and before long, Kate had shared most of the details of her life. Finally she laughed and held up her hand.

"Stop! You now know my entire life story and all I know is your name! It's your turn." Kate exclaimed. Tori said she was a widow and lived in Shelby where she had an apartment above her store.

"I sell a little bit of everything." She explained. "Including Montana made products, paintings and pictures, and second hand things on consignment."

"Good for you! But if you live in Shelby, what are you doing in Havre?" Kate wanted to know.

"Well, I like history too, so I've been learning all about Montana and this was on my list." Tori explained. That sounded like Tori wasn't a native Montanan, and Kate had more questions on the tip of her tongue, but she decided to wait while they paid the bill and walked back to the pickup. Just before they reached the end of the sidewalk leading to the parking area, a young man careened around the corner on a skateboard and crashed into Kate. The impact sent the two of them to the sidewalk in a tangle of arms and legs while the skateboard continued its forward momentum until it disappeared under a car. The young man untangled himself and jumped to his feet. He helped Kate up, apologizing profusely. Kate assured him she was not seriously hurt, and waved him towards the parking lot to retrieve his skateboard.

"How bad is it?" Tori asked worriedly, noticing Kate holding her left arm close to her body as they climbed into her pickup."

"My arm twisted under me when I landed. I'm pretty sure it's sprained." Kate said, ruefully. "I guess I'll be staying in Havre for a few days until I can ride again."

"I've got a better idea!" Tori exclaimed. "Come to Shelby and stay with me! I have plenty of room and I can haul your bike and trailer in the back of my pickup."

"I couldn't impose on you that way." Kate protested.

"I never pass up an opportunity to make a new friend." Tori insisted. "We have a lot in common, and I'd love the chance for us to get to know each other a little better. Plus I'm guessing Shelby was your next stop anyway." She raised her eyebrows questioningly and Kate nodded. "Well, my guest room is nicer than a motel. You can rest while I'm working in the shop, and we can take a few road trips so you can see the area. Oh! This will work out just great! Everything happens for a reason, you know." Kate heard the words like an echo of Sylvia telling her that exact same thing and since her arm was really starting to hurt, she decided not to argue and pointed the way to her motel.

Tori prevailed upon another motel guest to help lift Kate's bike and trailer into the bed of her pickup. Kate swallowed a couple of ibuprofen tablets, dropped her key off at the office and finalized her bill, and then they were on their way.

◆ ◆ ◆

TWENTY

"Tell me about Shelby." Kate suggested as Tori drove west on highway two. Her arm was throbbing and she needed a distraction.

"Let's see. In 1891 James J. Hill of the Great Northern Railroad decided to put a junction between the main east-west line and the north-south line between Great Falls and Canada. At that time, all that marked the place was a bunch of tents where the railroad workers lived. Later, a boxcar was placed on a side track at the junction and it was called Shelby Junction after Peter B. Shelby, who was the general manager of the Montana Central Railroad. A few years after that, they just started calling the place Shelby."

"If it wasn't for the railroad, this area probably wouldn't have been settled til years later." Kate commented.

"I'm sure that's true." Tori laughed. "Nowadays, Shelby gets over thirty trains a day, so the railroad is still a big part of the landscape. Thank you James J. Hill!" She gave a mock salute.

"Whatever else he was, he certainly had the vision and initiative that helped build this part of the country." Kate commented. "So a town was born?"

"You know how it went. Someone built a saloon. Then there was a small hotel, and it grew from there."

"What else goes on in Shelby besides the railroad?"

"It sits in the middle of a farming region called the golden triangle with a population of around three thousand people. Shelby hosts a four-county fair, which went on last week. There is a museum and of course we brag about famous people who either grew up here or graduated from Shelby High School….or spent more than a day here." Tori chuckled.

"All the towns I've visited do that, and every town seems to come up with someone who was famous for something." Kate searched her memory. "So, I know Jack Horner, the dinosaur guy, was from Shelby. Are there others?"

"NBA basketball player Larry Krystkowiak, author James Grady, and a scientist named Leroy Hood, who had something to do with DNA research." Tori replied promptly. "But Shelby is probably most famous for the Dempsey-Gibbons boxing match."

"Boxing match?" Kate asked. "There's got to be a story there."

"Oh, there is." Tori replied, and she launched into the tale. "Shelby is at the junction of two major highways and the railroad, but in the twenties that was about all it was – a junction. Then in 1922, oil was discovered nearby and the place became an instant boom town."

"I can imagine." Kate agreed. "That happened all over the state."

"People were moving into the area because of the oil, and businesses were springing up, including several new banks. So the movers and shakers of the community set out to make Shelby an economic center and a tourist attraction. They decided to start by bringing a world heavyweight championship fight to town, and to add a dash of patriotism they scheduled the fight for July 4, 1923."

"That has disaster written all over it if you ask me," Kate said, rolling her eyes. "What happened?"

"Well, Jack Dempsey was a big deal. He was famous all over the United States, and so were his manager Jack Kearns and his promoter Tex Rickard. I've heard people compare Tex to Don King, so that should give you an idea. Anyway, the Shelby officials figured that people would come to see any one of the three, and it might have worked, but whoever was in charge of such things picked Tommy Gibbons to challenge Dempsey. He was an okay fighter, but he wasn't famous. Nobody beyond the boxing world knew who he was and that made him a weak point in the plan.

Then Kearns, the manager, asked for an advance to cover traveling costs and a guaranteed purse, and threatened to take the fight elsewhere if they didn't agree. Gibbons demanded money too. The Shelby officials wanted the fight so bad that they agreed to everything and got the banks to provide the money to stage the event."

"I thought bankers were supposed to know better." Kate commented. "Go on."

"Well, they built an arena about the size of a football field; the place would seat over thirty thousand people. in order to raise the money that had been guaranteed to the fighters, tickets were priced pretty high and not very many people bought them. They say the place was only half full and some of those had stormed the makeshift barriers and gotten in without paying. Thousands more watched the fight for free from the rolling hills around the arena."

"So basically, the whole thing was an economic disaster." Kate commented. "I'm assuming the banks were left high and dry?"

"They were. Four banks closed, and the whole town was devastated. Oh, and I'm sure its no coincidence that the name of the weekly newspaper is the Shelby Promoter." Tori said with a smirk. Kate chuckled, looking around curiously as they drove down Shelby's Main Street.

"Good for them, I say. The town is still here, so we know the people who live here don't give up, and they aren't afraid to think big."

"That's true." Tori agreed as she made a left turn and pulled into a driveway. "This is my place." She touched the remote to open the garage door and drove inside. As the door closed behind them, Tori hopped out and flipped the wall switch so that light bathed the interior of an oversized two stall garage. Kate climbed down from the passenger seat and followed Tori to a large door, which turned out to be an oversized elevator. She raised her eyebrows at Tori before following her over the threshold.

"It's a freight elevator. I'll tell you the whole story tomorrow. Right now, let's get you settled." When they stepped out of the elevator, she led Kate down through the dimly lit kitchen and down a hallway to a doorway on the left. She turned the lights on and dropped Kate's bag on the queen sized bed. "You have your own bathroom through that door. Have a nice bath, take some more ibuprofen and get some rest. Yell if you need anything." She left and Kate gratefully followed her suggestions.

◆ ◆ ◆

Kate woke to the aroma of coffee, and it took her a minute to remember where she was. Her arm gave a painful throb as she sat up in bed and looked around at the details she had been too tired to notice the previous night. The walls were pale yellow. Both the bedspread and curtains had a cornflower blue background strewn with tiny yellow and white daisies. The adjoining bathroom was white with a pale blue shower curtain, and there were bright yellow towels and area rugs.

Kate dressed quickly, took more ibuprofen and found Tori seated at the island in the kitchen sipping coffee as she filled in the squares of the crossword puzzle from the newspaper.

"How's your arm?" Tori asked, looking up. "Were you able to sleep?"

"It's still swollen, but the ibuprofen kept me comfortable enough to sleep." Kate replied as she helped herself to a mug of coffee and glanced around the kitchen. "I love the daisies in the guest room and the bed was very comfortable!"

"Thanks." Tori grinned. "I love flowers! I did my room in roses, and the laundry room in lilacs." Kate took a seat at the table and looked around.

"This kitchen is great too!" She said admiringly. The walls were mint green with white trim. White appliances and cupboards with green countertops lined one wall. A large island provided both work space and dining area. She and Tori were seated on two of the wrought iron swivel chairs topped with green and white cushions.

The opposite wall had two large picture windows with white mini-blinds and green and white valances. One window was surrounded by built in oak cupboards, drawers and display shelves in a shade or two lighter than the floor. In front of the other window was an oval dining table with four chairs. The table was topped with a tea set on a lace table runner. A china cupboard with extra dining chairs on each side stood against the adjoining wall.

Kate glanced toward the elevator door in the middle of the end wall. On one side of the elevator was a stairway and on the other, sliding glass doors led outdoors.

"Aren't we on the second floor?" She asked with raised eyebrows.

"Come and see." Tori invited. She crossed the room and opened the sliding door so they could step outside. Kate followed and found herself on a large rooftop patio. She stopped in the middle of the space and turned in a circle, taking everything in. An assortment of flowers and strawberry plants spilled from the planters on top of the waist high wall that enclosed the entire rooftop. Three large green pots stood next to the wall on the left, two with tomato plants and another with cucumbers climbing on a trellis. Against the right wall was a pair of grow boxes, one filled with mixed salad greens and the other containing an herb garden. A round patio table and three chairs were grouped in one corner on the far side of the patio, while the other corner was taken up by a small hot tub and a cushioned lounge chair. Nestled between them was a cart with a hibachi on top and barbeque utensils underneath. Behind her, tucked out of sight beside the sliding glass door was a water spigot with a hose, a small workbench and a cupboard containing potting soil and garden tools.

"Wow." Kate said. "This is amazing!"

"Thanks." Tori smiled. "I spend a lot of time out here. Come and see the rest of my space." Tori led the way back inside and re-filled her coffee mug. "It's an old building that had been vacant for several years. Originally there was a television and radio repair shop on the ground floor and three apartments up here. I had the whole place gutted, and let me tell you that the freight elevator got a workout during the demolition and re-construction process!" She led the way through a white archway that led from the kitchen into a wide hallway.

"There is a powder room between the kitchen and the laundry room on the right. On the left are the two bedrooms, each with its own bathroom." Tori gestured as they walked. "You can check all that out later." As she spoke, they stepped through the arch at the other end of the hall into a huge room. Kate halted abruptly and looked around in amazement. The room was light and airy with cream colored walls, hardwood floors and four large picture windows. Both seating areas were filled with leather furniture, colorful pillows and cozy crocheted throws.

Between the picture windows on the far wall an antique mirror hung over a gas fireplace. A rectangular area rug in shades of cream, rust and dark green lay in front of the fireplace, bordered by a cream colored leather couch, two matching loveseats, pillows in earth tones, and a variety of occasional tables.

On the left side of the room, an L-shaped oak entertainment center filled the corner formed by the bedroom wall. It held a flat screen television, electronic equipment and an assortment of movies and CD's. An oversized dark green leather chair and matching loveseat, a cream colored glider chair and ottoman, each with a small table, anchored the square area rug in front of the entertainment center. The space on the other side of the window was filled with tall shelves crammed with books, a rust colored leather recliner, an end table and a floor lamp.

On the right side of the room, the wall next to the laundry room extended to form an alcove, which concealed an elliptical machine. Under the window was a cushioned bench with open shelves underneath containing hand weights, yoga bricks and rolled up exercise mats.

"You've created a wonderful home, Tori!" Kate exclaimed, admiringly.

"Thank you." Tori replied. "I had to do scale drawings for the rooms and each piece of furniture. Most of this is from the house my husband and I had. I sold a lot of things of course, but I kept my favorites." She shrugged and was quiet for a moment. "I've asked you all kinds of questions about your past, but you haven't asked me very many about mine. Why is that?"

"I grew up in a family who shared things, so I don't mind talking about my life." Kate shrugged. "But I've learned that everyone is different. My friend Amanda rarely shares her life stories. My friend Genny believes that everyone has the right to tell their story in their own time and in their own way, and I guess I believe that too." Tori stared at her for a moment and then took a seat on one of the loveseats in front of the fireplace and motioned Kate to the other.

"Here's my story then." She took a swallow of coffee, wrapped her hands around her mug and stared into it as if it were a crystal ball. "I was born and raised in Spokane. My parents just moved into a retirement community there last year. After high school, I lived at home and went to college at Whitworth. I met Brant my senior year while he was stationed at Fairchild Air Force Base and we married on Valentine's Day the year after I graduated." She finished her coffee and put her empty mug down on the coffee table. As if she needed something to do with her hands, she picked up one of the pillows. Hugging it to her chest, she continued.

"We traveled from one Air Force base to another for a few years, and then settled in Spokane where he ran the recruiting office. We raised both of our daughters there. Janie went to Gonzaga and married her high school sweetheart. Patti went to Whitman and married a young man from Seattle. We couldn't believe how blessed we were that the girls and their new husbands settled in Spokane. Everything was perfect -- until the day Brant had a massive stroke."

"Oh, no." Kate murmured.

"That's what I thought!" Tori nodded. "He was as slim and trim as the day I met him. We ate right and exercised and had regular checkups. We did all the things they say you should do, and one day he keeled over at work. He was fifty."

"I'm so sorry." Kate murmured. Both of them were silent for a few moments.

"I don't remember much about the next two years." Tori confided. "It was all I could do to get out of bed every day and keep breathing."

"Yes." Kate agreed. "I remember feeling that way too."

"On my forty-sixth birthday it occurred to me that I was alone in this huge house that we designed and built together, and it was full of memories. I didn't mind that so much. They were mostly good memories. But it was also full of dreams of the two of us growing old together. With Brant gone, I felt like I was merely existing in a shadow life, but not really living. I decided I had to do something to motivate myself to start living again, because I was too young to give up." She fell silent and Kate nodded in understanding. What Tori described was exactly what she had gone through after Charlie was killed. She, too, had looked for ways to motivate herself to keep going, and taking care of Karly wasn't quite enough.

"First, I took a couple of trips. I visited cousins in Portland and Seattle, and friends in Moses Lake, Sand Point, and Shelby. While I was here, I saw this abandoned building, and all of a sudden I could see myself living upstairs above a store. It was like having a vision. Or at least I think it was. I'd never actually had a vision before, so...." She shrugged.

"So you moved." Kate said, remembering how her friendship with Genny and Ben and her need for a change had been the catalyst for her own decision to move.

"I moved, and in the process I decided to change everything about my life that I could change. My name is Victoria and I'd always been Vicki. I decided to become Tori instead. I'd never bought or sold property, or even picked out a car on my own. Within a year I put my things in storage, sold my house and bought this building and started remodeling. When this place was ready, I had to decide which of my things to keep and move them, then sell or give away what was left. Sometimes I wondered if I would have anything to do when I got that all done. Once I had a place to live, I started on the store, and then I wondered if the store idea would work. I had no experience with working in, much less owning a store. I majored in history, planning to be a teacher."

"Did you ever teach?" Kate asked, curiously.

"No. First I had small children and we moved frequently, and then I just got busy doing other things."

"The store seems to be working out, right?" Kate asked.

"Yes, thank goodness! My girls were shocked, at first, over all the changes I was making. But I was so sure it was the right thing for me to do that eventually, they stopped fussing. I go to Spokane several times a year to visit my folks, my girls and their families, but I'm very comfortable here. And I feel good that I'm not a burden on them."

"Do you ever think about falling in love again?" Kate asked.

"I think the odds of that happening at my age and in a small town are pretty remote." Tori rolled her eyes and grinned. "But if I had a chance at love again, I'd grab it with both hands and hang on tight!'"

"You wouldn't be afraid?"

"Afraid to go through the loss again, you mean?" Tori asked. Kate nodded. "No. Definitely not. I wouldn't have missed the time I had with Brant, including having our girls, for anything. It was worth the pain of losing him." Both women were quiet for a few moments.

"I do get lonely, of course. But I think that's normal and I try to adjust by having work to do and friends and family to visit or call. That's one of the reasons I was in Havre the day I met you – I needed to get out and do something."

"Sounds like we're both taking one day at a time and doing the next thing." Kate commented.

"Exactly! I just kept doing the next thing and somehow I got the apartment re-modeled and the store set up. I made friends and got involved in the community, and traded my car in for a pickup with four wheel drive." Kate nodded, understanding exactly what she was talking about. They talked a little about how similar their experiences were. Tori completely understood that Kate's bike tour was a buffer between her old life and whatever would come next.

"I'm sure the next part of your life will become clear, eventually." Tori said. "Maybe you'll have a vision."

◆ ◆ ◆

The next day was Sunday, and while Tori caught up on bookkeeping for her shop, Kate decided to respond to her e-mail. It was a slow process trying to do most of the typing with one hand, and she ended up sending a group e-mail to her mother, Karly, Amanda, and Genny.

Ben sent a note to let her know that the Whitcomb family was relieved she would be willing to see them. She answered that with a smiley face, and then sat lost in thought for a few minutes, thinking that it was probably time to return the sapphire ring. Perhaps Charlie's brother had a son.

She had saved Logan's e-mail, written from Mt. Rushmore, for last. He thanked her for telling him about her history, and returned the favor by sharing some of his life story, which she read with great interest. He told her he'd grown up in Lewistown and that his parents, John and Jane Brown, still lived on the ranch. He and his siblings were named for mountain passes in Montana; Logan, McDonald, Marias, and Rogers. His brother McDonald had become Don, Rogers became Roger and Marias became Mariah.

"I didn't mind my name," he wrote, "but growing up, my siblings hated being named for mountain passes. We should probably have counted our blessings, given that it could have been worse. Some of Montana's passes have names worse than the ones our parents bequeathed to us - like Homestake, Eagle, Beartooth, Big Hole, Chief Joseph or Gibbons, for example."

He mentioned that his brothers and his sister were all married and living in and around Lewistown; Don helped his dad on the ranch, Mariah was a teacher and Roger was an optometrist. He was the oldest, had been married while still in college and divorced two years later, by mutual consent and with no children. He got his degree in engineering, landed a job with a large construction firm, and moved from one job to another, usually spending about a year in each place. Eventually, he got tired of moving around so much and decided to settle down, so he ended up in Billings working part-time for a small engineering firm. It was close, but not too close to his family. He closed by saying he would check in with her when he got back to Lewistown.

She sent an e-mail containing a summary of the past week, including her collision with the skateboarder, her sore arm, and her new friend, Tori. She told him she'd be staying in Shelby for a few days until her arm felt better. She sent another update to Sylvia though she hadn't heard from her, probably because they were still in Glacier Park, where there was no internet.

She took more ibuprofen for her aching arm and decided to call Amanda instead of sending an e-mail. They talked for half an hour, catching up on each other's lives, including Kate's sore arm and meeting Tori. Then Kate said the magic words.

"I met a guy." It took another fifteen minutes to relay all the details of meeting Logan and their e-mail correspondence to date. It was so good to talk to Amanda again! Kate had missed her.

TWENTY-ONE

The next morning after breakfast, Kate followed Tori to her shop on the ground floor of her building. They exited the spiral staircase next to the freight elevator. High windows bathed the area in light making it unnecessary to turn on the fluorescent ceiling fixtures. There was a mini-kitchen on the right, a large rectangular table with a dozen chairs in the middle of the room, and a roll top desk beside coat hooks and cubbies on the left. In a little nook on the other side of the elevator was a powder room, and the far wall contained storage shelves and cupboards. The walls, cupboards and shelves were a creamy white, while the desk, table, chairs, and floor were the same shade of medium oak.

"I host craft demonstrations at the table, and do my bookwork at the desk." Tori gestured vaguely as she led the way through the doorway in the middle of the storage wall. "This is my shop." Kate's eyes widened as she perused the variety of items. The floor was the same medium oak, but the walls were faded red brick that looked original, and the trim was white. Light poured through the two picture windows at the front of the shop and the smaller windows located high on the side walls. To the right was a tall circular clothes rack full of fancy dresses.

"Prom dresses." Tori explained. "When you need one, you need one, but nobody wears them more than once. I recycle them."

The corner beyond the dresses held shelves full of jewelry, soaps, lotions, candles, small pottery items, stained glass sun catchers and wall hangings.

"All locally made." Tori commented. "Tourists love them."

An upright piano occupied the middle of the wall, with a rack of sheet music on one side, and a variety of musical instruments in large cubbies on the other. There was an accordion, a flute, a saxophone and two clarinets.

"Just like prom dresses, people don't want band instruments after their kids are through with band. But someone else can always use them, so I sell them on consignment."

"What are those?" Kate asked, pointing to a row of long narrow boxes on top of the piano.

"Those are the music rolls that came with the piano, though amazingly enough, you can still buy them." At Kate's blank look, she said, "It's a player piano. They were really popular in the twenties. I got this one at an estate sale." She used her forefinger to slide the panel on the front of the piano to one side and pointed to the roll inserted there. It looked like a scroll with groups of holes punched into it. "The perforations represent notes that are read when they pass over what is called the tracker bar." She flipped a switch and after a few seconds, the sounds of 'This Land is Your Land' filled the shop.

"That's amazing!" Kate exclaimed. "Is it for sale?"

"Technically, everything in the shop is for sale." Tori shrugged. "But I put a pretty high price on this. It's an antique for one thing, and it's a Steinway, so it was well made, plus I like to play the piano myself, so I would hate to part with it." She grinned. "Unless the price was right, of course!"

The corner on the other side of the piano was labeled 'Book Nook'. The shelves were, indeed, full of books written about Montana or by Montana authors. Under the first picture window were shelves displaying Christmas ornaments and decorations.

"I keep the Christmas things on display all year, because tourists sometimes want them for souvenirs." Between the windows was a china hutch displaying tea pots, cookie jars, cups and mugs, punch bowls, and snack sets. There was an empty cedar chest under the second window, its lid propped open.

"Cedar chests are old fashioned, but some people still like them. Sometimes I sell one before my supplier gets another one made. They are great to store blankets or out of season clothes." Kate was impressed by the workmanship and decided she would like to have a cedar chest one day.

On the other side of the entry from the street sat a cash register on top of a three foot counter placed at a right angle to the door. There was a stool behind the counter, with space for bags and other supplies underneath it. In the other corner was an easel with a painting of the Sweet Grass Hills. The walls behind it held two more paintings and several scenic photographs.

"These are all by local artists, too. I'm amazed at how many tourists want artwork." Tori explained.

"How do they get stuff like that home?" Kate asked. Tori explained that she usually packed the smaller pieces for them to take with them, and shipped the larger ones to their home address.

The middle of the shop held a loveseat, a rocking chair and three mismatched tables. There were beautiful lamps on each table, and Kate moved to examine them in more detail. The first was an oval shape covered in cream colored pleats, trimmed at the top and bottom with bronze braid and three inches of fringe. Another had tulip shaped panels in pale yellow overlaid with lace and accented with decorative beading and tassels. The third one was umbrella-shaped, with alternating pink print and pale pink panels. There was delicate pink beaded fringe on the scalloped edges.

"Those are Victorian lampshades." Tori said, before Kate could ask. A local woman makes them. Aren't they gorgeous?" Kate nodded, still examining the details on the pink one.

"And everything is for sale?" Kate asked. "The furniture and the lamps, too?"

"Sure, for a price." Tori grinned as she unlocked the door and put up the 'OPEN' sign. Kate stepped outside to view the shop from the street. A weathered looking wooden sign hung from a black wrought iron frame above the door. Ornate black letters spelled out **Tori's Treasures** against a background the same color as the faded red brick of the building itself.

Tori did a brisk business with both tourists and local customers throughout the day, so Kate was somewhat surprised when she closed out the till and locked the door at three o'clock.

"I'm only open from nine til three." She explained. "How are you doing? You look like that arm is still pretty sore."

"It is." Kate frowned. "I've taken ibuprofen several times." She shrugged. "I'm sure it will be better tomorrow."

"If you are up for a distraction, we could go for a little drive." She offered. Kate readily agreed and soon they were in Tori's pickup heading north on the interstate.

"I thought you should see Sunburst while you are in the area. It is about thirty miles from Shelby and has a population of about three hundred." Tori said.

"The name is pretty." Kate commented, enjoying the view of the Rocky Mountains in the distance to the left, and the Sweet Grass Hills off to the right.

"The name describes the way the sunrise looks rising over the Sweet Grass Hills. West Butte is, strangely enough, on the west, Gold Butte is in the middle, and East Butte is on the east side." Tori explained. "There are other small hills in between, but Haystack Butte is the only one with a name that I remember. The hills have a rich history, beginning with the Blackfeet Indians who lived on both sides of the hills. Just north of West Butte in Canada there is a sandstone bluff with petroglyphs called Writing on Stone Park. I haven't been there, yet, but it is on my list of places I want to see."

"I know all about having a list of places you want to see!" Kate laughed. "What else do you know about the Sweet Grass Hills?"

"In the 1870's, white traders brought whiskey from Fort Benton to the Blackfeet in this area. That caused so much trouble that the government sent the Canadian Mounted Police to restore order to the area."

"That would be the famous Whoop-Up Trail?" Kate asked.

"Exactly. Then there was a coal mine on West Butte from the early nineteen hundreds until the late forties. Gold was discovered at Middle Butte in the thirties, causing a town named Gold Butte to spring up, with a population of about five hundred people. After that, Middle Butte became known as Gold Butte. The town is gone now, of course, but there is still a cemetery there. Every now and then someone from one of the old families is laid to rest there."

"Interesting. You probably couldn't find a more peaceful spot for a final resting place." Kate commented. "But why are the hills called Sweet Grass?"

"At about the same time gold was discovered; ranchers started settling in the area because of the abundance of tall, sweet, grass. Imagine how self-sufficient they had to be to live more than a day's wagon ride from the nearest town." Tori took the exit towards Sunburst and they drove down the main street and up around the high school.

"Refiners?" Kate asked, gesturing to the sign.

"I wondered if you'd notice that." Tori smiled. "Sunburst is mainly a farm and ranch community now, but when oil was discovered in the twenties, the town grew to about one thousand people, and the Texas Company, later known as Texaco, built a refinery here."

"It's funny to think of a refinery being in a town this size." Kate mused as Tori got back on the interstate and headed south.

"I suppose the refineries were smaller then than they are now. From what I've learned there were refineries in a lot of towns in Montana. Lewistown supposedly had the first operating refinery in the state in 1921. Most small refineries even had their own brands. Cut Bank refined Grizzly Gasoline which was made entirely from Montana crude oil. Shelby had a refinery in the early thirties and their gas was called Hi-Line." Tori exited the interstate and turned right onto a secondary road.

"Kevin, four miles." Kate read the sign aloud.

"The name of the town is spelled like the name 'Kevin' and pronounced 'Keevin'. Only the locals seem to know that." Tori informed her. "Kevin had a refinery, too. It was called The Big West. They marketed several brands, and the names are interesting."

"Interesting, how?" Kate asked.

"Well, the town was established in the early nineteen hundreds during the days of homesteading and named for Thomas Kevin who was a manager with the Alberta Railway. That railroad company ran an old narrow gauge railroad from Lethbridge to Montana on a track that was built in the late eighteen eighties. The Big West Oil Refinery was started in 1925, shortly after the discovery of oil in this area. The refinery marketed one brand of gasoline called 'Spur' and another called 'Big West'."

"Spur for the railroad and Big West for the refinery, huh?" Kate chuckled. "Clever!"

"The Big West Refinery closed in the late seventies," Tori explained, "but the clean-up is a slow process." She gestured to the old buildings and huge tanks that littered the area behind a chain link fence that sagged in several places. Crossing the railroad tracks, she turned right and drove down the main street.

"It its heyday, the town had a grocery store, a couple of bars, a gas station, a train depot and an elementary school. The post office is still here, but these days, I think the population is under two hundred." After a short trip around town, Tori drove back down the main street and kept going straight.

"Now where are we headed?" Kate inquired.

"This road goes across the prairie and up on the rim to Cut Bank, population not quite three thousand." Tori said. "The name comes from the description of the gorge of the Cut Bank Creek. The town has a penguin."

"Really? A penguin?"

"Yeah, Cut Bank claims to be the coldest spot in the nation, conveniently ignoring Alaska, of course. And because cold and penguins go together, they have a huge statue of a penguin."

"How big is it?"

"Twenty-seven feet tall. And on a good day, it talks."

"What does it say?" Kate asked with a laugh.

"I've never heard it." Tori admitted. "It always seems to be on the fritz when I stop by. But I think it says 'welcome to Cut Bank, the coldest spot in the nation'."

"Wow. It constantly amazes me that every town has something that they are famous for." Kate commented. "Small town people are good at finding things about their location or their history to celebrate, I guess." Tori drove around Cut Bank and then to the west edge of town so Kate could see where the railroad tracks spanned from cliff to cliff on an elevated track high above the canyon floor.

"Can you imagine how hard that was to build?" Kate marveled. "The railroad came through here in eighteen ninety one. I read somewhere that they laid an average of five to eight miles or track per day. I bet that particular stretch took a little bit longer!"

◆ ◆ ◆

The next day Kate walked several blocks to spend part of the afternoon browsing through the Marias Museum. The ten rooms of what had once been a private residence held a variety of displays and exhibits including Indian artifacts, antique toys, musical instruments, dinosaur bones and fossils, military memorabilia, historical photos, antiques, and items from the railroad, farming, and oil industries. She got back just as Tori was locking up.

"How was the Museum?"

"Well worth an afternoon." Kate assured her.

"I have another road trip in mind if you are interested." Kate said she was and within a few minutes they headed south on the interstate. They exited onto highway 44, the east/west route between the interstate and highway 89 that Kate had used when she went from Browning to Choteau.

Nestled on the shores of Lake Francis, the town of Valier boasted a population of about five hundred residents. It was named after Peter Valier, who supervised the building of the railroad line between Valier and Conrad.

"Imagine that - another railroad guy. What is Valier's claim to fame?" Kate asked as they drove through the tidy little community.

"Well, author Ivan Doig graduated from high school here. Also, they have a local airport with a grass landing strip, and water planes occasionally land on Lake Francis."

"It's a scenic spot, with the lake right here and the mountains on the horizon." Kate commented.

"Lake Francis was actually constructed before the town, mainly for irrigation, and the town grew up on its shores. It is still used for irrigation, but it is also a great place for fishing, boating and camping." Tori said.

"You know a lot about the area, don't you?" Kate asked.

"I love history." Tori said, simply. "I've been taking little trips to visit the surrounding area ever since I moved here." As she spoke, she turned north onto the Cut Bank highway. "I'll show you one of my favorite spots." After a few miles, the highway curved to the left but Tori continued to go straight on a gravel road. It was a very bumpy gravel road and Tori drove slowly in an effort not to jostle Kate's arm too much. Hay fields dotted with clusters of big round hay bales spread out on both sides of the road. Suddenly, in stark contrast to the prairie, a wide chasm appeared as if by magic. Spreading out from the edge of the canyon were hundreds of towering rock formations, some twenty feet tall. They had flat tops and were separated by numerous alcoves and pathways and a meandering river.

"This is Rock City." Tori said as they got out of the pickup to explore on foot.

"It's amazing! Do you know how it was created?" Kate asked, pulling her tablet out to take pictures, trying to ignore the ache in her arm.

"As it happens, I do." Tori replied with a smirk. "The formations were created when the rock was eroded from the bottom by the Two Medicine River, and from the top by rain."

"Okay, I'm familiar with rivers eroding rock, but rain? Really?"

"I know. Weird, but true. The formations are called 'hoodoos' and they are formed when water from cloudbursts runs over the brim and goes down on the underside. It is called the teapot effect, because it is similar to what happens if you pour tea too slowly and it runs down the spout instead of into the cup. Anyway, it takes centuries, but eventually it erodes the underside of the rock so they get that mushroom look. Some of the most famous hoodoo formations are in Bryce Canyon Nation Park in Utah. The ones in Montana aren't as famous, of course."

"So there are other hoodoos in Montana?"

"I haven't been to see them yet, but I've heard of two others, just in this area. There is a group of hoodoos southwest of Sweetgrass called Jerusalem Rocks, and west of Sunburst is a smaller group called Little Jerusalem." The two women explored for about an hour, before returning to the pickup and driving back to Valier and then to the interstate where they turned south towards Conrad.

"What do you know about Conrad?" Kate asked

"The original town was called Old Pondera and it was located a mile or so from present-day Conrad. It had a total of seven structures; one store, one rooming house, two saloons, a section house, a school house, and a water tank. It was the midway station between Fort Benton and Canada on the Whoop-Up trail. The mid-way station was also called Lucille's or Froggie's Stopping Place, and before you ask, I have no clue where those names came from."

"I bet Lucille owned the saloon, and Froggie was one of the wagon drivers who stopped there regularly and spent a good portion of his paycheck." Kate laughed.

"Probably." Tori chuckled. "At any rate, a dozen years after the town came into existence, the Great Northern Railroad laid tracks between Great Falls and Lethbridge, and by-passed Old Pondera by about a mile."

"Well that wasn't very nice of the railroad!" Kate declared. "Did they abandon Old Pondera and move to where the railroad was?"

"They did move, but they didn't abandon their town. They moved it, including all the buildings, to what is now Conrad. Today it is the county seat of Pondera County and has a population of about twenty-five hundred."

"Why did they call it Conrad?"

"I'm not sure, but maybe because the county was named Pondera. Conrad was named after the Conrad brothers, W.G. and Charles. They built a business empire that included overland trade, banking, ranching, mining, and real estate. Some of their descendents still live here." Tori parked on Main Street and they walked to the Home Café for dinner before returning to Shelby.

◆ ◆ ◆

By Wednesday, Kate's arm had not improved, and she reluctantly allowed Tori to make an appointment for her at the clinic. Her cell phone rang as they were leaving Tori's apartment. Truth be told, it rang so seldom that she almost didn't realize what it was. She had only purchased a cell phone because Karly and Madison insisted that she needed it on her bike trip. With the two of them standing over her, she had learned to operate it, but she was forever forgetting where she put it or letting the battery run down, and it was rarely her first thought as a means of communication. When she finally located the ringing phone in the bottom of her purse, she hurried to answer before it went to voice mail, without looking at the display.

"How is your arm?" It took her a minute to recognize Logan's voice.

"Oh, well, it doesn't seem to be improving. I'm actually on my way to the doctor right now." He said to let him know how that went and ended the call. She was still shaking her head when she joined Tori in the pickup.

"What's up?" Tori asked.

"That was Logan, one of the people from that bike tour I told you about? He didn't say hello or goodbye, just how is your arm and let me know what the doctor says." Kate rolled her eyes. "Weird."

♦ ♦ ♦

"Six weeks before I can ride again!" Kate said in disgust as she climbed into Tori's pickup nearly three hours later, her left arm cradled close to her body in a beige canvas sling. "They found a hairline fracture. No wonder it aches."

"Good thing you got it checked then." Tori soothed. Kate nodded, already thinking about who she could ask to drive to Shelby and get her and her bike and trailer. Lost in thought, she failed to notice the gray crew cab pickup parked at the curb in front of Tori's shop until a deep voice called her name. She stood motionless on the sidewalk as Logan walked towards her.

"Is it broken?" He asked, frowning down at the sling. When she continued to stare at him in shock, he turned to Tori and introduced himself.

"Nice to meet you, Logan." Tori shook hands and grinned up at him, then turned to Kate. "You two go on up. There's lemonade in the frig. I've still got a few things to do in the shop. Wordlessly,

Kate led the way upstairs to Tori's kitchen. When they were seated at the kitchen table with glasses of lemonade in front of them, she finally found her voice.

"What are you doing here?"

"I had a feeling you might need help." Logan replied calmly. "Is your arm broken?"

"Hairline fracture." Kate said, distractedly. "So you just drove to Shelby because you had a feeling?"

"We're friends, aren't we?" He asked. Kate considered the question as she gently rubbed her arm, trying to ease the ache. Finally, she nodded and Logan breathed a little sigh of relief.

"You said you were going to the doctor because your arm wasn't better, so I thought you might need a ride to Billings." Logan smiled. She had to admit that he had a very nice smile.

"I was going to call Amanda, or maybe Karly." Kate murmured. Her dad would have been her first choice, but her parents were on a camping trip.

"I'm already here, and I'm going to Billings anyway." Logan said logically, and Kate couldn't argue with that.

◆ ◆ ◆

"I take it you weren't expecting him?" Tori asked when Logan had gone, promising to return in the morning.

"No." Kate replied, shaking her head. "I've exchanged a couple of e-mails with him, but that's all."

"I think he likes you." Tori teased.

"He makes me nervous." Kate replied.

TWENTY-TWO

Kate found it surprisingly hard to say good-bye to Tori the next day, given that they had known each other for such a short time, but they promised to stay in touch and get together soon. Logan showed up at eight thirty, made short work of loading her bike and trailer, and by mid-morning they were driving south on the interstate. He had folded a blanket to cradle her injured arm and Kate was simultaneously grateful that it eased the ache, and irritated that he seemed to think she needed to be taken care of. She gazed moodily out her window, barely noticing the ripening fields of grain rippling in the breeze, or the Rocky Mountains in the distance. She should be grateful he had come to her rescue, but instead she dreaded the prospect of spending several hours in the close confines of the pickup with a man who made her uncomfortable. It was definitely going to be a long day. She leaned back and closed her eyes to discourage conversation. Within minutes she was sound asleep, lulled by the motion of the truck and the sound of the radio playing softly in the background.

Logan glanced over at Kate several times as he drove down the interstate, wondering why he was so drawn to her. She was pretty of course, with blue eyes in a heart-shaped face and thick dark hair. But pretty women didn't normally affect him this way. Even when he wasn't looking at her, he was aware of where she was and what she was doing. He couldn't believe it had actually irritated him when Greg flirted with her. His friend Greg, who automatically flirted with every woman he met, and meant nothing by it. He assumed that he would be able to stop thinking about her if she wasn't nearby, but when she left their group at Sidney he missed her, and worse than that, he worried about her. He knew his sister would say he was falling in love. Whatever it was called, he had never felt this way about a woman before and he wasn't sure he liked it. He sighed and admitted that what really worried him was that Kate didn't seem to be all that crazy about him.

"Where are we?" Kate woke and looked around groggily when Logan turned off the highway onto a gravel road.

"I hope you don't mind meeting my parents. I, uh, mentioned that I was going to Shelby to help a friend and Mom insisted we stop at the ranch for lunch." Logan said staring straight ahead. His fingers tightened around the steering wheel. "When I, uh, explained that my friend was a woman…well, to say Mom was curious would be an understatement."

"No problem." Kate replied, automatically. She was good with people and figured she could get through lunch with his parents. Besides, she realized that she was hungry. When they pulled into the yard a few minutes Logan groaned.

"What's wrong?"

"I figured Don would be here – he and Dad are getting the equipment ready for harvest. But it looks like Roger and Mariah are here too. Nosy brats! I wonder what their excuses will be."

Jane Brown was alone in the kitchen. She stood about five foot five, and was dressed in faded blue jeans, tennis shoes and a purple t-shirt. She was a bundle of energy with short curly brown hair and alert gray eyes. Before Kate had time to feel awkward or uncomfortable, she found herself welcomed and seated at a rectangular table with a glass of lemonade in front of her.

"What am I, chopped liver?" Logan asked as he poured his own lemonade and leaned against the island.

"You aren't company, and your arm isn't in a sling." Jane retorted. Kate glanced around as Logan and his mother bantered affectionately. The ranch kitchen was huge. The first thing she noticed was that there were two dishwashers, one on each side of a triple sink situated under the window. Three pies sat cooling on racks to the left of the sink. Opposite the sink was a large island with a tan marble countertop. At the moment it contained a white wicker basket of rolls, a tray of sliced ham and roast beef, and a platter with lettuce leaves, slices of tomato, onion, and two kinds of cheese. The cooking area was completed by an oversized refrigerator and matching upright freezer across from a six burner gas stove with double ovens. The tantalizing aroma of homemade soup wafted from the stock pot simmering on one of the burners.

When Jane insisted that they start on lunch, Logan helped Kate assemble a ham sandwich and carried it and a bowl of chicken vegetable soup to the table for her before he fixed his own plate. Just as he sat down, two men dressed in coveralls appeared in the kitchen, drying their hands on paper towels. Like Logan, both were tall and lean, with black hair, high cheekbones and dark eyes. The three of them looked more like brothers than father and sons, the only difference being that John's jet black hair had a touch of silver at the temples. Logan introduced his dad and brother Don to Kate and as they began to fill their plates a woman entered the kitchen from the hallway and a man came in from outside and set a box on the floor. Logan introduced them and then fixed his brother with a stern gaze.

"Isn't your office open today?" Roger was a carbon copy of his dad and brothers, except that he wore slacks, a dress shirt and a tie instead of jeans or coveralls, and his dark eyes were framed by black wire-rimmed glasses.

"I'm using my lunch hour to deliver parts for the combine." Roger said, failing miserably in his attempt to look innocent.

"Of course you are." Logan shook his head in mock disgust. Roger winked at Kate and grinned as he began filling his plate. Logan turned towards his sister and raised his eyebrows.

"Well? What's your excuse?"

"I'm just blatantly curious." Mariah said sweetly. "That's a sister's job, don't you know." She batted her eyelashes at him as she set her plate across from Kate and sat down. She was about Kate's height, with pewter gray eyes like her mother and thick black hair woven into a single braid trailing down the middle of her back. Everyone laughed, including Kate. The food was delicious and the conversation was casual and interesting.

"Thanks for being such a good sport." Logan said when they were on the road again, with his bike and trailer in the back of his pickup alongside Kate's.

"Your family is nice." Kate replied. "They were definitely curious about me, but they were nice." They had all been friendly and accepting, in sharp contrast to how Charlie's mother had acted those many years ago. Wondering where that thought came from, she pushed it out of her mind and focused on what Logan was saying.

"Yeah, well, I don't really have a lot of women friends." Logan paused, more than a little uncomfortable. When Kate didn't say anything, he plowed on. "The thing is, my marriage was a complete disaster, and it took me awhile to get over it."

"How long is awhile?" Kate wondered aloud. She was definitely curious about his marriage and divorce, but if he didn't want to elaborate, she wasn't going to ask. Logan was silent for a full minute and then he sighed and tightened his grip on the steering wheel.

"Over a decade."

"That's definitely awhile." Kate agreed, thinking that it had been over two decades since Charlie died, and she thought she had coped pretty well until her conversations with Sylvia had her thinking that she had emotional issues that she needed to deal with.

"My ex-wife had two affairs that I know of before we divorced." Logan said. He hated talking about it, but Kate had been candid about her background, so he supposed if he wanted to get to know her better, he needed to reciprocate. Since he did want to get to know her better, he forced the words out. "According to my psychologist, I came away from the whole experience bitter and distrustful of women."

"You had counseling?" Kate asked in surprise. "Did it help?"

"Yeah, it did, eventually." Logan said, surprised when Kate zeroed in on counseling instead of his short-lived disastrous marriage or his emotional issues. "I probably should have gone sooner, like Mom and Mariah nagged me to do. But I kept putting it off. I was busy. And I moved a lot." He shrugged. "I had a million excuses."

"I know how that goes." Kate agreed soberly. "I used the busy excuse too." She was quiet for several miles, lost in thought. Logan glanced at her several times but he did not interrupt her reverie. The realization that he liked everything about this woman still surprised him, and truthfully, it scared him a little bit too.

"I'm beginning to think I should have had counseling after Charlie died." She said thoughtfully.

"When I finally went in, my counselor said it was never too late."

"That's what Sylvia said, too." Kate replied.

"Who is Sylvia?" Logan asked, and Kate explained about meeting Sylvia and some of the things they had discussed, including, to her own surprise, that she was seriously considering getting some counseling herself. She had barely reached that decision herself and hadn't planned to tell anyone, least of all Logan. For some reason, he had become easier to talk to and soon they were talking about movies and books, and even politics. Before she knew it, she was directing Logan to her parents' home in Billings where he unloaded her bike and trailer, dropped her bag inside the door and said he'd be in touch. Then he drove away.

Since her parents were away for another month on their camping trip, Kate had the house to herself. She sent a text to Tori letting her know she was home, scrambled eggs for a light supper, then took a shower, swallowed a couple of Tylenol, fell into bed and slept clear through until morning. It was the best night's sleep she'd had since she hurt her arm. She awoke refreshed, spent the day catching up with her family and friends via phone calls and e-mail, and then drove her mom's car to have dinner with her grandparents. She parked in the driveway and used the gate into the back yard, stopping to greet her two grandfathers as they tended the grill on the patio.

"What's on the menu?" Kate asked when she let herself into the kitchen and gave each grandma a one-armed hug and a kiss. "Those two wouldn't tell me!"

"Pork ribs with apple-salsa." Vera grinned. "Your grandfathers have a grilling rivalry going and they are branching out from steaks, burgers and chicken. Last week, Mike did shrimp kabobs, so Ron scoured the internet and found this rib recipe he wanted to try."

"We're also having corn on the cob, buttered beets, new potatoes, and a tossed salad – all from our gardens." Grandma Carol added with a chuckle. "Not that we'll get any credit for helping with dinner, even though we actually grew the vegetables before we prepared them."

Dinner was delicious and it was good to catch up with her grandparents. Kate thought what a blessing it was that they were still in such good health in their mid-eighties. They wanted to hear all about her trip and she was glad she'd brought her tablet along so she could share her pictures.

♦ ♦ ♦

"So, big brother, what's wrong?" Mariah asked, leaning against the porch rail. Logan ignored her question and stared into the rain from his rocking chair on the porch. He had come to the ranch to help put up hay and worked long hours all week, just managing to finish up the biggest hayfield before the rain started. Thunder boomed and lightning flashed, in perfect harmony with his own black mood. Kate was not answering his calls or responding to his text messages, and he was going to be at the ranch for another week. It was driving him crazy! Mariah poked him in the shoulder and repeated her question.

"What's wrong?"

"What makes you think there's something wrong?" Logan asked, irritably, even as he knew he was wasting his breath. Mariah knew. She had an uncanny knack for knowing. It was one of the things that made her a great mother and a wonderful teacher. It probably made her an excellent wife too, he'd never asked. Unfortunately, in the little sister department, it usually made her a gigantic pain in the butt. He wondered if it was worth the effort to try dodging her questions, or ignoring her, and decided it probably wasn't.

"I bet it's about Kate." Mariah guessed shrewdly. "Did you screw things up with her?"

"I did not screw things up!" Logan snapped indignantly, realizing too late that he had fallen neatly into her trap. He closed his eyes briefly, then shook his head and gave in. "Hell, maybe I did, I don't know. She isn't answering my calls or texts, and I really like her."

"Yeah, I thought you did." Mariah said soberly. "I like her too. So do Mom and Dad. So what's the problem?" He shrugged.

"We've seen a lot of each other in the three weeks since I took her to Billings. We talk on the phone, meet for lunch, stuff like that. She seems fine as long as we're just hanging out, but if I do anything that crosses the friend line, she freaks." Logan said, miserably.

"Freaks, how?" Mariah asked.

"It's hard to explain. She goes real quiet and polite."

"Emotional withdrawal." Mariah said softly. "And this happens when?"

"First time it happened I took her hand while we were walking." Logan replied. "I thought maybe she didn't like holding hands in public. Then last weekend we were sitting on the couch at my place watching a movie, and I put my arm around her. She froze."

"Well, did you ask her what was wrong or talk to her about it?"

"No, I didn't talk to her about it! FYI, little sister, guys do not like to talk things to death." Logan said disgustedly. Mariah straightened away from the porch rail and stood with her hands on her hips glaring down at him.

"Logan!" Mariah snapped. "I grew up with three brothers. I have a husband and two sons. I am well aware that the male of the species doesn't like to talk about relationship stuff. But I am here to remind you that not talking about your feelings will complicate your life -- which you should know, because you've already been there and done that and it did not end well." She was right and Logan knew it. He sighed again.

"What if she likes me okay as a friend, but she doesn't want anything more than that." He blurted out what had really been bothering him and immediately wished he could call the words back.

"And you do?" Mariah asked, watching him carefully. "Want something more, I mean?"

"Maybe." Logan shrugged. "Yeah, I think I do, and it would be just my luck to be interested in someone who isn't interested in me, wouldn't it?"

"Honestly! Men are so dense, sometimes." Mariah shook her head and leaned against the porch rail again. "There could be something else going on, you know. You need to talk to her and find out. You can't just assume you know why she's doing what she's doing. She might not even know why she's doing what she's doing."

"Gee, Sis, that was not exactly enlightening!"

"Okay, listen." Mariah said impatiently. "Kate lost her husband right after they were married when she was quite young, right?" Logan nodded. "Well, since she never married again, maybe she never really got over that."

"So I have to compete with the memory of a dead guy?" Logan said sarcastically. "No thanks!"

"My dear, dense, idiot brother! There is a remote possibility that this isn't about you! Did you ever think she might be afraid of relationships?" Mariah asked in exasperation. Before he could answer, she snapped. "And in my not so humble opinion, you still have a few issues with trusting women!" Logan watched her stalk off the porch, get into her car, and slam the door shut. His little sister certainly knew how to make an exit. As she drove away, he considered her not so humble opinions. It had not occurred to him that Kate might be afraid of relationships. That would put a whole new light on the situation. Suddenly he was a little more hopeful.

◆ ◆ ◆

TWENTY-THREE

Kate turned off the vacuum cleaner and went to answer the door, but instead of the pizza delivery she was expecting, Sylvia stood on the porch, looking anxious.

"If you have a couple of hours, Tony can get some maintenance done on the motor home while we catch up."

"Sure." Kate replied, holding the door open. Sylvia turned towards the curb and waved, then stepped through the door as Tony put the motor home in gear and drove off down the street. When the pizza arrived a few minutes later, Kate poured them each a glass of Diet Coke, and the two women settled at the kitchen table. Kate toyed with the slice of veggie pizza on her plate. She hadn't eaten much in the past few days, and it was easier to order pizza than to go to the grocery store so she could fix something, but she really wasn't hungry. She consoled herself that at least she had something to offer Sylvia for lunch.

"So how are things?" Sylvia asked. When Kate shrugged, Sylvia fixed her with a knowing look. "I know something has happened, Kate. I told Tony that we needed to stop so I could make sure you are okay."

"Why do you think something happened?" Kate asked.

"Because once we were out of the park and found a place with internet, I read your e-mail updates. Now you aren't answering your phone." Sylvia explained.

"I dropped my phone in a bucket of water." Kate admitted.

"And you've been cleaning."

"Excuse me?" Kate frowned. "Why is cleaning a problem?"

"When we were discussing how you cope with stress, you mentioned that when you are really upset about something, you don't cry, you clean."

"Oh." Kate sighed and shrugged. "Well, that's true, I guess"

"So what is going on?"

"It's Logan. I've been spending quite a bit of time with him, but every time he gets too close, I freeze up, and then he gets remote and broody." She told Sylvia about her reaction to Logan putting his arm around her while they watched a movie. "So I think he was upset when he left and then he went to the ranch to help with haying the next day. I haven't heard from him since."

"Why do you think you freeze like that?" Sylvia took a bite of pizza and chewed while she waited for Kate to answer.

"I don't know!" Kate exclaimed. "That's what is so frustrating. I don't want to go all weird on him, but then I do. You're the psychologist; can't you tell me why I'm acting that way?"

"Since you asked, I think you started doing that as a defense mechanism when your grief was fresh and continued it when you were consumed with getting an education and raising Karly. I suspect that over the years, you have done it so often, and gotten so good at it, that now it is an automatic response."

"Well, how do I stop?" Kate asked in frustration. "I don't want to push Logan away."

"You do the next thing." Sylvia replied. "Right now that means eating your lunch." Kate rolled her eyes and took a bite of her pizza. She remembered Tori saying that she believed in doing the next thing too. Tori and Sylvia would get along great she thought, somewhat irritably.

"Do you think I need closure about Charlie in order to get on with my life?" Kate asked after she'd eaten some pizza.

"I prefer the term 'resolution' to 'closure' in this case. Sometimes tying up loose ends from the past can help you move forward."

"Like what?"

"Deciding to put your rings in the jewelry box was a wonderful first step. Giving the ring back to Charlie's family would be even better. Charlie will always be a part of your past, but he would want you to be happy, don't you think?"

"Yes, I think he would want me to be happy." Kate agreed. "I'm just not making much progress in breaking old habits."

"You can focus on trying to consciously change your responses, and talk to Logan about what's going on. If you can't change your behavior on your own, you might consider seeing a counselor."

Kate thought about Sylvia's advice throughout the weekend. She could remember urging Amanda to take a chance on Dave. Funny how the same advice that was so easy to hand out was so hard to follow. She thought about Tori's assertion that if she had the opportunity to love again, she would grab it with both hands and hang on tight. She wondered if it was already too late to try and talk to Logan about her issues.

◆ ◆ ◆

The next day, Kate stopped in front of the reception desk at the Whitcomb Law Office, fingers clutched tight on the strap of her shoulder bag and butterflies in her stomach. Her arm ached from her cleaning frenzy over the weekend, so she had the sling on today. She hadn't called, and now she wished she had made an appointment. What if Huck wasn't in, or wouldn't see her? That was silly, she scolded herself. According to Ben the family had contacted him because they wanted to see her. She wished she'd asked Ben to come with her, but he lived in Bozeman and that was a little too much to expect. She was a grown woman, she could do this. At least, she hoped she could.

"May I help you?" The receptionist asked with a smile.

"I'd like to see Huck Whitcomb, if he's available." Kate said politely.

"Do you have an appointment?"

"No." Kate shook her head.

"May I have your name, please?"

"Kate." The receptionist paused inquiringly, but when Kate did not offer a last name, she pressed the intercom button on her phone and spoke softly into the receiver. She seemed a little surprised when she put the receiver down turned back to Kate with a speculative look.

"He'll be right out." Huck materialized in the reception area almost immediately, both hands extended to clasp Kate's hand in welcome. His medium brown hair was turning white at the temples and he had a few more lines around his eyes, but otherwise he didn't look much different than he had on the night Charlie had introduced them. He ushered her into the conference room and offered her something cold to drink, then joined her at the table, inquiring first about the sling on her arm, and after she explained that, about the rest of her bike tour. Kate relaxed as she answered his questions. He was as easy to talk to as Charlie had been, and that gave her the courage she needed to reach into her shoulder bag, retrieve the maroon velvet pouch, and hand it to him.

"Charlie told me the history of this ring when he gave it to me, and I was honored to wear it, but I think the time has come to return it to your family so it can be passed on to the next generation."

"Thank you, Kate." Huck said, clearly touched, as he took the velvet pouch. "I remember giving the ring to Charlie. Even though we had just met, I had a feeling the ring would be perfect for you. I wish I had known you and Charlie got married. I truly regret not being there for you and Karly, all the time we've lost."

"I thought of contacting you several times," Kate admitted, "but…" her voice trailed off, uncertainly and she shrugged.

"I know exactly what you are too polite to say." Huck assured her, remembering how difficult Amelia had been. "Let's just say I'll be forever grateful to Mom's bridge buddy for sending that newspaper clipping. I'm hoping we can get to know you and Karly now – better late than never, as the saying goes."

"I'd like that, and I'm sure Karly will too." Kate assured him. "My friend Sylvia says everything happens for a reason, and that things have a way of working out."

"I believe that too." Huck smiled. "May I introduce you to George?" At Kate's nod, he picked up the receiver and pushed the intercom button on the phone. George looked a lot like Charlie except that he had his mother's blue eyes. Kate found him very easy to talk to.

"One of the reasons Grams was so blown away to find out about Karly is because she's the only girl in the whole family." He told her with a grin.

"Really?" Kate asked. George nodded, his blue eyes twinkling.

"Grandma and Grandpa had Dad & Uncle Will, then each of them had two boys, and now I have two boys and so do both of my cousins."

"Oh my! Charlie told me that everyone else in the family was a lawyer. Is that still true?" Kate inquired, and George nodded.

"Grandpa Chaz and his brother Levi are both retired now. Levi's sons, Jeff and James opened another law office in Great Falls. The two of them and their four sons work there. Dad and Uncle Will are senior partners here. Will's two sons and I all joined the firm after law school. All of our boys are pretty young yet." He shrugged. "If they chose law, we'll be delighted, and if they choose something else, we'll be delighted. Just so they are happy."

"It was only Amelia who pressured Charlie to go into law, Kate." Huck explained at Kate's look of surprise. "The rest of the family supported his decision to go into accounting. Unfortunately, Amelia could be very, ah, forceful with her opinions." Sometimes it was a struggle to be honest about Amelia without going into a rant about her, he thought ruefully. The woman had been extremely controlling, and she could hold a grudge forever.

"I only met her that one time." Kate said with a small smile and Huck hastened to change the subject.

"My parents are very anxious to meet you. Let's set up a time, shall we?"

◆ ◆ ◆

Kate thought Logan should be back in Billings by now, but he had not called or stopped to see her. She knew how her daughter would respond if she dared explain the situation to her. Karly would exclaim impatiently, 'just talk to him, Mom!' Amanda had already given her that advice, as had Sylvia when she e-mailed her about the meeting with Huck. Kate felt like a coward, because she probably owed Logan an apology, but she didn't have his number until her phone dried out. If it was going to dry out. Maybe it was time to get a new phone. Maybe it was already too late. She pushed thoughts of Logan out of her mind and made an effort to focus on the evening ahead.

She had rummaged through her belongings in the garage to find her photo albums so she could take them to show Charlie's grandparents. She was not quite as nervous about meeting Chaz and Emma as she had been when she went to see Huck at his office.

Huck picked her up at six. She hadn't asked where they were meeting Chaz and Emma for dinner, and was pleasantly surprised when they pulled into the parking lot of the same small Italian restaurant where Charlie had proposed. Once they were seated, she related that story as a way of breaking the ice. Between courses, she brought out the pictures of Karly's childhood, explaining about their relationship with Amanda and Madison in the process.

"I'm so glad you and Amanda and your daughters had each other. The wedding article said Karly and Madison were best friends, but they really grew up more like sisters, didn't they?"

"Yes they did, and Amanda is like a sister to me, as well." Kate agreed, and she told them that Karly and Madison both wanted to meet them. In fact, the two girls had already decided that a barbeque at Mitch and Madison's house would be the perfect spot for everyone to meet, because it was a central location between Helena and Billings, and would give the Whitcombs a chance to see where Karly had grown up. They were just waiting for everyone to agree on a date. Both Chaz and Emma hugged Kate good-bye and then Huck took Kate back to her parents' house.

Kate slipped out of her shoes as she locked the door and wandered into the kitchen thinking about how well the evening had gone. She was starting to make tea when the doorbell rang. Checking the peephole, she saw Logan standing on the porch. He looked tired and upset and judging by the stubble on his face, he hadn't shaved in several days. She opened the door, not sure what to expect.

"Who was that?" Logan demanded, his mouth a grim line and his dark eyes riveted on her face. She stared at him, not understanding his question until it dawned on her that he must have seen Huck dropping her off.

"That was Huck Whitcomb – Charlie's dad." She said, finally. "He took me to dinner to meet Charlie's grandparents, Chaz & Emma."

"Oh." He mumbled, and some of the tension left his shoulders. He sighed and rubbed the back of his neck. "Uh, can I come in so we can talk?"

"Okay." She stood back to let him in and led the way to the kitchen where the tea kettle was whistling. Logan took a seat at the table while she prepared tea, making a cup for Logan without asking if he wanted one.

"What did you want to talk about?" Kate asked as she put two mugs on the table and sat down opposite him, cupping her suddenly cold fingers around her mug for warmth.

"Us." Logan said. "If there is an 'us'. I've been calling and texting you for almost two weeks and you haven't answered." She closed her eyes and groaned.

"Oh, Logan! I'm sorry!" She exclaimed. "I dropped my phone in a bucket of water while I was cleaning, and I'm still trying to dry it out."

"Oh. I thought you were mad at me." Logan muttered.

"I'm not." She shook her head. "But I thought you were mad at me."

"And I don't see my name on your list." He nodded to the lined yellow pad on the table. He had noticed it while she made tea. Kate glanced at the yellow pad and fumbled for words.

"According to Sylvia, I have issues. Emotional baggage she called it. Whenever I'm under stress, I function better with a plan. That list is the start of my plan." Logan picked up the tablet and began to read aloud.

"Number one – Return the ring to Huck. Number two -- introduce Charlie's family and Karly. Number three – find a job. Bozeman? Billings? Somewhere else? Number four – rent an apartment." He glared at her. "I am not on this list, Kate. At all. Why am I not on this list?"

"I also have a problem with men." Kate sighed. "I know I've been sending you mixed signals...I'm sorry." Kate offered the apology while staring intently into her mug of tea.

"So which signals should I go by?" Logan asked. "The ones where you enjoy my company? Or the ones where you, uh, don't?"

"The ones where I enjoy your company." She muttered still not looking at him. "Look, sometimes I just kind of ... panic. I haven't dated much in the last twenty-five years and I'm completely terrible at it!"

"Good to know." Logan replied, his mouth twitching. "That you enjoy my company, I mean, not that you are terrible at dating." Logan took a sip of his tea and leaned forward. He waited until she met his gaze. "I tend to go after what I want, Kate. I want to be on your list. Are we on the same page here?"

"Yeah." Kate said softly. "As long as you understand that I have some stuff to work out." Logan picked up a pen and wrote his name at the top of her list in capital letters.

"There, now I'm at the top of your list." He said. "And, according to my sister, I have issues too, so we can work on that stuff together."

◆ ◆ ◆

Once Kate was able to take her sling off, she started doing exercises to strengthen the arm she'd been babying for six weeks, and got serious about looking for a job. Nothing piqued her interest until she saw a notice from a temporary employment service agency. She applied for it, listing her accounting and business management credentials and also her waitressing experience on her resume. Her new job was part-time and offered a variety of challenges as well as opportunities to meet new people.

Barb and Kent return from their camping trip and urged her to stay with them while she sorted things out. Kate helped her mother clean the camper so it would be ready for the next adventure. As they took inventory and made a grocery list, Barb suggested Kate invite Logan for dinner on Saturday so they could meet him. Kate readily agreed, but when the doorbell rang on Saturday afternoon, it wasn't Logan waiting on the porch grinning from ear to ear.

"Amanda!" Kate shrieked. The two women were still hugging each other and blinking back tears when Logan sauntered up the sidewalk. Dave turned towards him, smiled and offered his hand.

"You must be Logan. Dave Grant. Nice to meet you." He tipped his head towards Kate and Amanda. "Ah, Kate wasn't expecting us."

Eventually, Kate introduced Logan to Amanda and then to her parents. They were all on their way through the kitchen to the patio when the back door opened and two elderly couples appeared with their arms full. Ron set a pan of green beans on the stove while Carol opened the refrigerator to find a spot for her bowl of coleslaw, Vera's fruit salad and the two six-packs of soda Mike carried.

"Logan, you've been ambushed!" Kate exclaimed, as she went to hug her grandparents.

"You mean like when we stopped at the ranch for lunch and all three of my siblings showed up?" Logan laughed as he shook hands with everyone. "You passed inspection. I sure hope I do."

◆ ◆ ◆

On Friday of the following weekend, Kate and Logan drove to Bozeman so Logan could meet the girls and their husbands. On Saturday, Mitch and Madison hosted a barbeque for Chaz, Emma and Huck, inviting Ben and Genny and Amanda and Dave.

"Oh! You have Charlie's eyes!" Emma exclaimed holding both Karly's hands in hers and blinking back tears.

"Also his dimples!" Karly agreed with a smile to prove her point. "And you may have noticed the similarity in our names."

"We noticed that right away." Huck smiled. "I'm thrilled to meet you, Karly."

"It's wonderful to meet the other half of my family tree!"

"We are just sorry it took so long!" Chaz said, gravely. Everyone shared pictures and memories and Karly gave the Whitcombs a tour of the house she grew up in. Before the evening was over, Huck and his parents were planning a weekend in Billings to introduce the girls to the rest of the Whitcomb family. Madison looked startled and started to object, but Chaz held up a hand.

"You and Karly are sisters, just like Kate and Amanda. And all of you are part of our family now!"

◆ ◆ ◆

They spent Thanksgiving at the ranch so Kate could meet the rest of Logan's family, and Christmas in Billings so Logan could meet Kate's sister Julia, Jim, their sons, daughters-in-law and first grandchild. Logan surprised her with a weekend at the Yellowstone River Lodge in Columbus to celebrate New Year's Eve. Naturally Kate wanted to know all about the town. She discovered that it was first a trading post and stagecoach station called Eagles Nest. It was also the site of quite a bit of illegal whiskey trading with the Indians, and the whiskey had such a vile taste that people started calling the little settlement 'Sheep Dip'. Thank goodness that name didn't stick, Kate thought. Next it was called Stillwater, but there was already a Stillwater in Minnesota on the Northern Pacific Railroad line, so mail delivery became confusing. Finally the town was named Columbus, the county seat of Stillwater County.

With a population of less than two thousand people, Columbus managed to claim a few famous people. A professional poker player named Annie Duke had resided there, Dwan Edwards, drafted by the Baltimore Ravens in 2004, attended Columbus High School, and Jack Vaughn, who served as Assistant Secretary of State, Ambassador to Panama and Columbia and the second director of the Peace Corps was born there.

With a view of the river, a fireplace, and all the amenities of a luxury hotel, The Yellowstone River Lodge was the perfect place to unwind after the holidays. It was also the perfect place for a pro-posal on New Year's Eve, and Kate said yes. Two months later, how-ever, trying to plan the wedding was making Kate crazy.

"Logan? Could we just elope?" Kate asked tentatively.

"Our families would kill us." Logan replied.

"I just don't know where to start." Kate groused. "We should at least set a date."

"If you don't want the same kind of wedding you had with Charlie, we can do something different." They had been seeing a counselor to work through their emotional issues and had recently spent a fair amount of time discussing their individual feelings and memories about weddings. Logan knew that Kate was committed to marrying him, but she seemed to be having trouble with the cer-emony itself, so he had given the matter a lot of thought.

"Different, how?" Kate asked cautiously. She looked curious, but interested, so he explained the ideas he'd been mulling over.

"Well, you've talked about how a labyrinth symbolizes the paths we walk in our lives, and Lewistown is where we met, so maybe we should start the rest of our lives there. We could have an outdoor ceremony at the Labyrinth Gardens sometime this summer."Logan suggested.

"That is absolutely brilliant!" Kate exclaimed. "Lewistown is a central location, and I love the symbolism. Maybe some of our guests would even enjoy walking the labyrinth." With a definite goal in mind, Kate started to plan.

◆ ◆ ◆

The ceremony was at held at Lewistown's Labyrinth Gardens at ten in the morning on a Saturday, before the mid-July day got too warm. It was a mix of traditional and modern, with scripture readings, music and the vows they wrote themselves. All of the folding chairs arranged in neat rows on either side of the aisle were full of family and friends. Both of their families were there, including Dave and Amanda and Dave's parents. The entire Whitcomb family showed up. Sylvia and Tony had taken a weekend off from their campground hosting duties in Glacier Park to attend. Ben and Genny were there, and so was everyone from the bike group and their families, with the exception of Drew's son Andy.

Kate's pale yellow sundress, sleeveless with a scoop neck and a handkerchief hem, floated around her like sunshine. She carried a basket of miniature yellow roses and white daisies as she walked down the aisle on her father's arm. She appreciated the symbolism of having her old friend Amanda and her new friend Tori as attendants, both in mint green sundresses styled like Kate's and carrying baskets of wildflowers. Logan wore cream colored khakis and a pale yellow shirt, with his brothers beside him in khakis and mint green shirts.

Kate and Logan posed for pictures while the caterers set up round tables and the guests moved their chairs to form seating areas for dining. Two long tables held the buffet lunch of sandwiches, salads and fruit, and a smaller table held the tiered wedding cake with two miniature bicycles on top in lieu of bride and groom figurines. When everyone was seated with a plate of food in front of them, Kate and Logan posed for more pictures while they cut the cake. They had just finished eating when Greg approached and gave Kate a one-armed hug.

"You sure make a beautiful bride, darlin'." He said, dropping a kiss on her cheek.

"Stop flirting with my wife!" Logan growled with a mock frown. "Go get your own girl!"

"Excellent idea!" Greg retorted. Turning back to Kate, he asked, "Who is the strawberry blond over there?"

"That's my friend Tori." Kate replied. She didn't even need to look because she already knew Tori was the only strawberry blond in the crowd. "She's from Shelby."

"Is she seeing anyone?"

"Not that I know of." Kate grinned up at him. "Want me to introduce you?" Greg nodded, and Kate led him over to where Tori stood visiting with Ben and Genny. When she returned to Logan's side, he was watching Greg with a puzzled look on his face.

"What is it?" She asked, following his gaze.

"He flirts with everyone. He never asks for introductions. That's just weird."

"Maybe Tori is different. They seem to be finding things to talk about."

"Yeah." Logan shrugged. "I'd sure like to see him find someone again."

"What do you mean again?" Kate asked, realizing for the first time that she didn't know anything about Greg except that he was a lawyer, he liked cycling, he flirted outrageously and he played the guitar. "I thought he was single."

"His wife died of breast cancer when their kids were nine and twelve." Logan explained, still watching Greg and Tori. "He's a really great dad. Kristy graduated from college this year, and Greg Jr. just finished his freshman year."

When Kate and Logan took their leave two hours later, the crowd had thinned out, the caterers were packing up -- and Greg and Tori were still deeply engaged in conversation, as if they were the only two people in the park.